Praise for the novels of

# SUSAN WIGGS

"Wiggs is one of our best observers of stories of the heart. Maybe that is because she knows how to capture emotion on virtually every page of every book."
—*Salem Statesman-Journal*

"[A] beautiful novel, tender and wise.
Susan Wiggs writes with bright assurance, humor and compassion about sisters, children and the sweet and heartbreaking trials of life—about how much better it is to go through them together."
—Luanne Rice on *Just Breathe*

Praise for the novels of

# SHERRYL WOODS

"Sherryl Woods writes emotionally satisfying novels about family, friendship and home.
Truly feel-great reads!"
—#1 *New York Times* bestselling author
Debbie Macomber

"Sherryl Woods gives her characters depth, intensity, and the right amount of humor."
—*RT Book Reviews*

# SUSAN WIGGS
## SHERRYL WOODS
## SUSAN MALLERY

*Summer Brides*

MIRA

**MIRA®**

Recycling programs
for this product may
not exist in your area.

ISBN-13: 978-0-7783-2843-8

SUMMER BRIDES

Copyright © 2010 by Harlequin Books S.A.

The publisher acknowledges the copyright holders
of the individual works as follows:

THE BORROWED BRIDE
Copyright © 1996 by Susan Wiggs.

A BRIDGE TO DREAMS
Copyright © 1990 by Sherryl Woods.

SISTER OF THE BRIDE
Copyright © 2010 by Susan Macias Redmond.

For questions and comments about the quality of this book please contact us at Customer_eCare@Harlequin.ca.

MIRA and the Star Colophon are trademarks used under license and registered in Australia, New Zealand, Philippines, United States Patent and Trademark Office and in other countries.

www.MIRABooks.com

**Printed in U.S.A.**

# CONTENTS

# THE BORROWED BRIDE

## Susan Wiggs

Dear Reader,

This story, first conceived of fifteen years ago, has a special place in my heart for several reasons. It is the very first work I created for Harlequin Books and ultimately led to my very happy home publishing under the MIRA imprint. I'll forever be grateful to editor Marsha Zinberg for the opportunity.

*The Borrowed Bride* takes place in my adopted home state of Washington, and I hope it conveys the wonder and beauty of this region. Re-reading the novella was a glimpse through a different lens, and I was able to see how much of my current writer's voice was present early on, and how a story like this laid the groundwork for the novels that would come after. Still, the story needed updating in a few spots. And unfortunately for Washingtonians, but fortunately for my editors, there is still poor cell phone service in the area where the story takes place. Overall, I'm happy to report that my general worldview of the redemptive power of love is still in place.

I hope you enjoy this romantic journey and that your own dreams are coming true for you each and every day.

Happy reading,

*Susan Wiggs*
Rollingbay, Washington, USA
www.susanwiggs.com

To Mary Hyatt, my own dear mensch, with love.
Here's to long-distance friendships!

*Dance. Everywhere, keep on dancing.*
                    —Native American prophecy

# *One*

Isabel Wharton's dreams were finally coming true—or so she thought. Surrounded by a burst of springtime and eleven chattering women, she prepared to join their intimate circle, to become their daughter, sister, niece, cousin when she married Anthony Cossa.

The bridal shower, held in the garden of a cottage café on Bainbridge Island, was winding down. Isabel tore open the second-to-last package and peered at the gift, then beamed at her future sister-in-law.

"It's lovely, Lucia. Simply lovely." *What is it?* The thing resembled something she had seen in her ob-gyn's office. She bit the inside of her cheek to stop herself from asking. Lucia and Connie and Marcia would be the sisters she'd never had.

"A silver pasta server." Connie, Lucia's younger sister, set aside the package. "Leave it to Lucia to assume you want to cook pasta."

Ah, but Isabel *did* want to cook pasta. And cannoli and tiramisu and gnocci, all for Anthony. She wanted to do everything for Anthony. He would make the perfect husband, and better still, he came with a family that was so large, so boisterous and so loving that she was engulfed by a feeling of belonging.

They would warm the cold, empty places inside her. At least she hoped so.

"I saved the best for last." Connie perched on the edge of her white wicker garden chair.

Isabel caught Mama Cossa's eye and winked. "I'm not sure I trust your daughter."

"I haven't trusted Connie since she tried out for the seventh-grade wrestling team."

Isabel laughed and removed the slick, metallic gold wrapping paper. Female hoots filled the garden as she lifted a wispy silk garment from the box.

"Now *that*," Connie said with great pride, "is hot."

Isabel stood, holding the lacy red teddy against her. The silk felt as cool and insubstantial as mist. The lace plunged to her navel; the legs were cut sinfully high. Even held against her India-cotton skirt, the teddy felt wicked and wild.

"I figure Tony will have a heart attack when he sees you in it," Connie said. "But at least he'll die happy."

The women's laughter chimed like music in the garden. Isabel felt a wave of affection and gratitude, along with a feeling of contentment so sharp and sweet that her chest hurt. These women—Anthony's sisters and aunts and nieces, his beautiful mother—were to be her family. Her *family*.

Ever since she'd moved to Bainbridge Island and established her plant nursery, she'd begun to feel as though she really belonged somewhere. All that had been missing was a family, and now she was about to get that, too.

They began to drift homeward then; most of the guests were staying on the island, where the wedding would take place in just one week. Mama Cossa, good-humored but limping from bursitis, gave Isabel's hand a squeeze. "See you at the rehearsal dinner, dear."

Only a few women remained when a faint hum sounded in Isabel's ears. She gazed down the length of the garden. The flower beds and trees were drenched in the glory of sunshine. Just past the tops of the towering fir trees, she could see the sparkling waters of Puget Sound.

The island, she decided, was paradise on earth. She had built her life on a foundation of shattered dreams, but finally everything was falling into place.

The roaring grew louder. It was the sound of a boat motor or a car without a muffler—urgent, industrial, a faintly animalistic low grumble.

Connie and the others, who had been bagging up torn paper and ribbons, paused and turned. Isabel frowned. And then, right where the gravel driveway turned off from the road, he appeared.

He was an image out of her worst nightmare. Clad in black leather. A bandanna around his head. Inky, flowing hair. Mirror-lens sunglasses. The Harley beneath him bucking and spitting gravel like a wild animal.

"I smell testosterone," Connie murmured as the machine roared up a terraced garden path.

Isabel stood frozen, immobile as a block of ice. The apparition skidded to a halt, jerked the bike onto its kickstand and walked toward her. Long, loose strides. Tall boots crunching on the path. Tiny gold earring winking in one ear. Long brown hands hanging at his sides.

"Somebody call 911," Lucia whispered.

He yanked off the mirror glasses and stared at Isabel. Dark brown eyes dragged down the length of her. Then he reached into the lingerie box on the table and plucked out the red silk teddy.

"Very nice," he said in a rich drawl, inspecting the garment. "You were always a great dresser, Isabel."

She snatched it away and thrust it into the box. "What are you doing here?"

He gave her the old cocky grin, the expression that used to make her go weak in the knees.

It still worked.

His looks had attracted her in the first place. She had been drawn to his aura of seductive danger, the faint sulkiness of his full lips, the powerful body as well tuned as his Harley. The long hair so thick and gleaming that she yearned to run her fingers through it.

The direction her thoughts had taken ignited a blush in her cheeks. "This really isn't a good time."

"There never was a good time for saying the things we should have said to each other," he said with that lazy, Sunday-morning, stay-in-bed-all-day drawl. "But I figure it's now or never."

Her blush intensified. "Maybe you could come back later, after…" She let her voice trail off. Her mouth was dry, her thoughts scattered.

"Nope, Isabel, won't work. We've got some unfinished business." He hooked a thumb into the top of his black jeans and shifted his weight to one leg. "I figure you'd rather settle things in private, so you'd better come with me."

With a force of will, she was able to drag her gaze from him. "Connie, this is Dan Black Horse."

"Perfect," Connie whispered helpfully. "Just perfect." She sent Dan an adoring look. "I have all of your albums. I've been a fan for years. Too bad you've quit."

"Pleasure to meet you," Dan said with effortless gallantry.

Connie gave Isabel's shoulder a nudge. "Go ahead," she said with sisterly wisdom. "If you've got something to settle with this guy, take care of it now, because next week it'll be too late." She lowered her voice and said, "If you weren't my friend, I'd kill you for not telling me you knew Dan Black Horse."

Isabel stooped to pick up her woven straw purse. "I won't be long." She forced her lips into a smile. "I'll be all right, really."

Dan Black Horse pivoted on a boot heel and led the way down the garden path. When they reached his bike, he eased it off the kickstand and held out a black, slightly battered helmet.

"No way," she said, stiffening her spine. "I'll follow you in my car."

"Nope." He plunked the helmet on her head and fastened the strap. "Where we're going, you don't want a car."

She clenched her jaw to keep from screaming. *Priorities, Isabel,* she reminded herself. *Keep the priorities straight.* The most important thing was to avoid making a scene.

She heaved a sigh, hitched back her cotton skirt and got on the bike.

"Way to go, girl," Connie murmured, not far behind her.

"We'll go to the Streamliner Diner," she told Dan tautly. "And I mean to be back by—"

The thunder of the large engine swallowed her words. He rolled forward, then opened the throttle. The bike jerked into motion.

Instinctively, her hands clutched low on his hips. A feeling of the forbidden seized her. She gritted her teeth, moved her hands to the cargo bar behind her and held on for dear life.

He wasn't wearing a helmet, she observed as they turned onto the narrow wooded highway that bisected Bainbridge Island. Maybe a cop would pull them over.

*Officer, I've been kidnapped by a man I swore I'd never see again.*

But as they roared southward toward the quaint little township of Winslow, even the stoplights turned green, conspiring against her.

Craning her neck around his bulky shoulder, she saw the diner up ahead, looming closer…and then farther away as they veered past it, down the hill toward the ferry terminal.

"Hey," she shouted in his ear. "You said we'd have our little talk at the diner."

"*You* said that, sweetheart." He tossed the words carelessly over his shoulder and passed the tollbooth.

The last straggling cars were pulling onto the ferry. A female attendant wearing a bright orange smock was about to cordon off the loading platform.

Dan thumbed the horn. It emitted a chirpy beep. The

attendant grinned and waved him through. He drove up the ramp and parked. Immediately, a horn blew. Too late to get off.

As the ferry eased away from the terminal, he turned around to face her. "Damn, Isabel," he said, "you're one hard woman to find."

The second he killed the engine, Isabel struggled off the bike. "You're crazy," she said, "but I suppose you know that."

"Maybe." He favored her with a look she remembered well, the one of sleepy arousal that used to make her happy to dive back into bed with him for long, languid weekend mornings.

"This is ridiculous," she said in exasperation—both at him and at her wayward memory. She braced her hand on the iron wall to steady herself as the ferry headed for downtown Seattle.

When Dan didn't reply, she turned and stomped up the stairs to the lounge. The spacious waiting room, flooded with April sunshine, was crowded with islanders heading to the city for shopping or an evening on the town. She spotted a familiar face here and there and managed to nod a greeting.

*Great,* she thought. All she needed was for the bank clerk or the hardware store owner to see her going to Seattle with a sinfully good-looking man.

She went out on deck, where the wind caught at her skirt and hair. Gulls wheeled and sailed along beside the ferry. In the distance, a sea lion splashed in Puget Sound.

It didn't take Dan long to find her. Within minutes,

he joined her on the open-air deck. "Here." He pushed a paper cup of café latte into her hand. "Skim milk, one sugar packet, right?"

She took the cup and sank to a bolted-down bench. "I hope you know you've ruined the afternoon for me."

He sat beside her, resting his lanky wrists on his knees. A dark fire smoldered in his eyes, and she sensed a tension about him, a coiled heat that disturbed and fascinated her. "Couldn't be helped. Besides, it's better than ruining the rest of your life."

She almost choked on a mouthful of hot coffee. "What's that supposed to mean?"

He reached forward and caught a drop of latte with a napkin before it stained her India-print skirt. "You can't marry him, Isabel." His voice, with the unforgettable low rumble of masculine passion that had filled the airwaves for two years, was harsh. "You can't marry Anthony Cossa."

"Since when do I need your permission?" she retorted. The breeze plucked at her hair. Her permed curls were now a deep chestnut color, thanks to an expensive salon job. She pushed a thick lock behind her ear and glared at him. "How did you find me, anyway?"

He sent her a hard-edged grin. "Through Anthony."

"Oh, God." She set down her cup and folded her arms across her middle. "What did you do to Anthony?"

Dan stretched out his long legs and crossed them at the ankles. He leaned his head back against the wall. The movement and pose were graceful, vaguely feline, subtly dangerous. "I don't remember you being this suspicious."

"I'm generally suspicious of men who kidnap me from my own wedding shower."

"Fair enough. I had business with Anthony. And what do I see when I get to his office? Your smiling face in a silver frame on his desk."

She tried to picture it. Dan, all in rebel black, with his long hair and earring, facing Anthony, immaculate and trying hard to look laid-back in his Banana Republic chinos.

"He's a good guy, Isabel," Dan said expansively. "He's real proud to be marrying a gorgeous, successful woman."

"He's no slouch in the looks and success departments," she argued. "Maybe I'm real proud to be marrying him."

"Maybe," Dan said, jamming a thumb into his belt and drumming his fingers on his jeans.

Isabel jerked her attention from the insinuating pose and glared out at the Sound.

"That's what I thought at first," Dan went on. "I was going to blow the whole thing off, wish you a happy life with your upright, square-jawed bachelor-of-the-month, and bow out."

"I wish you had." She took a gulp of coffee. She probably shouldn't ingest caffeine. Being with Dan made her jumpy enough. "Why didn't you?"

"There are things I've always wondered about, Isabel." He sat forward, gripping the edge of the bench. It was there again, the pulsing rhythm in his voice, the mesmerizing glitter in his dark eyes. "Five years ago, you walked out on me and never looked back."

*I couldn't look back, Dan. If I had, I would have gone running into your arms.*

She gave up on the latte and rose from the bench to drop her cup into a waste barrel. "What do you want from me?"

"Just a little of your time."

Her eyes narrowed. "How much?"

He sent her the same lazily sexual smile that had cast a spell on her five years earlier. She had been twenty-one, a terrible driver, and while backing out of a parking space in front of an ominous-looking nightclub, she had knocked over a large black motorcycle.

Terrified but determined to do the honorable thing, she went into the club to find the owner of the bike.

He was performing that evening, playing to a small, grungy but clearly appreciative crowd. The lead singer of a local band, he strummed a wild, primeval tune on a battered Stratocaster guitar. To Isabel, he looked like eternal hell and damnation in the flesh. He was gorgeous. She was spellbound.

He forgave her for the damages, took her out for a latte that had stretched into an all-night conversation, and stole her heart.

She backed warily away from the memory, for it was still as dark and seductive as that moonlit night had been.

"How much time, Dan?" she asked again, telling herself she was older, wiser, immune to his devilish smile.

"That depends," he said, "on how long it takes for you to realize you're marrying Anthony for all the wrong reasons."

"Oh, please." She turned away and gripped the rail of the ferry. "I'm a big girl now. And I'm not stupid. I don't want you back in my life."

The boat was nearing the downtown pier. Good. The minute they got to the terminal, she would call Anthony at his office. The situation was bound to be awkward. Best to explain this to him before Connie got started.

A flash of electric awareness came over her. She felt Dan behind her, although he wasn't touching her. Despite her anger, a vital tension tugged at her.

"Turn around, Isabel," he whispered in her ear. "Look me in the eye when you say you don't want me."

Her entire body felt slow and hot, as if she were swimming through warm honey. She forced herself to turn to him, pressing the small of her back against the iron rail.

He clamped one hand on the bar on each side of her so that she was trapped. She looked at him, really looked at him, and her throat went dry.

He had hardly changed at all. Still the same magnificent face that made women stop and stare. Same velvet-brown eyes with gold glinting in their depths. Same lean, unyielding body, filled with a hard strength that made his tender touch all the more astonishing. Same perfectly shaped lips...

His mouth was very close. She could feel his heat, could feel the clamor and clash of panic and desire inside her.

"You were saying?" he whispered. His lips hovered over hers, and she felt a fleeting reminder of the wildness that had once gripped her whenever he was near. "Isabel?" His intimate gaze wandered over her throat now, no doubt seeing her racing pulse.

"I was saying," she forced out, "that I don't..."

"Don't what?" His thumbs brushed at her wrists, lightly, gently.

"...want you..." she tried to continue.

"Go on," he whispered. His tongue came out and subtly moistened his lower lip.

"…in my life again."

His hands stayed on the railing. Yet he moved closer, his hard thighs brushing hers, searing her through the wispy fabric of her skirt. She felt every nerve ending jolt to life. By the time he grinned insolently and pushed back from the railing, she was dazed and furious, and the ferry was unloading.

"Just checking," he said.

"You bastard," she whispered.

A pair of women with straw shopping bags passed by, sending Isabel looks of rueful envy.

Dan stepped back, smiling his I'm-a-rebel smile.

"I need to make a phone call," Isabel said. "And then I'm taking the next ferry back to Bainbridge."

"We haven't settled a damned thing."

"We settled everything five years ago. It didn't work then, and it won't work now."

"Five years ago was only the beginning."

"No." The word sounded strangled as she headed for the stairs. "It was the end."

He caught her wrist, and she froze. There was not a trace of a smile on his face when he brought her around to look at him.

"Don't you think you owe me one more chance?" His voice was a low rasp that reminded her of the smoky, yearning love ballads he used to sing to her. "After all, you almost had my baby, Isabel."

# *Two*

Dan Black Horse couldn't believe Isabel had agreed to come with him. But then, he couldn't believe he had said such a blatantly manipulative thing to her.

She had even called the clean-cut Anthony and told him not to worry; she'd be in touch.

And so here they were—a couple of hours southeast of the city, at his guest lodge in a wilderness so deep and untouched that there weren't even roads leading to the property.

He looked across the timber-ceilinged lounge at her and could not for the life of him think of a damned word to say.

She stood at a window, one slim hand braced on the casement, gazing out at the dense old-growth forest that rose like a sanctuary around the lodge. In the green-filtered glow of the afternoon sun, she looked fragile and lovely, the shape of her legs visible through the thin, full skirt, her back straight and proud, her hair flashing with burnished light.

A wave of tenderness washed over him. Always, she managed to look isolated and alone, even when she was in a crowd of people. It was one of the first things he had noticed about her.

"You changed your hair," he said at last, then grimaced at his own inanity. Boot heels ringing on the floor, he crossed to the bar and took out a can of beer for himself and a soda for her.

She turned around to face him. Her full breasts strained against her cotton jersey top. "You changed your life."

Her face was more striking than he remembered. Large doe eyes. High, delicate cheekbones. A full mouth that drove him crazy just thinking about it. An air of winsome uncertainty that made him want to take her in his arms and never let her go.

Ah, but he had let go. Five years earlier, he had not been brave enough, smart enough, to hold her.

He handed her the soda and gave her a lopsided grin. "Yeah, I guess you could say I made some changes."

"A few, it would appear." She strolled around the rambling room. "Where's the phone? I had no idea you were taking me *this* far away. I should check in with—"

"No phone," he told her quietly.

"What?" Liquid sloshed out of the can, but she didn't seem to notice.

"There's a radio for emergencies, but the phone lines don't come up this far, and it's too remote for cellular."

She sagged against the back of an armchair. "Whatever happened to the city boy? Didn't you find fame and fortune with the Urban Natives?"

"Depends on your standards for fame and fortune.

The band did okay. The last album went gold, and it got me into this place."

"I noticed the name of this place on the door—The Tomunwethla Lodge." She brushed her hand over a woven wicker bean jar on a side table. "What does that mean?"

Ah, she had trained herself well. He had always hoped she would acknowledge the past, maybe even come to cherish it as he did. But given Isabel's background, that wasn't likely.

"Cloud Dancer Lodge," he said. "'Cloud Dancer' is a song I once wrote. A really bad, crying-in-your-beer song. Probably the most popular thing I ever did."

Isabel rose and stood on a braided oval rug in front of the massive hearth. "So what's the point?"

"Of the song?"

"Of everything."

He set down his beer and took her hand, leading her to the huge sofa facing the fireplace. A moose head with baleful glass eyes stared down at them.

"The point of everything," he echoed, blowing out his breath. He tried another grin on her, but she remained solemn. "Lady, you asked a mouthful." He half turned, hooking a booted foot over his knee. God, he wanted to touch her, *really* touch her, to wake up the passion he knew was only sleeping inside her. But the way she was looking at the moment, he was afraid she might shatter.

Just as she had five years ago.

"First, my granddad got sick," Dan said after a moment. "I moved to the town of Thelma to help look after him. And damned if I didn't start to like it out here again." He linked his hands behind his head and stretched out his legs. "Used to be, I couldn't wait to get away from the rez, from the country." Through half-lidded eyes, he watched her for a reaction. There was none. If anything, she seemed even more subdued. More withdrawn.

*Well, what did you expect, Black Horse?*

"My granddad died."

"Dan, I'm sorry."

"He was eighty-three. He left me a grant of land that's tied to a treaty with the government dating back to the 1880s. Right around the time of his death, a timber company approached the tribal council, wanting to make a deal on clear-cutting."

"But this area is sacred ground," she blurted out. Then she looked surprised at herself and fell silent.

"Exactly," he said. "But the deal was real tempting. When you don't know where your next meal's coming from, lunch with a grizzly bear looks pretty appetizing."

That coaxed an extremely small smile from her.

"So I did some research. The lands are protected, but the council was leaning toward the timber company. I made a counteroffer. Got a special grant to develop a recreational area, sank everything I had into it and built this place. Just put the finishing touches on it a week ago."

"It looks as if it's been here forever," she said. "The lodge is really beautiful, Dan."

"It's supposed to have that rustic flavor." Flipping his wrist outward, he did a perfect imitation of Andy, the band's former keyboard player, who had switched careers to interior design. "Without skimping on creature comforts."

Isabel laughed softly. The sound gripped Dan where he felt it the most—in his heart.

"So that's the short version," he said. "If this is a success, I could open lodges in Alaska, maybe Belize or Tahiti in the winter—"

"Why?" Her question was sharp and humorless.

"Because I know what I'm doing." *Sort of.* "Somebody else would come in and build a theme park. Probably stick totem poles up everywhere and sell shaman baskets for yard ornaments. I wanted something better. I wanted to do it right."

She stood and crossed the room, inspecting a cloth wall hanging and the tuber mask beside it. "This is just right. Really." Even as his chest filled with pride, she paused. Maybe she was beginning to unbend a little. "I take that back. The snowshoes hanging on the wall are marginal. And the antler ottoman has got to go."

"It's my favorite piece of furniture."

She sat back down on the sofa. "So now I know why you're here. Why am I here?"

He paused. "A picture's worth a thousand words?" he offered.

"Fine. I came. I saw. I'm impressed. Now take me back to the city."

"I can't exactly do that," he said in a soft, slow voice.

"What do you mean?"

"We have a lot to talk about. I need time."

She shot up again. "I don't *have* time. I'm getting married exactly one week from today. I have to meet with a caterer. A florist. A dressmaker. Photographer, videographer—" She counted them off on her fingers and turned on him in frustration. The pale skirt floated around her slim legs, and for a moment, she looked as exotic as a gypsy dancer. "Sorry, Dan. I just didn't schedule in being abducted by an ex-boyfriend."

He'd had no idea she was so bitter. This was going to be harder than he had thought. A lot harder.

"In other words," he said, "you want me to say what I have to say and then get the hell out of your life."

She blew out an exasperated breath. "That's putting it a little bluntly." Then she looked defiant. "I don't have time to play games with you."

He crossed the room in two strides and clamped his hands around her upper arms. She felt delicate and breakable. He used to marvel at her softness, her femininity, the way it contrasted with his own hard edges and roughness. But when she flinched at his touch, he grew angry.

"Is that what you think this is, lady? A game?"

"Tell me different." She glared up at him.

"I brought you here because you ran away, and I was fool enough to let you go. Well, not this time."

"What?"

He stared into her eyes, seeing his reflection in their depths and, in his mind, seeing the dreams and desires that used to consume them both, feeling the ache of an unfulfilled promise.

"I can't let you go, Isabel. I can't let you just walk out of my life again. You're making a big mistake, marrying that guy, and I can prove it."

"How?" she challenged, lifting her chin.

"Like this." He lowered his mouth to hers and cupped his hand around the back of her head. This was not how he had treated her aboard the ferry. He was not teasing her or, in some mean-spirited way, trying to assert his masculine power over her. This was a kiss designed to bring back the wildness and passion they had once shared. To remind her—remind them both—of all they had lost and all they could be once again if they tried.

She held herself rigid. At first, she made a resentful sound in the back of her throat. He softened his mouth on hers and skimmed his thumb down her temple to her jaw, lightly caressing. A small sigh gusted from her, and her clenched fists, which she had put up between them, relaxed. Her palms flattened lightly against his chest.

Ah, he remembered this, the thin, keen edge of desire he felt only with her, and the way she swayed and fit against him. Her mouth was soft, and the taste of her— one that had lingered for years after she left—was as familiar and welcome as the springtime.

His tongue traced the seam of her lips, and she opened for him, almost shyly, her trembling hands over his heart.

Finally, when it was all he could do to keep from making love to her right then and there, he lifted his mouth from hers. She looked up at him, and he down at her, at the sheen of moistness on her lips.

The sheen of tears in her eyes.

"Isabel?" His voice was low and rough.

"I can't believe you'd do something so cruel."

He dropped his arms to his sides. "What the hell is that supposed to mean?"

She drew an unsteady breath. "You're just trying to manipulate me. To make me feel unfaithful to Anthony."

"What about being faithful to yourself?" He pivoted away, furious at her, furious at himself for wanting her. "I guess you never learned that, did you?"

She caught her breath as the dart struck home.

Though Dan knew it wasn't her fault, she had turned away from the part of her that was like Dan—the Native American part.

"I moved on, Dan," she said. "I moved past that. It's known as growing up."

"I'm sorry. I didn't find you again to hurt you. I did it to ask you for a second chance."

She brushed at her cheeks with the back of her hand. "It's no good. I can't. You—you bring up a darkness in me. I get all twisted around inside when I'm with you. I can't live like that."

"There are those who say you should seek out your darkest places. Explore them. Find the sunshine that will burn the shadows away."

"Don't you see? That's what I'm trying to do."

"You're running away, Isabel."

She crossed to the door and went out onto the porch to stand, glaring at a magnificent view of Mount Adams. "It's my choice."

He came out and stood behind her, placing his hands lightly on her shoulders. She didn't pull away.

At length, she said, "Take me back to the city, Dan."

"I'll take you back this instant," he said, "if you can say you really mean it when you tell me it's all over between us."

He turned her in his arms. He saw the truth written all over her face. She had been just as aroused by the kiss as he had.

But he could see that she was close to breaking. It was time to back off, to give her space, to let it all sink in.

"I have to feed the horses," he said. "They've got

internal clocks that tell them exactly when five o'clock rolls around."

"I can't believe you have horses. You wouldn't even keep a goldfish in your apartment in Seattle."

He grinned and spread his arms. "Hey, I'm a responsible citizen now."

She eyed his earring, his black ponytail, his T-shirt with the slogan Question Authority. "Yeah, right."

Whistling, Dan jumped down the porch steps and headed for the stables. "Believe what you like. You're stuck with me for one more night."

# Three

Isabel watched his long, lanky frame disappear down a wooded path. He strode gracefully, showing the same ease with which he used to walk onto a stage in front of a crowd of fans. He didn't look like a crazy man.

But she knew better. And he made *her* crazy when she was with him.

She touched her lips and closed her eyes while warm pulsations of remembrance passed through her. Why did he have to kiss her? Why did he have to bring back all the glory and pain and messy, magical moments that used to make each day with him an adventure?

Why did he have to remind her that she felt none of this savage, dangerous passion with Anthony?

The thought of her fiancé jolted her into action. She pushed open the screen door and grabbed her purse from the bar. Slipping the strap onto her shoulder, she marched down the steps.

If Dan wouldn't take her off this mountain and back to the city, she would do it herself. Rope-soled espadrilles notwithstanding, she would walk to the nearest phone, wherever that was.

Why hadn't Anthony just said no when she had called him from the ferry terminal? As in, *I think it's a lousy idea to spend the day with your old boyfriend. Get the hell back here right now.*

But no, not Anthony. "Sure, babe," he'd said in his breezy way. "If it's something you think you need to do, go for it."

Part of her wished he had just enough of the caveman left in him to stake his claim. To sling her bodily over his shoulder and take her off to his lair.

As Dan Black Horse just had.

But Isabel had to remind herself that Dan's methods had been worse than primitive; they'd been downright manipulative. Mentioning their lost baby had really hurt.

She tossed her hair back and continued down the path—if this faint indentation was indeed a path. The cleared area around the lodge gave way to old-growth forest so dense and primitive that she felt like Eve in the Garden of Eden.

She tried to get her bearings. They had arrived on Dan's Harley. She still had the grass stains on her hem from the bouncing cross-country ride. But there had to be a path to follow, maybe a logging track or the road the builders had used to haul materials to the lodge.

Dan had explained that lodge guests would typically arrive by helicopter, landing on the helipad a short hike uphill. That had a lesser environmental impact than clearing the woods for a road.

Muttering under her breath, she continued down the

hill, thinking that if she just kept going down, eventually she would reach the dirt road and then the highway.

Within half an hour, she had decided that bridal-shower clothes were not appropriate for treks through trackless wilderness.

In another half hour, she paused to note that the sun was to her left. That was west. Seattle was to the northwest. But another hour after that, she realized the sun was setting, and if anything, she had wandered into even denser woods.

Finally, to top off a really good day, it began to drizzle.

The foul word that came out of Isabel surprised even her. The hem of her skirt trailed over a spray of thick fern fronds.

*That is the* nokosa *plant,* said an almost forgotten voice in her mind. *Our people use it to heal wounds.*

"Sure thing," Isabel muttered. "So what do you use to keep from getting lost in the wilderness?"

Not that she would heed any advice from that voice. It was the voice of the first man who had betrayed Isabel: her father.

She clenched her teeth. This was outrageous. She saw the headlines now: Prominent Businessman's Bride Found Dead. *She just wasn't herself that day,* Connie would helpfully recall for the press.

Isabel plodded on, keeping despair at bay with sheer stubbornness. The shadows grew longer, the forest floor wetter. With every step she took, she devised a new torture for Dan.

The light rain misted her hair, then plastered strands of it to her forehead and neck. Her skirt and cotton jersey top were soaked through. Her espadrilles absorbed moisture like a pair of sponges.

Miserable, wet, lost and furious, she shook her fist at the cloudy twilight sky. "Damn you, Dan Black Horse!" she shouted.

A few minutes later, she spied a movement in the distance. Low branches of Sitka spruce nodded and bobbed as something huge and menacing stirred beneath them.

Another choice headline popped into her mind: Bainbridge Bride-To-Be Butchered By Bear.

Isabel screamed.

When Dan came back from feeding the horses, he assumed Isabel had gone to look around the place.

Good, he thought. He had worked hard to build the lodge. Harder than he had ever worked at anything. Making it in the music business had been a cakewalk compared to this—to wresting a working enterprise out of a virgin forest without disturbing the very essence of that wilderness. The property consisted of the lodge and outbuildings, a central yard with a spectacular view of Mount Adams, the stables, garage and helipad. It would have been quicker to bring in bulldozers and cement mixers, but he had done everything the hard way. By hand, with local labor. Native American labor.

He hoped Isabel liked it, hoped she realized what it meant to him. Maybe she would open her mind to the past, and her heart to the tribe she'd been made to leave so long ago.

He sat on the cedar porch swing, waiting for her to return and planning what he would say to her tonight.

First, dinner. Grilled salmon from the river, some greens and herbs from Juanita's garden and a nice Washington State wine. Then he'd tell her everything. Almost.

He figured it was a little too soon to tell her he was on the verge of bankruptcy. And maybe too late to tell her that he loved her.

After a while, he grew restless. He got up and paced the porch. He called to Isabel. He walked the length and breadth and circumference of the entire property.

Finally, the sick realization sank into his brain.

Isabel was gone.

"Lady, you look like you seen a ghost," said the stranger.

"A bear." Isabel's legs felt wobbly. She leaned back against a large rock. The surface was soaking wet, but no wetter than she already was.

"A bear?" He looked around, his long hair whipping to and fro. "Where?"

"You," she said, fully aware that hours of exposure had probably addled her brain. "I thought you were a bear."

"Cool." He pushed back a low-hanging branch. In every respect but one, he appeared a typical American teenager—oversize hiking boots, baggy, low-slung jeans, a plaid shirt with a hood trailing down his back.

He stood high and dry beneath a broad fiber mat supported by three straight sticks. The design woven into the mat was a tribal bear crest.

"I'm Isabel Wharton," she said, "and I guess you could say I'm lost."

He grinned—the half shy, half cocky smile of a

teenage boy. "Gary Sohappy," he said, "and I figured you were."

"You…" Her pulse was finally returning to its normal rate. "How did you know to come looking for me?"

"Dan radioed down." He held out the woven shelter so that it protected her. "He said to keep my eyes peeled for a real good-looking woman with a chip on her shoulder." Gary took her elbow and started down the slope. "Watch your step here." He glanced at her, still bashful, still full of mischief. "I don't see no chip."

"I left it with Dan Black Horse," she said through gritted teeth. "I take it he's a friend of yours."

"Yep." He continued to lead her down the slope. It was almost dark now, and she could see no discernible path, but the boy seemed to know where he was going. "My uncle and I and a lot of guys from the rez helped him build the lodge. He said you were his first guest."

A tiny dart of guilt stung her. She had not paused to look at it that way. Dan had built a virtual woodland paradise, and she had shown little appreciation for his hard work.

"He caught me at a really bad time," she said with wry understatement.

The woods seemed to be thinning. Rain pattered down almost musically on the mat umbrella.

"Guess so," Gary said. "I hope the Seahawks like it better than you did."

She frowned. "The Seahawks? As in Seattle Seahawks?"

"Yep. He's been trying to get a contract to bring the whole team up for R & R. Like a wild-man weekend or something."

Realization clicked in Isabel's mind. Anthony was a

promoter for the Seahawks. *That* was how Dan had come into contact with him and figured out how to find her.

But if Dan needed the contract, then why would he jeopardize it by dragging her back into his life at this critical moment? Anthony was a tolerant man, but maybe not *that* tolerant.

Darkness had fallen by the time they reached a level clearing. Isabel saw a cluster of buildings hunched against the side of a hill. She made out the shapes of an antique tractor and a battered pickup truck.

"How far are we from the nearest town?" she asked Gary.

He stopped beneath an awning at the back door of the main house and shook off the umbrella. "Probably ten miles to Thelma. Maybe Dan'll take you there Monday night. There's a dance at the fire hall."

"Dan's not taking me anywhere," she muttered. They entered the house, and the world seemed to tilt on its axis.

She had never been here, had never seen this place, but she knew it. There was a place like this in her heart. She had been running from it for years.

She stood on a fiber mat in a small kitchen. The linoleum floor was cracked but swept clean. The yellow countertops had a boomerang design in the Formica, circa 1960. A butane-gas stove held a battered teapot and a large cast-iron dutch oven. A curl of steam, redolent with the fragrance of herbs, seeped from beneath the lid of the pot.

On the wall was a gas-station calendar with a photo of Mount Rainier. The picture was fading, and the calendar had not been turned since February. In the doorway stood a small, slim woman whose smile showed no surprise, only welcome.

"Hi, Gram." Gary parked his hiking boots on a rubber mat just inside the door. "Found her."

"That's good. Supper'll be ready in a minute."

Gary left the room, and the woman inclined her graying head. "Juanita Sohappy."

"I'm Isabel Wharton. I guess Dan told you about me."

Juanita nodded, then lifted the lid of a basket. "Here. Take off your shoes and wrap up in that. Sit down at the table. I'll get you some stew."

"I'm not hungry, thank you." Isabel pulled the blanket, worn soft with age, around her shoulders.

Juanita's black eyes glinted with warning. "Everybody eats when they come to my house."

Isabel sat down, instantly obedient and secretly delighted by Juanita's aggressive hospitality. In the kitchen, she observed a poignant collection of poverty and pride. Four dishes stacked just so in the cupboard. A collection of World's Fair 1962 tumblers. Juanita's apron had been made from a flour sack with intricate, beautiful embroidery at the edges.

Isabel took it all in with a lump in her throat, and a stark truth hit her.

She had built her life in Bainbridge. But she had left her soul in a place like this.

# *Four*

Petunia swung her head to the side and cast a baleful glare at her rider. She was the best horse in Dan's stables, but he knew she deeply resented getting wet and wasn't too fond of the dark, either.

Dan made a sound of sympathy in his throat and urged her down the hill. Horseback was the best way to find Isabel. Elevated, he had a broader range of vision—at least until it grew dark. Unlike the bike, the horse was quiet, and he could hear Isabel if she answered his calls.

The rain hissed through the woods, spattering onto the broad, lush tongues of primeval ferns and drumming dully on the hood of his poncho. He ought to check with Theo and Juanita. If Isabel wasn't with the Sohappys, he would radio the forest search service.

In the meantime, he yelled until his throat ached.

Damn it, where *was* she?

In one way or other, he thought, heading north toward the Sohappys' settlement, he had been searching for Isabel Wharton for the past five years.

Only now he knew what it took to hold her—if he could get her to sit still long enough to listen. If he could get past that wall she had built around her heart. If he could find the words he had never bothered to say to her.

He remembered the first time he had ever seen her. The scene was branded on his memory. He had been twenty-three, cocky as hell, driven by a need to escape and rebel and shock people. The ponytail, the leather, the earring, the attitude—all were donned with calculated purpose, and he wore them like a second skin. His appearance tended to scare nice people.

He liked that.

When Isabel came into his life, Dan was playing his guitar and singing to a crowd as dark and ominous-looking as he. His music had already gained him some startled praise from area critics—not that he cared. He just sank into the sharp, rough rhythm, letting it surge around him like the constant, broken pulse of the sea. Through his music, he expressed the wildness and mystery inside him, expressed it with an insistence and a precision that was profitable, but ultimately destructive.

He spotted her through the heated, angry glare of stage lights. Only a vague impression at first, but totally mind-blowing given the usual crowds at the Bad Attitude. She was dressed all in white with a burnished halo of sable hair framing a troubled face and the largest, saddest eyes Dan had ever seen.

He stepped back from the mike, doing idle riffs while he watched her. She bent to speak to Leon Garza, the sound man. Her hair fell forward, obscuring her face. She tucked a lock behind her ear then, with a quick, nervous motion of her hand.

Leon lifted his eyebrows, skimmed her with a hungry expression Dan suddenly wanted to pound from his face and then nodded toward the stage.

Dan let his riffs trail off and signaled for Andy to take over on the keyboard. She looked up as Dan approached. The expression on her face would live in his heart forever. She showed the usual nice girl's shock and fear. Her slim hand clutched tighter around her purse strap. But it was her determination that caught his attention.

That, and the quick, unmistakable signal flare of sexual interest. She probably wasn't even aware that her breath caught. That the tip of her tongue briefly touched her lips. That her eyelids dropped to half-mast.

Yeah, she was a nice girl, but her soul was wild.

"My name is Isabel Wharton." She handed him a business card. "I think I just wrecked your motorcycle."

That was the beginning. He felt it then, and so did she—the heart-catching awareness and a wanting that tore at his gut.

It was so powerful it should have—could have—lasted forever.

"I won't lose you again, Isabel," he said under his breath as he rode on.


The sitting room was small, tidy and shabby. Gary was in the next room playing the air guitar with the headphones on. Isabel could hear the tinny rhythm even from a distance. It was one of Dan's songs.

Juanita sat in a fading armchair, knitting a muffler of red wool. On the sofa sat her son, a soft-spoken man called Theo, who had come in shortly after Isabel. His booted feet were propped on a stack of farming and forestry journals.

"I figure Dan'll be here pretty soon," Theo said. "It only takes about twenty minutes on foot."

Isabel sent him a rueful smile. She was warm and dry, and her curls were now a thing of the past. *It's that Indian blood,* her foster mother used to say. *Makes your hair straight as a board.* Isabel had spent three weeks' allowance on a permanent that very day, and had worn her hair curly ever since.

"Twenty minutes?" she said. "I was out walking for at least two hours."

Theo kept his face solemn and impassive, but his eyes twinkled. "Guess you took the long way. You must've been plenty mad."

She blew out her breath. "Not mad. Just impatient."

Juanita made a light, noncommittal sound in her throat.

Isabel winked. "Well, maybe a little mad." She felt unexpectedly—almost reluctantly—comfortable with this family. And there it was. The operative word. *Family.*

She had never really had one. She remembered a few happy times on the reservation back before her daredevil father had gotten himself killed. After that, she recalled only a murky haze of formless months. Although she'd still had her mother, an Anglo, the woman had only been there in a physical sense. After her husband's death, she had severed all emotional connections with Isabel.

Eventually, with a sort of dazed resignation, she had surrendered her daughter to foster parents.

The O'Dells had been older, excruciatingly kind and

absolutely convinced that Isabel's dark moods were caused by her ambivalence about being half Native American. They hadn't meant to make her reject her heritage, but their subtle emphasis on Anglo ways had changed her. With the very best of intentions, they had scoured her soul, emptied her mind of the ways of her father's people.

When Isabel graduated high school, the O'Dells had retired to Arizona. They still exchanged Christmas cards and the occasional letter.

*Family.* Without consciously knowing it, she had gone off in search of one.

With Dan, she had almost found what she was looking for. She remembered staring in awe and cautious joy at the results of the home pregnancy test. She remembered rushing off to the club where he was playing that night, practically bursting as she waited for him to finish the set, then leaping into his arms to tell him the news.

His reaction was the beginning of the end. He looked panicked, muttered a choice swearword, then gave her a fake smile and false words of hope. They would marry, of course. Get a little house in West Seattle. Shop for furniture and dishes. Build a life together.

Two weeks later she lost the baby. Two weeks after that, she lost Dan. He was away on a gig when the bleeding started. By the time he made it to the clinic, it was too late.

He held her and wept with her, but even through a fog of painkillers she saw it. The look of guilty, sad relief in his eyes.

"You're a million miles away," Juanita said. She had

a wonderful smile, her creased face a relief map of a long, well-savored life.

Isabel smiled back. "I guess I was."

Juanita set aside her knitting and wrung a steaming, fragrant cloth into a basin next to her chair. She wrapped the cloth around her right elbow. "Arthritis," she explained.

"Ma, the doc at the clinic said to take the pills and use the heating pad," Theo said.

"My way's better." She looked directly at Isabel. "I use an old Indian salve. Bethroot and wormwood steeped in hot water."

"It smells wonderful," Isabel said. But it was more than that. Just being in this house caused a deep fluctuation inside her. These people didn't question or accuse, but just accepted who she was, what she had done. As Juanita had bustled around the kitchen, getting supper and then steeping her herbs, the old folkways seemed to seep back into Isabel's bones. And to her surprise, it didn't hurt.

The rain stopped as softly as it had begun. Isabel excused herself and walked out onto the rickety front porch. Stars of searing brightness shone over the dark hulks of the mountains. The air smelled of evergreen and fresh water. It was cool at this elevation, and she wrapped the warm shawl tighter around her.

She heard Dan before she saw him. Or rather, she heard the horse. The damp thud of hooves, the occasional ripple and snort, the creak of saddle leather.

It wasn't every day a man came for her on horseback.

He appeared in the darkened yard, a slick, hooded poncho enshrouding him. "And I thought," he said in his rich, silky voice, "that going to Bainbridge to get you was a pain in the ass."

Theo came out on the porch. "You okay, Dan?"

"Yeah. Petunia's good and mad at me, though."

"Petunia?" Isabel asked.

"She came with the name. Won't answer to anything else."

"You can put her up in the barn for the night," Theo said. "Gary'll ride her to your place in the morning. You want to stay here?"

"I'll borrow your truck if you don't mind."

Isabel opened her mouth to protest. Then she thought about the small house, the meager supplies. It wasn't fair to impose on the Sohappys.

But the prospect of spending the night alone in a luxurious wilderness lodge with Dan Black Horse didn't thrill her, either.

Or maybe it thrilled her too much.

# *Five*

"You mean there's a road leading to your place?"

Dan smiled into the dark and ground the pickup's gears a notch higher. "It's an old logging trail. Real old. You have to know where to look for it."

She clutched at the edge of the seat as they bounced over a rut. "Good," she said. "Then you'll have a way to get me home tomorrow."

He said nothing. He didn't want her to go home tomorrow. More than that, he didn't want her to insist on going home tomorrow.

Finally, he asked, "Did you like the Sohappys?"

"Very much."

"They're my nearest neighbors."

"I was lucky Gary found me."

"He's a good kid. Wasn't always, but he is now."

"He told me you hope to get the Seahawks up here. Why didn't you tell me?"

He drove to the front of the lodge and parked. "Because now it might not happen."

"Why not?"

Dan killed the engine and draped his forearms over the steering wheel, turning his head to look at her. The rain had ruined her fancy hairstyle and made it glossy and straight. He liked it better that way.

"'Cause I stole their promoter's girlfriend," he said.

"Oh, please." She jerked the door open and jumped out, climbing the porch steps to the front door.

"Go on in," Dan said. "It's not locked."

She hurried in. He'd built a fire in the hearth of the main lounge, and the leaping flames seemed to draw her. He stood behind her, watching her tense movements and feeling such a surge of tenderness and passion that his chest hurt.

"Look," she said, staring as if mesmerized by the fire. "Number one, I wish you'd been straight with me and told me about your business with Anthony. And second, you didn't 'steal' his girlfriend."

"Borrowed, then?" Dan suggested.

"I don't belong to either of you. He was amazingly understanding when I called him today."

"Then he's a fool." Dan took her by the shoulders and turned her to face him. "Like I was a long time ago. I never should have let you go, Isabel."

Just for a moment, she swayed toward him.

An unbearable tension seized him; he wanted to cover her mouth with his, to taste her and plunge his hands into her hair.

Then she seemed to catch herself and pulled back. "There was never a question of you 'letting' me go. I left. That's all there is to it."

"Then why are you crying, Isabel?" he whispered.

She lifted her hand to her cheek and seemed surprised to feel tears. "It's been a long day," she said in an unsteady voice.

He took her hand, the one that was wet with her tears. "Come on. Your room's ready."

She seemed a little dazed as she followed him upstairs. He gave her his favorite room, the one Juanita had done in timber green, with a wall hanging depicting a dogwood blossom.

A man's flannel pajama top lay folded on the bed. Isabel looked at him questioningly.

He grinned. "It's one of mine."

"But you never—" Her face flushed as she broke off.

"Nope, not when I lived in the city. It gets cold up here. I didn't get the heaters up and running until a few months ago." He handed her the nightshirt and pointed her toward the massive bath and dressing room done in gleaming green tile and chrome-and-glass brick. "I'll go make you a pot of tea. Okay?"

Her brief smile was weary and resigned. She disappeared into the bathroom, and he went to make the tea.

When he returned with a tray a short time later, he stopped in the doorway, propped his shoulder on the doorjamb and grinned. She was already in bed, fast asleep.

Isabel awoke amid snowdrifts of eiderdown comforters. This was, she decided with an indulgent stretch, the most decadent bed she had ever slept in. It was also the most restful night she'd had since she could remember.

Then, peevishly, she figured that walking for miles in the rain was bound to make anyone sleepy.

She bathed in the sunken oval tub with the massage jets turned on full blast. She left it only when she realized how hungry she was. Wrapping herself in a thick terry-cloth robe that had been draped over a towel warmer, she finger combed her hair and helped herself to a new toothbrush that lay on the counter.

Then she went in search of her clothes, not relishing the thought of putting on the damp, muddied skirt and top. She was amazed to find the clothes, along with her espadrilles and a cable-knit cardigan sweater, on a luggage bench just inside the door. Everything had been cleaned for her.

She found Dan in the kitchen, locked in a staredown with a can of biscuits.

Unable to stifle a laugh, she said, "You just have to press a spoon on the seam, and it'll pop open."

He glanced up and grinned at her. She blinked, and for a moment her legs felt wobbly. Dan had always had a dazzling smile, one that caught at her heart and made her fiercely proud to be the object of it.

He handed her a spoon and the can of biscuits. "I've never been big on breakfast."

"I remember."

His gigs had kept him out late every night. The next day, he usually staggered down to the espresso stand on the corner for latte and biscotti.

As she popped open the can, he watched with amazement and asked, "Is that legal?"

Laughing again, she peeled apart the biscuits and put them on a baking tray. He slid it into the oven and poured them each a mug of coffee. "It's good to hear you laugh, Isabel."

"I slept well last night."

"Pretty quiet up here, isn't it?"

She added cream and sugar to her coffee. "I can't believe you washed my clothes."

"As survival skills go, laundry isn't too much of a challenge."

"I remember a time when you couldn't toast bread."

"I've figured a few things out." His voice dropped, and his strong brown hand closed over hers. "Isabel."

She knew she should take her hand away. She knew she should insist on going back to the city immediately. She knew she should not be feeling this overwhelming attraction to a man who had broken her heart.

Yet she simply sat there in the bright, sunlit kitchen alcove, sipping coffee and holding hands with Dan Black Horse.

It was wrong. So why didn't it feel wrong?

She felt warm and dreamy and relaxed. She loved the way he looked in the sunlight through the window, his long hair gleaming, his denim shirt parted at the throat to reveal his tanned chest, his dangerous smile and his deep brown-black eyes.

*I've missed you.*

She almost said it. Then the oven timer went off, and they jumped simultaneously. Dan retrieved the biscuits and brought them to the table with butter and honey.

While they ate, he talked. "I always thought I'd have no trouble handling the band's success," he said. "But when it started happening for us, it never quite felt right. I guess you could say it messed with my internal chemistry or something." He ran a hand through his loose hair. "I didn't fit into my own life anymore. The tours, the schmoozing, the politics, putting up with Jack and Andy and all their problems…" He shook his head. "I kept waiting to feel like myself again. To do something real."

A faint smile curved his mouth. "'The great mother calls home her own.' That's how my grandfather explained it. Once I found this place again, there was no way I could ever go back to what I had before."

"I read about your departure from the band," she said. It had been all over the local arts journals.

He waved his hand. "We hung together for as long as we could. Had a few laughs, made some good money. I pick up the guitar now and then when I'm in the mood. That's enough for me now."

She looked out the window and saw a bird land on a tangled marionberry bush at the edge of the yard. "What time is it? I really need to be getting back."

His eyes hardened almost imperceptibly. He had never been big on clocks and schedules. It was one of the things she had found so charming about him at first, so exasperating later.

He squinted at the clock on the stove. "Looks like around noon."

"Noon!" She almost choked on her biscuit as she shot to her feet. "I can't believe I overslept."

"No such thing as oversleeping at this lodge. That's a house rule."

"But—"

He stood and pressed a finger lightly to her lips. She tried to ignore the frankly sensual feeling that simmered inside her.

"Listen," he said, slowly taking his hand away. "I

remember what you said about your busy week. But you can't get any of that done on Sunday. At least take a look around, Isabel. See what I've done with the place."

She remembered how petty she had felt yesterday for ignoring his accomplishments. After he took her home, she would never see him again. The least she could do was admire what he had built.

The rain had washed the forest clean. Everything was a rich, glistening green. A light breeze shivered through the trees. Isabel felt a piercing sense of connection with this place, and she understood Dan's affinity for it.

They walked along a path to the stables. The long, low building, surrounded by a fenced yard, housed four horses, three of whom put out their heads to see who had come. Isabel patted one hesitantly on the nose.

"You never did care for horses, did you?" Dan asked.

"You know why. My father died—killed himself—in the Yakima Suicide Race." She winced at the memory. She had been ten years old. With a gang of other men from the reservation, he had joined the dangerous cross-country race on horseback, hurtling down almost vertical ravines, leaping streams and fallen trees. Her father had plunged off a ninety-foot cliff to his death.

The next year, an animal-rights group had outlawed the use of horses in the race, and it was presently run on motorcycles. Of course, that was too late for her father—and also for her mother and Isabel.

She stared at the big bay horse. "It wasn't the horse's fault any more than a car wreck is the car's fault."

"The race is different now," Dan said.

"And how would you know?"

"I know," he said simply. "The local wineries are really big on sponsoring the race. It's—" He broke off, as if he thought better of what he was going to say. "Come on." He took her hand and continued the tour, showing her the best places to fish for salmon and trout, a shed where the white-water kayaks and rafts were stored, an equipment barn crammed with a tractor, an off-road motorcycle, a mower, a snowmobile, cross-country skis, fishing and rain gear.

She studied him, leaning against the rough-cedar building, surrounded by soaring trees, and she couldn't suppress a smile.

"What?" he asked.

"How does the saying go? 'The difference between men and boys is the price of their toys.' You have every toy."

He laughed. "No golf clubs yet."

"This all must have cost you a fortune."

He pushed away from the wall. "Everything I had. People are supposed to want to come here and play."

"So you're counting on getting this contract with the team."

"It'd keep me out of debtors' prison." He sent her a devilish grin. "Do they still have debtors' prison?"

As they started back up toward the lodge, she thought, what an adventure this was. It made her plant nursery on Bainbridge seem dull.

But safe. Very safe.

Dan showed Isabel the beginnings of the garden Juanita had started for him. Tiny herb, flower and vegetable seedlings sprang from rows of damp black soil.

Isabel surveyed the area, cordoned off from deer and rabbits with electrified wire. Here was something she knew, something quiet and orderly like the life she had made for herself.

She walked along stepping stones between the rows, enchanted by the old-fashioned homeyness of the garden. The foxglove were the sort raised a century ago, antique strains she rarely saw these days.

She stooped to pinch off a sprig of fragrant Yakima tea, used for brewing or making potpourri. "This is a little more familiar territory."

Dan leaned back against the garden gate. "How did you get into selling plants, anyway?"

"The temp agency I was working for sent me to Bainbridge to set up work files for a nursery. I ended up staying on, eventually taking over the management of the whole business."

He moved toward her, plucking the tender cutting from her fingers and dropping it to the ground. "And you're happy growing plants, selling them?"

"Well, of course," she said. His proximity raised a tingling awareness in her. She stepped back, feeling a little defensive. "I guess it doesn't compare with grunge-rock tours and wild-man adventures, but it's perfectly fine and I'm good at it."

"And your plans to marry?" A dangerous edge crept into Dan's voice. "Also perfectly fine?"

"Yes," she said too quickly.

"So you're not looking for anything better than 'fine.'"

Somehow, without her realizing it, Dan had backed her against the garden gate. He was so close that she could see him in sharp detail—the regal sweep of his cheekbones, his coal-black lashes like individual spears around bottomless dark eyes.

Isabel had always known Dan Black Horse possessed a special magic. The critics and music fans knew it, too; in a matter of a few short months, they had boosted him from obscurity to stardom. And then the rest of the country discovered him—on the covers of trade and fan magazines, on CD and concert posters.

Even those who had never heard his music were drawn to him. It was that aura he had, a subtle yet wrenching wounded look that made people stare and wonder and ache for him.

"I can't do this," she said in a choked whisper.

His hands rested easily on the top of the gate on either side of her. He wasn't touching her, but he was like the electric fence—falsely benign, waiting, ready to administer a hot shock if she dared to touch.

"Can't do what?" he asked.

"This… Be with you, damn it! Be near you."

"Why not?"

"I can't think straight," she blurted out. "You're playing games with me, and it's not fair."

He didn't move a muscle, but his eyes and mouth hardened almost imperceptibly. "I wish you'd listen to yourself, Isabel. You're standing there admitting you still have feelings for me."

The words hit her like a punch in the stomach. For a moment, she couldn't breathe, and her eyes watered as a tearing pain swept through her. His image blurred and softened, and she felt as if she were drifting toward him, closer, her hands already anticipating the rough-denim, hard-muscled texture of him.

But before she could move or speak or make sense of what was happening, Dan shoved back from the gate and stalked away. Stricken, she stared at his long, slim, retreating form. Then she saw that Gary Sohappy was riding into the yard on the horse called Petunia. He and Dan spoke for a moment. Gary held a parcel wrapped in a hooded sweatshirt under his arm. He handed it to Dan and dismounted.

Isabel left the garden to say hello to Gary and to thank him again for finding her last night. When she reached them, she stopped short and gasped, spying the bundle in Dan's hands.

"What happened?"

"Not sure," Gary said. "I found her on the way up here."

*She* was a bald eagle. Only her head was visible, sharply defined in line and color. The great hooked beak was vivid yellow, the eyes bright obsidian, the distinctive head sleek and white.

Gary's hands were covered in scratches. "She was pretty hard to catch," he said with a grin.

Dan held the bird under his arm. "Get inside and wash up, Gary. Use the disinfectant soap. We'll be in the barn."

Isabel picked up the trailing reins of the horse and followed Dan.

He stared at the bundle. "Ever seen a bald eagle close up before?"

"No." She was riveted. The bird was watchful, almost brooding. "I had no idea they were so large. How did Gary know it was a female?"

The bird pecked at Dan's arm. He winced. "Her temperament?"

"Sexist," Isabel muttered.

In the barn, she tethered the mare in cross ties and went with Dan into a small tack room. Barrels of feed stood along one wall beneath an array of reins. Dan set the bird carefully in a dry sink. The eagle struggled, fighting the makeshift bandage. There was something heartbreaking about seeing such a majestic creature floundering and helpless in an alien environment.

But apparently Dan's voice worked on the bird, too. "Shh," he said, and spoke a patois of English and Yakima in a mesmerizing singsong. He used his hands with a light, knowing touch, stroking the smooth feathers and even the sharp beak with one hand, while the other hand unwrapped the bird. She still acted edgy, as if ready to explode into flight at any moment.

Except that she couldn't fly, and as soon as Dan set aside the sweatshirt, they saw why. One wing hung limp. Isabel could see a little blood.

"Must've been wounded in the storm," Dan said. "I don't think the wing's broken, so that's something." He kept up his singsong patter as he opened a metal wall chest to reveal a selection of horse liniments, containers with handwritten labels, jars with rusting lids, a few giant syringes. Dan selected a plastic bottle of antibiotic powder and dusted the wound with it.

The bird erupted into a panic. Dan gathered it awkwardly to his chest and held it there, grimacing as a set of talons sank into his forearm.

Isabel bit her lip. "What can I do?"

He shrugged. "Hell, I don't know. We should probably immobilize this wing."

"Let's try that."

Even with Gary helping them, it took over an hour to bind the wing. The bird had the temper of a pit bull, with razor talons and a can-opener beak to back it up. By the time they had fashioned a bandage of gauze, all three of them bore a few nicks.

Gary lined a crate with straw and positioned it under a single lightbulb for warmth. He placed the bird inside, and they stood back, watching. The bird still had fire in her eye and a haughty air, and her chest rose and fell rapidly. Gary went to put up the horse.

"I guess we should feed it something," Dan said.

She shuddered. "Don't eagles eat raw meat?"

"I think so," he said.

"Couldn't we try a can of tuna fish or something?"

As they walked up to the house, Dan draped an arm across her shoulders. The movement was so natural and felt so right that before Isabel even thought about it, she leaned her head into his shoulder. His knuckles grazed her cheek, and she shivered.

"I should get my purse," she said, wondering why her voice sounded so lifeless and flat. "I guess we'd better get started for Seattle."

"Nope." His stride didn't falter as they mounted the steps.

Isabel stopped and looked at him. "What do you mean?"

He gave her a smile that raised a hollow ache in her chest. "Too late, Isabel."

"Anthony said to take all the time I needed. I'll never be too late for—"

"I mean too late in the day. It's dark out."

She blinked, then looked around. Through the black-leafed trees, the sky was deep purple with twilight.

"You're stuck with me for one more night, Isabel," he said unapologetically, then turned and went inside.

# *Six*

The next morning, Dan caught his breath when Isabel walked into the kitchen. He had probably, at some point, seen a more beautiful sight, but for the life of him, he couldn't remember when.

Her face was scrubbed clean, her hair slightly damp from the shower. She wore a gray sweat suit with the University of Washington seal on the front. The soft folds of fabric enveloped her small frame.

She helped herself to coffee. "I found the sweat suit in the closet in my room. I hope you don't mind."

"'Course not, Isabel. It's chilly this morning." He rose and handed her the sugar bowl.

She smelled like every warm, fragrant dream that haunted a man in the dead of winter. When she didn't fuss with her hair, it relaxed into a long waterfall of silk he wanted to bury his fingers in.

"Did you check on the bird?" she asked.

"A couple of times in the night, and then at the crack of dawn."

What he didn't tell her was that he had also stood in her room in the dark, watching her sleep while wave after wave of tenderness and regret rolled over him.

Five years ago, she had slipped into his heart through a side entrance when he thought he had barred all the doors. He set his jaw and clenched his eyes shut, remembering.

The day she had told him about the baby was branded on his memory. She was so thrilled and so scared. So was he. No, he was terrified.

His feelings for her suffered from some sort of paralysis. Too young and too thickheaded to understand that the first bloom of love needed to deepen and ripen and mature, too stupid to see that responsibility wouldn't stifle him, he'd panicked.

Her grief and rage over the miscarriage provided him with the opportunity to escape. Like a fool, he took it.

"Dan?" Her voice intruded on his thoughts.

He opened his eyes and blinked at her.

"Is the bird okay?"

"Yeah." He couldn't stop staring at her.

She took a sip of her coffee, regarding him over the rim of her mug. "Are *you* okay?"

His grip on the edge of the tile counter tightened. He had to anchor himself somewhere, to something, or he would explode. "Yeah. Only—"

"Only what?"

"I always thought you were the one who left five years ago, Isabel."

"And now what do you think?" She seemed to have no trouble switching into his train of thought. He could almost believe the past was on her mind, too.

"Physically, you left, you walked out. But I didn't give you many options. Stay in hell with me or save yourself. Not much choice there."

She started to move away. "We were young—"

"*Were* young," he echoed harshly, grasping her wrist. "We're different now, and you know it."

She was breathing hard with some inner struggle. Dan made himself let go of her hand. "Sorry." He carried her cup to the table for her.

Both of them were edgy and emotional this morning. Dan's nerve endings felt raw with desperation. All he knew for certain was that he could not stand the thought of her getting married to someone else. He had no idea what alternative he could offer her, but he had to make her see that what they had shared was not over. It would never be over.

"Did the eagle eat the tuna fish?" she asked, shifting gears again.

"Some. It didn't seem to be to her taste." Dan forced himself to release his need for her at the moment. There was an intensity to his feelings that she would probably find frightening. He had to back off, get a grip. "I tried canned salmon this morning. She picked at that. I was thinking we could try to get her some fresh fish today. It'd probably be better for her."

"We should," Isabel said quickly.

He grinned. "Any excuse to go fishing."

She grinned back. "Any excuse."

Dan felt as if a time bomb were ticking somewhere at the back of his mind. If he mentioned it to Isabel, it might go off. If he didn't mention it, it might go off anyway.

Armed with rods, a creel and a picnic lunch, they plodded in hip boots down to the lake. Isabel looked vibrant, as beautiful and understated as a doe in a forest grove—and as fragile.

*All right,* he thought. *Say it.*

He stopped walking and touched her shoulder. "I meant to ask you earlier. If you need to make a call, I can radio someone in town—"

"It's okay." Color stained her cheekbones. "Anthony said I should take all the time I need."

"Anthony is a first-class fool," Dan said, "and I thank God for that."

She started walking again, so he couldn't see her reaction to his words. "He's always been very understanding. And I've always been moody. So it's a perfect match."

"Yeah, right."

At the lakeshore, they waded in, flailing their arms to keep from falling as the mud sucked at their boots. After they tired of standing, they slogged ashore and took off their boots. Dan rolled out a thick fiber mat so they could recline. Isabel baited her own hook, arguing volubly about the merits of canned corn versus salmon eggs. She looked gorgeous, fitting the scene like an emerald in a perfect setting. Before Dan's eyes, she seemed to relax, the inner tightness he sensed in her uncoiling.

Mother Earth doing her sacred duty, he decided whimsically. As he lay back on the mat and let the warmth of the sun bathe him, he imagined he could feel the slow, steady heartbeat of the earth beneath him, a subtle, comforting rhythm that he had ignored for too long. He had been deaf to it until his grandfather, filled with a dying man's reflective wisdom, had awakened him to it once again.

Perhaps that was what Isabel was feeling now, that sense of homecoming.

She glanced at him. "What are you thinking?"

He sent her a lazy smile. "That it's a perfect fishing day." He touched her slim thigh with one finger and traced it gently, teasingly. "Enough nibbles to keep things interesting, but not so many that it starts…to feel…like work."

She laughed—a little nervously, he thought—and shifted away from him. "You're a bad influence, Dan. I don't think I've spent so many hours doing nothing and—" She bit her lip.

"And loving every minute of it?" he asked in a low voice. "To an outside observer, it might look like not much is going on." He touched a lock of hair at her temple. "But there's plenty happening here, Isabel. We'd both be lying if we said otherwise."

Isabel had no idea how long she had been sleeping. The excitement of fishing again—something she hadn't done since her father had taught her—must have worn her out. But she hadn't realized a nap in the fresh air could give her such a sense of renewal. She awoke to blink at the late-afternoon sun, squinting through breeze-blown leaves, listening to the soft lapping of the lake on the shores and to the quiet cadence of Dan's breathing.

He had fallen asleep, too. In his faded jeans and plaid shirt and hiking boots, a John Deere cap pulled down over his eyes, he was the consummate woodsman—

wholly masculine, with a rugged splendor that made him a part of the forest and mountains.

Something still existed between them, some magnetic attraction. She could no longer deny that. But for now, she refused to shape the idea into words. She was simply taking the time she needed—

Needed for *what?* asked the wary cynic inside her. To rediscover that, yes, Dan Black Horse was still the sexiest, most fascinating man she could ever hope to meet? And to rediscover that he still had the power to break her heart?

Helping herself to a long drink of lemonade from the thermos, she scowled at him. "You're not doing me any favors, Dan Black Horse."

He awoke with a luxurious, long-bodied stretch that made her hormones jolt into overdrive. "What's that?" he asked in a sleepy voice, taking the thermos from her.

"Nothing," she snapped. "You—" A buzzing sound interrupted her. With reflexes tuned perfectly by instinct, she pounced on her rod and set the hook. Moments later, she reeled in a plump, silvery trout, by far the best catch of the day. Laughing, she said, "I *told* you I was right about the corn."

He laughed with her, and the tension dissolved. They packed up their gear and hiked back to the lodge.

The eagle snapped up a small fish in her big yellow beak. She scarfed another, then cocked her head, waiting for more.

"She likes sushi," Dan said.

Isabel clutched his arm and nodded. "I think we're spoiling her. She won't know how to survive in the wild after this."

"She's a grown bird. I don't think a few days with us will make her lose her taste for the wild." His finger traced a shivery line down the side of Isabel's throat. "Right?"

Stung, she lurched away. "I need a bath," she said hastily. "It's been a long day."

He winked at her. "It's not over yet."

She luxuriated in the tub, letting the massage jets pummel her muscles. She loved the sense of unreality that enveloped her here at Dan's lodge. She was remote, detached from the rest of the world.

*Free.*

But *free* was just a nice word people used instead of *lonely,* or maybe *desperate.*

What Isabel had wanted—had *always* wanted—was a sense of connectedness. To know that she belonged.

Anthony was perfect for her. He came fully equipped, a package deal with a large, loving family that surrounded and enveloped her like a hand-stitched quilt. *He* was what she needed.

Not Dan Black Horse with the heartbreak in his eyes and a body that promised enough forbidden pleasure to make her legally insane.

She realized she had been in the tub brooding for far too long. Feeling sheepish, she got out and dressed in her skirt and top and the cardigan sweater Dan had loaned her yesterday.

She stood in front of the mirror wishing for mousse and a curling iron until she realized what she was doing, what she was thinking.

It shouldn't matter how she looked for Dan.
But oh, God. It did.


"That smells heavenly," she said, a soft smile curving her mouth. "When did you learn to cook?"

"It's not cooking, it's grilling." Dan grinned at her as he set down a platter of trout and vegetables. His long, glossy hair was still damp from the shower, and he smelled of soap and wood smoke.

He served a chilled local wine and even lit candles on the dining-hall table. They sat across from each other and lifted their glasses.

For Isabel, the moment froze in time. In the blink of an eye, she was hurled back to the night she had told him about the baby. After she'd told him the news, she'd had ginger ale and he'd had beer, but they had laughed and clinked their glasses and made promises with no idea how to keep them.

The soft *chink* of his glass against hers brought her back to the present. "Isabel?" he said in his low, rough voice. "What'll we drink to?"

"The eagle's health?" she suggested, pleased that her voice did not sound as wobbly as she felt.

He chuckled and made the toast. Isabel grew warm and flushed with the good food and the chilled wine, and the moments slipped past.

She glanced out the big bay window to see violet shadows streaking the mountains. "I suppose," she said, "you'll tell me it's too late in the day to start for Seattle."

"Isabel?" His large hand covered hers.

"Yes?" The wine and his nearness gave her a pleasant, floating sensation.

"It's too late to start for Seattle."

"What a surprise to hear you say that." She forced herself to stop smiling. "Tomorrow, then," she said decisively. "First thing."

"Seeing as how you've been getting up at the crack of noon, that shouldn't be a problem."

"It's easy to sleep here," she blurted out.

His hand lifted to her face, knuckles grazing the curve of her cheek. "I'm glad you like the lodge."

"I didn't say I—"

"You didn't have to." His finger made a tender exploration, finding the shape of her chin and then tracing her lips until she almost cried out for mercy.

"Dan—"

"We could go somewhere," he said lightly.

"Where?"

He didn't answer, but got up and took her hand. He held out a leather jacket, and when she slid her arms into the slick lining and felt its comforting weight on her shoulders, she nearly wept with the poignancy of her memories.

He had owned the leather jacket for as long as she had known him. Its shape was his shape. Its scent was his scent. It seemed to carry the very essence of him, to envelop her with the intimacy of a lover's embrace.

He seemed not to notice the effect it had on her as he took her hand and led her out to the shed where he kept his Harley.

She asked no questions, and he offered no explanations. She simply got on, wrapped her arms around him, closed her eyes and leaned her cheek against his back. She felt protected and alive as never before.

The bike roared down the mountain, headlights

sweeping the wooded slopes. She had complete faith in his driving. Even at night, he knew the wilderness like an old song memorized in his youth.

After a while, they came to a dirt road, and a few miles beyond that, the paved one. Isabel was startled and intrigued when they rolled into the town of Thelma.

# *Seven*

"I can't believe you brought me to a dance," Isabel said, standing in the foyer of the fire hall.

Dan grinned and slid his leather jacket off her shoulders. "We used to go dancing a lot."

She turned her head and sent him a wry look. "Getting crushed in the cramped space of some seedy concert hall was never quite my idea of a good time."

"You should have said something. Shouldn't have let me drag you along." He exchanged greetings with Sarah Looking, who was in charge of the coat check, and handed her the jacket.

Isabel gave a little laugh, though he noticed the strained sound of it. "I wanted to be where you were, Dan."

*Do you now?* he wanted to ask her. *Do you want to be where I am now?*

"I guess I didn't really know where I wanted to be," he said, leading her into the dance hall. "But I never meant to force you to do anything that made you uncomfortable."

"You never did, not really."

He drew her against him for a dance. The ersatz country swing music was whiny and slow, but somehow satisfying. It was, he conceded, more than likely the fact that he was dancing with Isabel. She felt like heaven in his arms, her frame supple and willowy, her soft hand cradled in his, her face shy and shadowy in the dim light.

"Care to ditch that no-count Indian for a cowboy, ma'am?" someone asked.

Isabel gasped in outrage, but Dan stepped back, laughing.

Clyde Looking, head of the tribal council, lifted his ten-gallon hat in greeting, and Dan made the introductions. Within moments, Clyde danced away with Isabel, and Dan eased back to the refreshment table to help himself to a drink.

Lucy Raintree served him. Theo Sohappy stopped by. People were easy with one another, chatting and joking, some just smiling and tapping their feet to the overdone percussion from the cheap keyboard. The music should have made Dan cringe, but instead it was as comforting as a greeting from an old friend. Later, he would perform a song or two; he always did.

Dan felt—had felt from the start—an unexpected sense of community with these people. The feeling had always eluded him in the city. He'd had friends, sure, but with them he had never found this level of comfort, this quiet settling of the soul.

Dan had never known he was missing it, but maybe it was part of the reason he had been so savage inside, had made mistakes on important matters. Like Isabel.

Had he ever told her he loved her?

"So she's still here." Theo watched Isabel dance with Clyde Looking. "And you didn't even have to tie her up to make her stay."

Dan laughed, his eyes following the dancers. Clyde was the perfect host, pausing in his two-step now and then to introduce Isabel to someone new. She looked flushed and bright-eyed. Dan had feared she would feel awkward here, that her laughter and conversation would seem forced, but he could tell her enjoyment was genuine.

"Nope," he said, "I didn't tie her up, not that the thought didn't cross my mind."

"Don't blame you. God, she's a looker. Part Indian?"

"Yeah, but she was raised in an Anglo foster home."

"Ma told her she had to step out of the shadows, be herself. You know how Ma is."

"If anybody can thaw out Isabel, Juanita can," Dan said.

Theo clapped him on the shoulder. "Looks like you did a pretty good job of that yourself. Is she going to stay for the race?"

Dan felt a twinge of apprehension. He was signed up to ride his motorcycle in the Yakima Suicide Race. He owed it to Isabel to tell her, but he just hadn't found the right time. She'd try to talk him out of it. And he already knew he wouldn't listen.

"I don't know, Theo," he said. "I guess that's up to her." His gaze was riveted to Isabel. The song ended, and she excused herself from Clyde and made a beeline for the pay phone in the corner of the hall by the drinking fountain.

Dan's gut sank like a stone. Quite obviously, nothing had changed, and she couldn't wait to call her boyfriend and tell him so.

Everything had changed, and Isabel knew she could no longer put off calling Anthony. Her fingers felt cold as she lifted the receiver and dialed his number, punching in her credit-card code and then waiting with growing impatience through six rings.

The answering machine kicked on. She listened to the bland, cheery message, then said, "Anthony, it's me, Isabel. If you're there, pick up. We need to talk. You see—"

"Sure, babe." Anthony Cossa's real voice interrupted her. "What's up? Are you ready to return to civilization yet?"

"The lodge up here doesn't have a phone. I'm in a town called Thelma."

"Listening to lousy country music, if I'm hearing the background noise right." He laughed easily.

"I was planning to come back sooner, but something came up. A couple of things." She had no idea where to begin, what to tell him, what was fair. An injured eagle? An unresolved past? A sudden need to look into a part of herself she had kept in the dark for years?

"Having second thoughts, babe?" Anthony asked.

She could discern no inflection in his voice. She tried to picture him—he was probably wearing khakis or jeans, in his pristine Santa Fe–style condo on Western Avenue, drinking a beer from a microbrewery and being paged every sixty seconds while channel surfing on his forty-eight-inch TV.

She tried to remember the last time they had shared a bottle of wine and just listened to music for a few uninterrupted hours. She tried to remember the last time they had gone dancing.

"Isabel?" he prompted.

"Anthony, I just don't know. Saturday, I saw our whole lives rolling out ahead of us like a giant red carpet. But now—"

"Now what?" Still she heard no sharpness in his voice, just curiosity.

"Maybe the red carpet took a left turn somewhere. I'm having to take a good look at myself, Anthony, and—"

"Just a sec. I have another call coming in." He clicked off.

She stood staring at the telephone keypad, wondering whether or not she had a right to be irritated.

"Okay." Anthony was back. "I've got someone on hold. Long-distance."

She was leaning heavily toward being irritated now.

"So what do you want to do?" he asked. "Postpone the wedding? Call it off?"

She felt the burn of tears in her eyes. "Your family has everything all planned—"

"My family," he said. "That's really what all this is about, isn't it? That's what it's always been about."

"I adore your family, Anthony. I'd hate myself if I disappointed them."

"Yeah, well, look. You do whatever it is you have to do to get your head straight, and call me tomorrow, okay, babe?"

"Yes, but—"

"I better take this other call. Talk to you soon." He was gone with a gentle click.

Isabel stood with the receiver still held to her ear and

leaned her forehead against the cold, shiny metal of the pay phone. She'd believed she belonged with Anthony. She had thrived on the fast pace of his lifestyle, and he had seemed eager to move to Bainbridge Island in order to be with her.

But his abruptness and bland reaction had seemed exaggerated in their phone conversation. Perhaps it was the odd juxtaposition of hearing Anthony's voice in a fire hall in Thelma. Or perhaps it was the things Clyde had said about Dan still echoing in her ears.

According to Clyde, Dan had saved the tribal council—the whole town, for that matter—from financial collapse. The lodge enterprise had employed people who hadn't had jobs in years.

Of course, Clyde had said cautiously, Dan had run through a lot of his own money getting started. A *lot* of money.

The rapid-fire beep of the off-the-hook-phone signal startled her. She quickly replaced the receiver in the cradle and turned.

Dan stood a few feet back, watching her.

The sight of him made the breath catch in her throat. He had always been easy in his tall, broad-shouldered frame, and he seemed so now, with his weight shifted to one leg and a thumb stuck into his belt. He was backlit by the muted lamps in the hall so that she could not see his face, only the inky waves of his long hair.

He was too far away to have heard her conversation, yet she felt a heated blush rise in her cheeks as if she had been caught doing something wrong.

Ridiculous. *He* was the whole reason she was in this dilemma. If it had not been for him, she would still be in the bosom of the Cossa family, getting ready for her wedding.

Moments passed. They both stood unmoving. Some part of Isabel yearned for him so fiercely that she nearly wept. Then, before she could decide whether or not to go to him, he turned on his heel and strode away.

She felt a deep, invisible agony rip through her, but she stood there mute and helpless. She wanted to be angry, wanted to blame him for her doubts, but he was ignoring her, stalking past dancing couples and groups of people chatting together.

She should not have been surprised when he stepped onto the low platform and picked up an acoustic guitar. But she was. Somehow, she had managed to forget that Dan was a musician, a performer. An artist.

The lights dropped even lower, and the other musicians tapered down the tune they were playing. The fiddler set a mike in front of Dan.

He was surrounded by shadow, alone in a pool of light as he had been when she had seen him for the first time. As perhaps he had always been. When he lifted an unseeing gaze to the listeners in the room, her heart lurched. How well she remembered that unfathomable look.

His long brown hands worked magic on the battered old guitar, drawing out chords of melancholic sweetness. It was the music of lonely places in the heart, of chances missed, of lost souls looking for a welcome somewhere.

Dan's gift with music had not diminished since his retirement. Instead, Isabel knew instantly that his talent had intensified and deepened. He had come back to the place where his soul had been made, and she heard a new awareness in his mesmerizing voice.

The words were simple, a refrain that rang true, that made women reach out and sidle closer to the men beside them, and made the men gently take the hands of their partners.

Through it all, Isabel stood alone, stricken, watching, knowing only one thing for certain.

She had never stopped loving Dan Black Horse.

There. She admitted it to herself. And it was the truest thought she'd had in years. She had let anger and fear eclipse her love and darken her heart, but the love had never gone away. It had just been obscured by a hundred other things. And she had allowed it. So had Dan.

But somehow, he had found a way to look back at what had happened and to learn from what he saw. That was what it was all about. His song, and his abduction of her, the whole crazy weekend.

The song ended with a smattering of applause. Dan grinned and chatted for a few minutes with the musicians. Then he walked straight to Isabel.

"Now what?" he asked, keeping his distance, watching her, waiting.

"Now—" Isabel's mouth felt dry as dust. If she followed her heart, there would be no turning back. Yet she had never felt more certain of anything in her life. "Now we go home."

# *Eight*

Dan wasn't sure what she meant, but he knew what he wanted her to mean. He said, "I'll get your coat," and then nothing more as they rode back to the lodge.

After putting up the bike, he took her hand and started walking across the yard. The moon was up, and spidery shadows crept across the damp ground. The quiet was all pervasive, pierced only by the hollow hoot of an owl.

Dan stopped walking and looked down at her, at the fine, silvery light in her hair. Her breathing was quick and uncertain. He gently brushed a stray strand of hair back from her cheek. He wondered about that phone call she had made, but he didn't ask. He'd find out soon enough.

"Now what?" she asked, echoing his own question to her. She gazed up at him, looking as lost and lonely as she had the first time he'd seen her.

He felt a surge of tenderness as he slid his arms around her waist and pulled her close.

"Now this," he murmured, and settled his mouth on

hers. He kissed her in a way that left no question as to his intent. The pressure of his lips urged her to open for him, and his tongue plunged inside, hungry, possessive. His body was so racked with desire that by the time he lifted his head, he could barely speak.

If she said no, he would back off. He had made that promise to her the first time he had kissed her, and he knew he would still honor it now.

When she spoke, it was a breathy whisper. "Yes." And nothing more.

But it was all he needed.

Hand in hand, they walked into the darkened lodge and up the stairs to her room. She had been here only two days, but already her presence was strong in the soft, soapy fragrance that hung in the air, in the overturned paperback book she had left on the bedside table, the shoes she immediately kicked off.

He knew there were things he should say to her, things he should ask her, but talking distracted him from the way he wanted to touch her. He stood behind her and took off the leather jacket she wore, letting it slither to the floor beside the bed. He bent and brushed aside her hair and kissed the tender flesh at the nape of her neck.

A soft sigh slipped from her, and she tilted her head to one side. His lips trailed across her heated skin, tongue flicking out to touch her earlobe, hands moving to her waist to release the front buttons of her knit top. He freed her of the shirt and slid his hands up over her breasts. He slid her skirt down and watched her step out of it. He ran his open-palmed hands up and down the length of her, feeling the contours of her body as if for the first time. She had not changed; she was still petite and slender and soft. So utterly feminine that she made him feel large and clumsy.

She gasped, reaching up and back with her arms and winding them around his neck to bring his mouth down. He turned her and kissed her then, and she brushed against him with an intimate, suggestive movement. She slipped out of her lacy underthings while he undressed, and neither felt awkward, for it was an inevitability that had been waiting for them for years, lying dormant and unacknowledged in their hearts until this searing instant.

They lay back on the bed, cool sheets and billowy eiderdown sighing beneath the weight of their bodies. Dan braced himself up on one elbow and let his caresses ripple down the length of her while he gazed into her face. She wore a slumberous look, moist lips slightly parted, eyes half-closed. Her hands reached for him; then her palms drifted down his sides to his hips. He had to set his jaw and squeeze his eyes shut to regain control.

Not until this moment did he realize the power she had over him. He bent his head and kissed her, drinking from her lips, his hands circling her breasts and then dipping lower, parting her thighs, finding her so ready for him that he could hold off no longer. He moved over her, their mouths still joined. Wanting her pleasure even more than he wanted his own, he lifted his head and waited, muscles straining, for some sign from her. She stared up at him, her shadowed expression unreadable.

"You're not…" he said through clenched teeth, "making this easy."

"Am I supposed to?" she whispered. But there was

a smile in her voice, and her hands drifted down and clasped and guided him, and they were suddenly together as if they had never been apart.

He found a rhythm they both remembered, a dance of the heart that had endured despite the passage of time. She lifted and tilted herself, as giving as the earth in springtime, and her dulcet acceptance filled him and brought him such a shattering pleasure that he saw stars. When a soft cry slipped from her and she arched upward, he knew the reunion was complete, knew that neither of them would ever be the same.

Still their silence persisted, and it was a comfortable stillness, an abatement of worry. Neither spoke; they did not have to. Nor did they want to. That would mean entering the world again, entering reality, facing up to the unresolved matters that hung over them.

Dan gathered her close and made love to her again, slowly this time, lingering over every part of her as if getting reacquainted with an old friend. She gave herself to him with a sigh of surrender. He found all the little delights of her, the hollow of her throat and the tender inside of her wrist, the backs of her knees and inner thighs where the skin was softer, smoother than anything he could imagine. With hands and mouth, he brought her to ecstasy again—and again—until she was sweetly exhausted, snuggling against his chest and growing warm and heavy limbed until, just as dawn tinged the sky, she slept.

She awoke slowly, hovering in a delicious realm somewhere between sleep and waking. Her mind was filled with memories of Dan—his voice, his touch, the taste of his mouth, the shattering power of the passion she had found with him.

Only him.

Willfully, she thrust aside the thought. Just for now, she would not worry about the future. Just for now, she would let herself be warm and lazy and slightly dazed by all that was happening to her.

"Dan." She whispered his name and opened her eyes, but he was gone. He must have gotten up to make coffee. She stretched, feeling interesting aches in certain parts of her body, then went to brush her teeth. Rather than pulling on the terry-cloth robe, she slipped into Dan's leather jacket. Wearing it, feeling its voluminous weight drop from shoulder to midthigh, she felt closer to him.

The jacket should have evoked bitter memories, for she had also worn it the afternoon she had come home from the hospital. Both she and Dan were so silent that day, neither knowing what to say. They both cried and held each other and looked at the doctor's pamphlet explaining how a high percentage of early pregnancies ended in miscarriage; it was generally a natural process and there was no reason they could not try again....

Somehow, they both knew they would not try again. The first time was an accident, but a second time would be deliberate, would force them to commit to permanence in their relationship, no more drifting through the days toward a hazy, shapeless future.

He had not been ready. And when Isabel finally realized that she could no longer wait for the full commitment of his love, she left.

Last night changed everything. Dan had never touched her so deeply, so intimately. He was different now. Settled. Responsible. Ready to love her. She was falling in love all over again. This time, it was for real. This time, it was for keeps.

As she walked bare legged and barefoot down the steps, she felt wicked and wanton. Dan had plucked her out of her controlled, rigid life and plunged her into a world of sensation and emotion. It was scary and sometimes it hurt, but she had never felt so alive.

Her hand encountered a folded piece of paper in the pocket of the jacket. She pulled it out—a flyer of some sort. As she read the words, she stopped on the second-to-last step. The blood froze in her veins. Her heart turned to a block of ice.

"No," she said in a low voice, forcing her legs to start moving again. Surely this was just something Dan had picked up and forgotten to discard. Surely… She forced herself to calm down and made her way to the back of the lodge.

The kitchen was warm and cheery with the scent of coffee. Dan was out on the back porch, leaning against the railing, holding a mug in one hand and an envelope in the other. He was looking out at the mountains.

He wore only jeans, no shirt or shoes. His muscular shoulders and chest gleamed in the muted morning sun, and his hair flowed down his back. The subtle shadow of whiskers softened the harsh line of his jaw.

There was such a stark beauty in him that for a moment Isabel felt completely inadequate. He could not possibly be hers. He was too perfect, too desirable.

Then she remembered her purpose and stepped out onto the porch. The screen door tapped shut behind her, and Dan turned.

His slow, easy smile held every memory of the splendor they had shared the previous night. "Damn, Isabel," he said, his eyes smoldering, "you always were a great dresser." He set down his mug and held out one arm. She went into his embrace, and he kissed her, his mouth tasting of sweet coffee.

"Did you sleep all right?" he asked her.

"Sleeping is about the only thing I can do right around here," she said.

"I can think of a few other things." His hand slipped into the jacket, and his eyebrows lifted. "*Damn*, Isabel. You're naked in there."

She couldn't stifle a laugh as she moved away. His expression told her he had every intention of whisking her back to bed. She welcomed the prospect, of course, but first she had something to ask him.

"What about this?" She held out the flyer.

He hesitated for a heartbeat. The piece of paper dropped from her fingers.

Dan propped one hip on the railing. His face was inscrutable. "The Yakima Suicide Race," he said.

She drew her hands into the sleeves of the jacket. "It has nothing to do with you, Dan. Right?" When he did not answer, she said again, "Right?"

"It's this afternoon," he said, not looking at her. "And I'm entered."

Isabel leaned back against the door and squeezed her eyes shut, hoping against hope that she'd heard wrong. Just the thought of grown men on motorcycles jolting down near-vertical slopes, leaping gullies and skirting cliffs made her nauseous.

"Dan," she said, dragging open her eyes. "My father *died* in that race."

"I know."

"Don't do it, Dan."

"One of the local wineries made the purse worth winning. It could keep me afloat through the summer, long enough to get the cash flow started."

"You won't need any business if you die in the race," she said fiercely. "I can't believe you'd do this to me."

"Will you listen to yourself?" Dan rounded on her. "Your father didn't do a damned thing to you. You've always regarded his death as a deliberate, personal affront. A reason to pretend you're not Indian at all, a reason to hide with your sterile Anglo foster parents and grow flowers on your sterile Anglo island."

His words sliced like cold metal into her. "I don't need this, Dan. I don't need you to say these things to me."

He advanced on her, anger blazing in his eyes, and braced a hand on the door behind her. "Maybe it's time someone *did* say them. Your father's death wasn't about you."

"And this race isn't about me, either," she retorted, glaring up at him, trying to tamp down her feelings of dread. "You're doing this because you blew the deal with Anthony, right?"

Dan said nothing. She took it as an affirmation. "You know," she said softly, "there's a sort of crazy gallantry in what you did. But there's nothing gallant about putting your life at risk."

His jaw tightened dangerously. "Isabel, don't do this. Don't make me choose."

"I can't make you do a damned thing," she said. "I never could."

# Nine

"Why are we stopping here?" Isabel asked, noting a string of triangular colored flags stretched across the road in Thelma. Yakima Suicide Race, the banner proclaimed.

Resting his hands on the steering wheel of the pickup truck, Gary Sohappy held in the clutch and looked back at the straw-lined crate in the bed of the pickup truck. "I was just trying to decide what would be the best place to let the bird go."

"I don't think it can fly yet."

"Dan said it could." Gary shifted gears and continued down the only paved road in town.

"Dan's been wrong before." She looked at her watch. After their quarrel, she had insisted on coming to town to call Anthony. He had groused a little about having to reschedule a meeting, but he had agreed to meet her in front of the fire hall and take her back to the city.

The prospect left her cold and empty.

Dan had prepared for the race in stony silence. Like a knight of old, he had strapped on armor of black leather, adding shin guards, pads at his knees and elbows and a helmet. He tried to kiss her goodbye; she turned away. Then she turned back in time to see him walking off with long, angry strides.

She opened her mouth to call to him, but no sound came out. He rode off on the motorcycle just as Gary arrived to take her to town, then to take the eagle into the wild and let it go.

One passenger into the wild, one back into her cage. The thought struck Isabel like a blow in the dark, and she gasped.

"Something wrong?" Gary asked.

*Everything,* she thought.

"Where does the race end?" she asked suddenly.

"Huh?"

"The race. I want to see the end of it."

"Same place it does every year. But I thought you had to meet somebody."

"Gary," she said, "I need to see the race."

He grinned. "Okay by me."

Her hands, clutching the door handle, were like ice as the truck bounced off-road and uphill. When the terrain became impassable, Gary parked and they got out. Tall grass swished and sighed in the breeze. Gary went around to the bed of the truck and opened the eagle's crate.

"Is she all right?" Isabel asked.

"I think so—ow! Her talons work just fine." Gary set the eagle on a large rock. The bird perched there, looking haughty and fierce, the breeze ruffling her feathers. Slowly, her wings unfolded.

Isabel held her breath. *Fly,* she thought. *Fly. You can do it.*

The bird let the wind sift through her feathers, then folded her wings back up.

"Not ready," Gary mumbled, clearly disappointed. "I brought my camera and everything." He scooped up the bird and began to climb the hill. "We'll have the best view of the race from Warrior Point," he said over his shoulder.

The cold numbness froze her hands once again, and no matter how hard she tried to drive the dark memories out of her mind, they came at her, as steady and inevitable as the tide.

She knew exactly where Gary was heading.

Because she had stood there and watched her father die. Her memories were as sharp and clear as slides viewed through white light. Her father and his friends were drinking beer. Not a lot—just the usual amount for an afternoon. Her mother laughed with them when her father teased his wife about her concern for his safety.

He kissed them both goodbye, his wife on the lips, his daughter on the top of the head. Isabel saw mirth in his eyes, but something else, too, something too subtle for her to grasp. Now she realized it was a restless hunger. A deep dissatisfaction.

Her father had never held a steady job. Running off on dangerous adventures seemed to be a way of proving himself. Defining who he was—not some reservation idler, but a man.

She understood none of this when she was a girl. She understood only that she had seen her father die.

A group of observers had gone out to the point, Isabel

and her mother included. Isabel was standing, holding hands with her mother. The riders appeared in an explosion of dust and thundering hooves, pouring down a near-vertical gully, leaping a narrow, deep chasm before swinging in a hairpin curve down the side of the mountain.

Only, instead of making the hairpin curve, her father went over a cliff. Isabel stood in disbelieving silence, staring down at his broken figure and the unmoving horse beside him. She remembered one other detail of that moment in time. Her mother—quite deliberately and quite without malicious intent—dropped Isabel's hand.

Isabel's mother completely shut down. She had moved to the city and willingly surrendered Isabel to a foster home.

From that moment onward, confused and angry, Isabel pretended that the past did not exist. She eradicated from her character all Native American values and sensibilities.

Until Dan.

The thought of him drew a gasp of anguish from her.

"We're almost there," Gary said over his shoulder.

"I know," she muttered.

Dan had filled her with his passion and pride and vitality. She had been afraid of the tribal part of him, and perhaps she still was, but he had awakened her to the ancient songs and rhythms she had never quite been able to banish from her heart.

She had loved the tender, whimsical side of him. But she had never understood the dark side, the danger-loving side, the part of him that hungered for tests of his strength, his endurance, his mortality.

She saw the point looming ahead. Little had changed. A line of evergreens grew along a ridge. The valley was a deep cleft formed by the two mountains, with a rushing stream in between, and by gazing across the velvety green gorge, she could see the course the race would follow. It was more like the bed of a waterfall than a path, steep and curving and littered with rocks. And of course, there was the cliff, brooding and sheer, too stark to grow anything but the most tenacious of plants.

She stood and watched. Gary set the bird on the ground. The day was bright and sharply clear. The sound of the wind filled the air. And then she heard it.

The animal rumble of motorcycle engines. The riders were approaching the last and most dangerous leg of the race.

A curious thing happened. The eagle grew restless, bowing out her wings and rushing into the wind; then the bird flung herself off the end of the point. Isabel gasped and Gary laughed in wonder and lifted his camera to his eye. At first, the bird appeared to be falling, helpless, a horrifying sight. Then an eddy of wind caught her beneath her wings. With a high-pitched cry, she was soaring, soaring across the valley that was already alive with the thunder of the race.

Dan felt a little silly wearing the windbreaker bearing the label of a Yakima Valley winery. It was white, and he never wore white, and besides, the zipper was faulty. But in return for their sponsorship, he got a few perks, including deep discounts on his supply of wine for the lodge.

Other riders were similarly garbed, their numbered windbreakers shouting ads for everything from motor oil to masa harina flour.

He knew he would win the race today. Number one, he needed the winnings. Number two, he was riding like the wind. There were simply days when this was true.

Smaller and more nimble than his Harley, the off-road motorcycle seemed an extension of his body, slanting and skating with elastic responsiveness beneath him. He could almost forget the look on Isabel's face when he had tried to say goodbye, hoping she would wish him luck.

She hadn't.

The flavor of danger filled his mouth with a sweetness that turned bitter when he remembered Isabel.

She seemed to think plunging into danger was his way of recoiling from intimacy, that after last night it was no coincidence that he was here today, putting his life on the line. She believed it was his way of avoiding emotional commitment.

He wanted to say she was wrong. But was she?

He set his jaw and prepared for the last and most treacherous part of the race. The windbreaker flew loose, the flimsy zipper breaking as he bolted down a rock-strewn ravine.

A movement caught his eye. He chanced a lightning glance upward and was amazed. A soaring eagle was circling the valley.

He wondered if it could be the eagle they'd rescued. If it was, that meant Isabel was *here*. Watching.

The loose jacket flapped madly. Dan swore under his breath and gritted his teeth, clearing his mind. He had to jump a gully and make a turn before he was in the clear.

He braced himself to soar across the gully. But then the unthinkable happened. The windbreaker caught a gust of wind and flew upward, obscuring his face, blinding him.

He never found a footing on the other side. He just kept going like a stone flung from a sling.

# Ten

There was no hospital in Thelma, so Dan was taken to the tribal clinic across the road from the fire hall. There was no regular doctor, either, but an emergency-room physician from Olympia was on hand for the race.

Isabel did not even recall the frantic drive to town. The clinic personnel had barred her from seeing Dan; she had only glimpsed him as he was whisked past on a gurney. His eyes had been closed, his face pale.

They had promised to report back to her. With panic clawing at her insides, she paced the cool, antiseptic corridor, then finally stepped outside to lean against the cinder-block building.

She thought about praying, but no words would form. She thought about cursing, but that seemed so useless, like throwing stones at the moon. And so she covered her face with her hands and shuddered, wishing hard, wishing with all her might, that he would recover.

"Isabel?" A man's voice penetrated the swirling panic.

Her eyes flew open. "Anthony."

"Hey, I've been hanging around waiting for over an hour." He did not look angry. She had never known Anthony to get angry. He looked pleasant and smooth and artlessly handsome as always.

"Are you about ready?" he asked.

"I…" Her mouth felt like sawdust. "I can't go anywhere, Anthony. There's been an accident." She practically choked on the word. "I have to wait and see if—" She broke off and regarded him helplessly. "I can't go with you."

He raked a hand through his abundant dark hair. "Look, Isabel, this is getting ridiculous."

"I know," she said softly. "I know. You don't deserve this. You go back to town, Anthony. Never mind about me."

He held her lightly by the shoulders. "Babe, I'll wait."

Juanita Sohappy joined them, hurrying to Isabel. "Is there any news?"

"No," Isabel said faintly. "Not yet."

"I hope the white-eyes doctor knows what he's doing," Juanita said, using the language Isabel had never quite forgotten. She squeezed Isabel's hand, then went inside the clinic.

Anthony stared after her for a moment. "A friend of yours?"

"Yes. We just met, but she reminds me of the past, of people I used to know."

"This is really wild. People you used to know? Native Americans?"

She blinked. Her thoughts seethed and scattered like storm clouds. "I'm half-Indian," she said simply.

His hands dropped from her shoulders. He stared at her as if she had just sprouted antlers.

"Is that a problem?" she asked.

"Of course not." But his voice was taut, strained. "The problem is that you never told me."

"No. No, I didn't."

"Why in the world—" He made a fist and pressed it against the gray cinder-block wall. "What is it, Isabel? Did you think I'd find you weird or something?"

"I guess I didn't think much at all. I never told anyone."

"This is insane. We're supposed to be married Saturday. And here I am finding out things—important things—about you that you should've told me months ago. What else haven't you told me?"

Ah, so much, she thought sadly. About her father, her mother, all the things that had turned her into what she was when she had first met him—a bashful woman frightened of her past, intimidated by passion, seeking a way to belong.

And she wondered—she *made* herself wonder—if it was fair to expect Anthony to answer all those needs.

And that, after all, was the key. Neither Anthony nor Dan nor anyone could *give* her happiness. How naive she had been to think they could.

"Anthony," she said, her voice more steady than she could have wished. "I'm sorry. After I hear about…" Her voice broke. "About Dan, we'll talk."

"I'm not sure we need to." His lips thinned, and she could tell he was annoyed, but to the core of his being, Anthony Cossa was a kind and patient man. Kinder and more patient than she deserved.

A moment later, Juanita pushed open the clinic door.

She did not say a word. She did not have to. The expression on her face said it all.

His grandfather would have called it a "true dream." Wispy images and sensations in Dan's head pulsed with vivid color. Drumbeats sounded in his ears, and he felt the heavy thud at the base of his neck.

Right where it hurt the most.

A coldness seized him, and he tried to dive back into the dream, into the colorful oblivion behind his eyes. But he could not will himself to slip away again. A horde of thoughts and regrets battered at him. He thought about asking for more of the painkiller that had gotten him this far, but that would only postpone the inevitable.

He had to open his eyes and face what had happened to him.

Correction, he told himself. What he had done to himself.

*Minor lacerations,* the doctor had reported. A few cracked ribs. It was a good thing he had been wearing a high-quality helmet. Too bad none of his safety precautions could protect his spine.

*Possible nerve damage,* the doctor had said with a look on his face that chilled Dan to the center of his chest. The physician claimed he could not render a prognosis until Dan was transported to a major hospital for extensive neurological evaluation.

But the doctor's expression, so studiously bland and gentle, said, *Sorry, buddy. You'll never walk again.*

Dan insisted on two things. That the doctor keep his condition strictly confidential. And that Dan receive the largest legal dose of painkiller the doctor could, in good conscience, administer.

The physician agreed to both requests without hesitation.

But now, Dan was emerging from his narcotic fog, and he had some decisions to make. First, the lodge. The tribal council would help him. Maybe the winery would keep things afloat until the guests started coming. And hell, if it came to that, Dan still had his voice. He could record something new, though he'd look pretty ridiculous singing flat on his back.

And then there was Isabel… The pain lanced like lightning through him. He barely had time to compose his thoughts before she stepped into the room.

He hated himself for putting that expression on her face—that look of terror and pity and shattering grief. Her skin was pale and looked tautly drawn across her cheekbones. Her hair was mussed as if she had passed her fingers through it repeatedly in agitation. Her narrow hands were held clasped in front of her.

"Hi," he said. "I just woke up."

She nodded and stood at the foot of the bed, her gaze moving slowly over the apparatus that held him immobile. He was reminded of a time when their roles had been reversed, when she had been the patient. That was the beginning of the end for them the first time. Now, once again, their parting would take place in a hospital room.

"I would've waited all night if I had to," she said. "Would've waited a lifetime."

Dan let out a slow sigh. The bitter irony of it all ate at him. He had brought her here to make her see that they still loved each other, that they could make it together. And she had realized it, but the revelation had come too late. He knew she would stick by him through whatever ordeals he had to face in the coming months.

But he would never let her shackle herself to him now.

"I guess I deserve an 'I told you so,'" he said.

"I'd never say that." She moistened her lips.

The thought of never again tasting that beautiful, kissable mouth nearly drew a roar of anguish from him.

"How are you?" she asked, as he knew she would. "No one will tell me a thing. Exactly what's hurt? What's broken?"

"Nothing that can't be fixed," he lied. "Next year at this time, I'll be back in the race."

"You can't mean you'd do it again."

"Sure I would." He troweled on more lies, saying anything—*anything*—to drive her away, to save her from loving a broken man. "I never should have come to see you again. You were right all along. I can't change. I'll always be wild and reckless. I'd drive you crazy."

She looked stricken. Tears brimmed in her eyes. "You're making me crazy now. I came to tell you I'd stay with you—"

"It's no good. It didn't work for us the first time, and it won't work now. It was stupid of me to think it would."

"But—"

"Go back home, Isabel," he said in a hard-edged voice. "There's nothing for you here."

She stepped back from the bed, clutching her stomach as if he had struck her. She swept him with a horrified gaze, taking in the huge iron device holding his head, the stiff cage around his middle. "I'm not leaving you," she whispered.

"I won't let you stay. We can't make it together. What happened today just proves it."

The pain that flashed in her eyes made him want to reach out, to beg her to stay, but he forced himself to say, "I never should have found you again in the first place. I'm sorry for that."

She looked at him for a long time. He thought she might cry, but she didn't. She squared her shoulders and lifted her chin, looking both fierce and fragile. "I won't force myself on you."

"Goodbye, Isabel," Dan said.

And when she turned away and walked out the door, he added in the faintest of whispers, *"I love you."*

# *Eleven*

"It's wonderful to see all of you," Isabel said, and she meant it. Sitting at her favorite garden café, enjoying a perfect Indian-summer afternoon, she truly did mean it. Six months after the disastrous bridal shower, Connie and Lucia had come over to Bainbridge Island for lunch.

Connie handed her a cream stock envelope. Somehow, Isabel knew before opening it what she would find.

It was an invitation to Anthony's wedding.

"We figured you'd want to know," Lucia said.

"You're right." Isabel smiled at them. Even after she had broken off the engagement with Anthony, his sisters remained friends with her. And Anthony surprised her by coming through with a contract for Dan's lodge. By all reports, the team had a spectacular weekend, hosted by Clyde Looking and Theo Sohappy while Dan was still laid up.

"I'm pleased for Anthony," Isabel said with conviction. Connie touched the rim of her wineglass to the rim of Isabel's. "We figured you would be. But what about you, sweetie?"

In an odd way, Isabel cherished the hurt that she lived with night and day, the hurt she had endured since last April, when Dan had ordered her out of his hospital room, out of his life. Sometimes, that pain was the only thing that reminded her she was alive. Early on, she had tried to call, but again and again he refused to speak to her.

"I'm all right," she said, looking down, tucking a silky lock of hair behind her ear. She'd gone natural with her hair for the first time since high school, letting it grow in straight and stark black instead of using chemical perms and colors. Idly, she noted the blast of the one-fifteen ferry horn.

Summer sales at the plant nursery had broken records. Of the three new staff members she'd hired, two were Native Americans, and one was an expert on traditional Indian herbs.

In a burst of energy, she had totally redone her cottage. Over the bed hung her pride and joy—a Yakima mat woven with the design of a soaring eagle crest.

On a good day, she avoided thinking of Dan for whole minutes at a stretch.

But most days, she dwelled on the time she had spent at his lodge, remembering every moment, polishing it up in her memory until it gleamed with the soft patina of a lost dream.

She had stayed in touch with the Sohappys. They told her little of Dan, only that he had gone to a hospital in Olympia for therapy and then returned home. The lodge was prospering thanks to the winery that had

sponsored the race and to record summer visitors.
Word-of-mouth recommendations kept the place booked
solid.

From Dan, there was nothing but silence.

Isabel gulped back her wine and tried to focus on
what Lucia was saying, but a faint sound kept humming
beneath the murmur of conversation.

She gazed down the length of the café garden. Most
of the plants had come from her nursery. The flower
beds and trees burst with fall color.

The roaring grew louder, more urgent. Lucia stopped
talking. Isabel stopped breathing as unbearable anticipation built in her. And then, right where the gravel
driveway turned off from the road, he appeared.

He was an image out of her most intimate dreams.
Clad in black leather. A bandanna around his head. Inky,
flowing hair. Mirror-lens sunglasses. The Harley beneath
him bucking and spitting gravel like a wild animal.

"It's Mr. Testosterone again," Connie murmured as
the machine roared up the terraced garden path.

Isabel stood, clutching her wineglass in fingers numb
with shock. The apparition skidded to a halt, jerked the
bike onto its kickstand and walked toward her. Long, loose
strides with a limp that favored his right leg. Tall boots
crunching on the path. Gold earring winking in one ear.

"This sort of déjà vu I can live with," Lucia whispered.

He yanked off the mirror glasses and stared at Isabel.
His dark eyes dragged down the length of her, and she
felt the touch of his gaze like a caress.

The wineglass slipped from her fingers, struck the
grass and rolled under the table. "What are you doing
here?" she asked.

He gave her the old cocky grin, the expression that used to make her go weak in the knees.

It still worked.

She was still drawn to his aura of seductive danger, the faint sulkiness of his full lips, the powerful body as well tuned as his Harley. The lean hips and broad shoulders that made her body flush with memories.

"I came to see you," he said. "And to say I'm sorry."

Her cheeks heated with stinging color as she moved away from the table. "'I'm sorry'?" she echoed. "You banished me from your life, and you think two words will cover it?"

"No," he said in a low, rough voice. "It'll take me a lifetime to make it up to you."

"You can start now," she said, folding her arms over her middle, not daring to let herself hope.

He gave her that lazy, Sunday-morning, stay-in-bed-all-day grin. "I figure it's now or never, Isabel."

She felt the rapt fascination of her friends, and from the corner of her eye, she saw Connie jerk her head, urging her to go with Dan.

Still uncertain, she took his hand, and they walked toward the Harley. She felt the unevenness of his gait. Rather than detracting from his physical grace, the limp shifted his weight in a way that was somehow wildly sexy.

He held out a helmet for her. She stepped back, dropping his hand and studying him. For the first time, she noticed a few extra lines around his eyes and mouth and a leanness in his face that had not been there before.

"I won't go with you until you tell me the truth, Dan. I want to know the real reason you stayed away so long.

Why you never called." She eyed his right leg. "Just how bad were your injuries?"

He started to put on his mirror glasses, then seemed to think better of it. "Not so bad they didn't heal, Isabel."

"What about what you did to us?" she asked, forming the words around the ache of tears in her throat. "Will that heal?"

"Saying I'm sorry is only the beginning. When I sent you away, it was like cutting off an arm. Cutting out my heart, maybe. It was stupid, running you off when I had never needed you more."

"Then why?" she persisted. "I need to know."

"I thought I'd never walk again. I didn't want to saddle you with that."

She remembered the way he had looked in the hospital bed, immobilized by a stainless-steel scaffold. Realization hit her like a thunderclap—it hadn't been anger she'd seen in his eyes, but fear. "I can't believe you thought your physical condition would make a difference in the way I feel, Dan."

"Like I said, it was stupid. *I* was stupid. But I've had a lot of time to learn a few things."

"What sort of things?"

"That I don't need to take risks, to go looking for danger, to hide from my feelings. My reckless rebel days are over."

A rush of elation rose through her, and her mouth curved into a smile. "Well, it's about damned time. I'll hold you to that."

"I know." Without warning, he set down the helmet and pulled her against him so that she was engulfed by the textures and scents that had haunted her dreams all summer.

From the corner of her eye, Isabel saw Connie briskly fanning her face.

"Forgive me," Dan said, brushing his lips over hers, "for wanting to make sure I *could* heal before I came back to you."

"That *is* stupid," she whispered, entranced by the way he was kissing her, so lightly and gently that her head swam. "You should've told me."

"I'm telling you now," he said, still kissing her almost senseless.

"Telling me what?" she managed to ask.

"That I love you. That I want us to get married. Have babies. Grow plants and build picket fences and plan fundraisers and go fishing—"

"Yes," she said, sliding her fingers through his long, silky hair, letting the bandanna drift to the ground.

"Yes to what?" he asked.

"To all of the above."

\* \* \* \* \*

# Acknowledgments

Special thanks to Steve Butterworth,
a real-life wild man.

Thanks to the usual suspects:
Barbara Dawson Smith, Betty Gyenes
and Joyce Bell; and to Barbara Samuel,
Anne Stuart and Brenna Todd.

Thanks to Marsha Zinberg, for a new opportunity.

# A BRIDGE TO DREAMS

## Sherryl Woods

# One

The fog rolled in, gray and thick, but not nearly
dreary enough to dampen Karyn's enthusiasm. She
could barely see the Golden Gate Bridge in the gloomy
twilight, but beside her she had shimmering, golden
sunshine in the form of at least a dozen travel brochures
for Hawaii, from the exciting, sun-drenched beaches of
Honolulu to the more private but equally tropical sands
of Maui. She'd spent the past hour in the travel agency
sorting through the colorful, tempting photographs of
places she'd only seen on television. Finally the impatient travel agent had grown weary of her dreamy expression and her indecision and had handed over the
entire assortment, suggesting that she take her time
before making her reservations.

Karyn intended to do just that. She was going to
spend the entire weekend savoring every minute of
planning the first real, away-from-home vacation she'd
taken in her entire twenty-six years. She was choosing
far more than a destination. She was searching for ro-

mance and adventure and a dash of excitement all rolled into one seven-day vacation.

As her car began the steep climb up the narrow, winding road to her apartment, the engine coughed and sputtered.

"Come on, Ruby, you can do it. You climb this hill every night," she reminded the aging engine. The response was a wheeze that would have put a human in the hospital. Karyn felt the first pang of panic. "Don't you dare give up on me now," she ordered. "It is cold and wet outside."

Ruby responded with an apologetic murmur, then choked and died. Karyn yanked on the emergency brake as the car started to roll backward. Then with a familiar sense of resignation, she put the car into Neutral and tried to restart it. Tonight, however, the red Volkswagen did not respond. After several futile attempts to encourage the ancient car back to life, Karyn sighed and rested her head against the steering wheel.

"Why now, Ruby?" she said, admitting that the signs of a permanent collapse were all too ominous. "Couldn't you have waited another month? Another year? What did I ever do to you except feed you oil and wax you? Is this any way to repay me for taking you off the junk heap and giving you a new coat of paint?"

On the off chance that the car would react favorably to her pleas, she turned the key one last time. Nothing. Not even a muted grinding noise to indicate that there might be a hint of life stirring under the hood. Resigned, Karyn let the car roll to the curb, reset the emergency brake, then got out and went to hunt for a pay phone so she could call a tow truck. Thanks to Ruby's growing number of quirks, she knew the number at the garage by heart.

"When are you going to give up on this old heap?" her gray-haired mechanic grumbled when he had the car hooked up and Karyn was bouncing along in her all-too-familiar spot beside him.

"One more year," she said wearily.

Joe, who'd bandaged every part in the car half a dozen times over the past eight years, shook his head. "It'll never make it. It's getting too dangerous for you to be out in this thing, especially at night. One of these days you're going to get stranded after the shop's closed. Then what'll you do?"

"Abandon it. Call one of my brothers. Take the bus. Whatever," she said. It was exactly the same thing she'd said last week and the week before. "Joe, you know I can't afford a new car now."

"But you can afford some expensive trip?" Joe knew all about Hawaii. He didn't approve. "What's more important? Your safety or a few days away from home in some foreign place where you don't know a soul?"

"Hawaii is hardly foreign."

"Might as well be. You have to cross a mighty big ocean to get there, don't you?"

Karyn sighed. Joe had considered his own move from Oakland to San Francisco risky business. He was even more protective of her than her family was, something she hadn't thought possible. "I am going on this vacation," she said with a stubborn glare in his direction. "I have waited a lifetime to save enough money to get away on my own and see another part of the world. I will not give up this trip. Please, Joe, just fix the car this one more time."

Still grumbling under his breath, he chomped down on his unlit cigar. "Okay. Okay. I'll do the best I can."

But on Saturday when Karyn returned to the garage to pick up Ruby, the car was sitting forlornly at the back of the lot in a spot obviously chosen because it wouldn't block traffic. Joe wore a funereal expression. Even his cigar drooped at a downcast angle. Karyn's heart plummeted.

"The engine's blown," he said. One thing about Joe—he didn't waste words or sympathy.

"Can't you fix it? You're the best. There must be something you can do."

"Not worth it," he said, poking his head back under the hood of a car that apparently had more of a future.

"It is to me. Please, Joe."

"It'll cost you more than the car's worth."

"How much?"

"Five, maybe six hundred. More if I can't find the parts in some junkyard."

The figure represented half of her savings, half of the money she'd set aside over the past year and a half for the long-dreamed-about trip to Hawaii.

"I know you was counting on taking that vacation, but it ain't worth it." He even managed to sound vaguely sympathetic, which told her far more than she liked about the state of the car. Joe was a genius with engines. He never willingly sent one to the junk heap. If he couldn't fix Ruby, then Ruby was beyond repair.

"Use the money to put a down payment on a new car or at least a good used one from this decade," he urged. "Pick one out and I'll go over it for you. You can take the trip next year."

Karyn knew the advice was well-meant and probably sound, but it sent her spirits sinking straight down to her toes. More dejected than she'd ever been, she walked over to the scarred red VW. She wanted badly to kick the tires, but couldn't bring herself to do it. Unlike Ruby, she still had a certain amount of loyalty.

"How could you do this to me?" she said plaintively, taking one last resentful look before gathering the Bay Area maps, sweaters and umbrellas that had accumulated in the backseat. She started across the parking lot. As she reached the gas pumps in the center, she opened her purse, took out the travel brochures for Hawaii, ceremoniously tore them into shreds, then dumped them into the oil drum that served as a trash can. They were only pieces of paper, but as they fluttered away she felt as though she were destroying her dream.

It took Karyn until the following Friday after work to accept the inevitable. With a sort of grim determination she went to a car dealership she'd passed every day. She walked past the sporty new convertibles, past the serviceable sedans, beyond the new car showroom to the used car lot. She tried very hard to tell herself that buying a replacement for Ruby was going to be exciting, that it would be terrific to drive something that didn't quit at stoplights and balk at hills. All she could see, though, was the dimming vision of Diamond Head.

"May I help you, miss?"

Karyn sighed heavily and returned to reality, which in this case happened to be an eager salesman who was practically rubbing his hands together in glee at the prospect of making a sale before the day ended.

"I'm looking for a car," she said without enthusiasm.

He chuckled as though she'd made a terrific joke. "Well, you've certainly come to the right place," he said with so much forced enthusiasm that Karyn reconsidered the possibility of taking the bus for the rest of her natural life. Only the fact that she often needed her car for work kept her standing right where she was.

"Now, we have a real beauty over here," he said. "Take a look at this convertible. Only a couple of years old, real low mileage. Just right for a pretty little thing like you. It's flashy. Sexy. It projects a certain image, if you know what I mean."

Karyn glanced at the bright red car that reminded her all too vividly of Ruby in color, if not in style. Used or not, the car looked expensive. She didn't want to get her hopes up so she shrugged indifferently. "How much?"

"Well, now, I guess that's something we'd have to discuss. Why not take it for a test drive and see how you like it?"

"How much?"

"Just look at this interior. All leather and it's like new. Not a mark on it. Only twenty-five thousand miles on her, too."

"How much?"

"You have a trade-in?"

She shook her head.

"Hmm."

"How much?" she persisted.

"What sort of budget do you have?"

"Limited."

His enthusiasm staggered after her terse response. "I see. Perhaps we ought to take a look at something a little more basic. We have a classic right here, a good solid car. Dependable. That's important." He led her to a dull blue two-door the size of a large can of tomato sauce. There was rust around the edges of the door. A dent marred the left front fender. "Nothing fancy, mind you, but reliable transportation. I'm sure we can bring this in on your budget."

Karyn studied the car without interest, then glanced back at the convertible. If she was going to blow her vacation on a car, why not get something with a little style? Why not go for something that suggested the owner was a daring adventurer, instead of a recently graduated paralegal, who dutifully watered her geraniums every Thursday and took her vitamins every morning?

"Tell me again about the convertible."

The salesman's eyes lit up. "Absolutely. Let me get those keys and you can take her for a little spin. Get the feel of her. Once you've driven that beauty, nothing else on the lot will do."

Of course that was exactly what Karyn feared. Her nervousness increased when the salesman put the top down and settled her in the bucket seat behind the wheel. The engine turned over on the first try. The damn thing purred. As the rare, late-afternoon sun caressed her shoulders and the gentle breeze whispered through her hair, a spark of excitement was born. She recognized that spark. She'd felt it gazing at pictures of Waikiki and dreaming of tall, dark, handsome strangers. That spark was very likely to be her downfall.

Back in the salesman's office, she braced herself to negotiate. He ran through the car's virtues as lovingly as a proud father trying to pitch his daughter to a blind date.

"You don't have to sell me," she said. "Just give me a price."

He looked crestfallen. Apparently it was not going to be that simple.

"Why don't you give me a figure," he suggested. "We can start from that."

*Start from?* The phrase had an ominous ring to it. Why not start with the bottom line? "A thousand dollars," she said finally.

The salesman appeared to be suitably aghast. He shook his head and swallowed hard. "I'm afraid that's a little out of line. I don't dare take it back to my manager. He'll laugh me off the lot."

"Then it's your turn. I've given you my starting figure."

"Come on," he pleaded, beginning to sweat. "Give me something to work with here."

"I just did."

"I can't take that to the boss. A thousand dollars is nothing for a car like that."

Karyn stared at him and her apathy began to return. She wasn't going to get the convertible. She would not go into debt for a car, not when she was finally getting on her feet financially. Growing up as she had on the cutting edge of financial disaster had taught her the dangers of living on credit. "Maybe we should just forget it." She stood. The dealer was surprisingly alert and swift for a man at least thirty pounds overweight. He moved to block her way.

"Wait a minute. Don't be too hasty." He flashed another of his thoroughly insincere smiles at her. "I'm sure we can reach an agreement on this, if we go about it right."

"I don't think so," she said, slipping past him.

"But, miss," he began frantically, running along behind her.

She cast one last, regretful look at the convertible, then turned—straight into a rock-solid wall.

"What's the problem, Nate?" To her amazement, the wall talked. She glanced up and discovered it also had shoulders. Very broad shoulders, in fact. A deep dimple slashed one tanned cheek at a rakish angle. A scar knit a tiny white thread through one dark eyebrow. The result was uneven, unique and totally devastating. Even though she had no experience with car salesmen, Karyn recognized at once that this had to be the dealership's top gun. This man could have sold Fords to stockholders at General Motors. Those dark green eyes could have seduced her eighty-year-old spinster aunt. His hand rested at the small of her back, presumably to steady her after their encounter. It felt as though she had been touched by lightning. She simply stared, while Nate tried to explain the difficulty.

To Karyn's dismay tears welled up in her eyes. All she'd wanted was a car. The process should have been no more complicated, if slightly more costly, than buying a toaster. Instead, she'd discovered that it required the skills of a nuclear-summit negotiator and the patience of a saint. She had neither, nor was her purse exactly brimming over with the third necessary ingredient—cash.

"Look, I really think this was a bad idea. I'll come back another time."

"You like the convertible," the wall said, studying her expression.

She nodded.

"What did you offer?"

"A thousand dollars," she said with a trace of defiance.

Brad noted the stubborn tilt of her chin, but, more important, he caught the shimmer of tears in her huge blue eyes. He was a sucker for a woman's tears. It had gotten him into trouble more than once. He had a hunch this was going to be another one of those times.

"I see," he said very seriously. "Can you make it twelve hundred?"

"But…" Nate protested, only to be silenced by Brad's fierce look. He watched a spark of excitement return to those wide, innocent eyes and felt his heart do an unexpected flip. She glanced longingly at the convertible.

"If I live on peanut butter sandwiches for a while," she said slowly.

"Fine," Brad said before she could change her mind or Nate could start whining about the loss of commission. "Nate, take care of the paperwork. Miss…"

"Chambers."

"Miss Chambers and I will be in my office having coffee. Come and get us when the car is ready. Make sure it's washed and waxed and that the inside is vacuumed."

"Certainly, Mr. Willis."

He watched as recognition dawned on her face. "As in Willis Motors?" she said.

"Heir apparent," he confirmed, taking her arm and steering her back into the main showroom, down a corridor and into an office that was decorated with plush carpet, mahogany furniture and a wall that featured too many photographs of him standing beside various race cars.

Brad glanced at those photos, which were a taunting reminder of a past he'd only recently had to give up. The sacrifice still hurt. Left to his own devices, he'd have stripped the walls of every last picture, but they were his father's pride and joy. Ripping them down would have shown his father just how much sacrificing his racing career had meant. Since that would only cause his father pain, there was no point in it.

Brad focused his attention on the petite, dark-haired imp before him. Before she could vanish like a woodland sprite, he settled her into a chair and gave her a cup of coffee. She was probably in her mid-twenties, but she seemed so young compared to the sophisticated women he usually met. He wondered fleetingly if he ought to be offering her milk instead. He perched on the side of his desk and studied her with blatant interest. The fact that she was obviously flustered by the intense scrutiny fascinated him.

"You won't get rich making deals like that," she told him sternly. "Not that I'm not grateful, you understand, but it's bad business."

"I'm already rich," he confided. If his father hadn't seen to that, his own success on the racing circuit would have ensured it. He'd discovered long ago that money was useful, but it didn't solve all the world's ills by a long shot.

"Plan to stay that way?" she said, obviously still worried about his rash decision to make a deep slash in the price of the car.

"Absolutely. Another few hundred dollars from you won't make that much difference in our bottom line for the year, so don't worry about it," he said, minimizing the cut. He had a hunch if she knew exactly how much he'd subtracted, she'd have demanded to know what he expected in return and bolted from his office in a huff.

"But why'd you do it? For all you know I could make a habit of going around, conning men into giving up their cars at rock-bottom prices."

He laughed at the idea of anyone with a face that innocent being a con artist. "I doubt it."

"Why?"

"I saw you get off the bus. I watched you walk through the lot. You obviously needed cheering up. You looked as though you were on some sort of grim mission." In fact that was what had brought him out of his office in the first place. He'd been drawn by that aura of dejection. He probably should have lived a few centuries earlier, so he could put on his armor and ride off to save damsels in distress. The knight-in-shining-armor syndrome was definitely out of step in this day and age. Most women had no interest in being saved from much of anything—except maybe dragons, but they were in short supply.

"Very perceptive," she was saying with a hint of surprise.

"You didn't really want to buy a car?"

"I wanted a trip to Hawaii."

He nodded sagely. "There aren't many of them on the lot today. Did you think of trying a travel agent?"

"I did," she said with a heartfelt sigh. She held up her hand, her finger and thumb a scant inch apart. "I was this close to going. This close," she repeated mournfully.

"What happened?"

"Ruby died."

She sounded so sad again that he felt instantly sympathetic. No wonder she'd looked so forlorn. No wonder he'd wanted to rush to her rescue. "I'm sorry. Ruby was your...?"

"My car."

"Oh." His sympathy waned, but not his fascination. "So you're buying a car, instead of taking a trip you'd badly wanted to take."

"Exactly."

"You can always take the trip next year. Hawaii will still be there."

"That's what Joe said."

The mention of this Joe unsettled Brad in a surprising way. For some reason it bothered him that she ran around quoting some other man as though his opinions really mattered to her. "Joe?" he said cautiously.

"My mechanic. We've been on very friendly terms the past couple of years."

He scowled. It was worse than he thought. "I see," he muttered.

"I doubt it, unless you've had a '68 VW recently."

"Good heavens." With understanding, there came an astonishing sense of relief.

"Exactly. I'd hoped to keep it alive one more year, just until I had a chance to take this one little vacation." She gazed at him wistfully. "Was that so much to ask?"

"It was a lot to ask of a '68 VW. Why was the vacation so important to you?"

"I'd never taken one."

He regarded her disbelievingly. "You mean to Hawaii?"

"I mean ever, to anywhere. I am twenty-six years old and I have never been south of San Francisco. North, east or west, either, for that matter. With seven kids in the family, we're doing good to get everyone together on Sundays for church. We went on a picnic once. It rained."

"But you just said you're twenty-six. Surely you've been on your own for a few years now."

"I have never been on my own, not the way you mean. I am the baby in the family. I have six older brothers who regard the idea of my being out after dark as worrisome at best. When I finally got through school and started earning enough to get my own apartment, they took turns standing guard at night until I threatened to call the cops on them. Now they just keep calling until I get in. Heaven knows what they'd do if I ever…" Her voice trailed off in obvious embarrassment. "Well, you know."

He chuckled. "I certainly do. I think I understand why you wanted to get away."

"Don't be mistaken. They're really great brothers. I just wish they all had a couple of dozen kids of their own so they'd leave me alone."

"You're very loyal."

"Yeah, that's what I told Ruby." Suddenly she blushed. He loved it. "You must think I'm an idiot talking about my car as though it were a person."

Actually, Brad liked that about her, too. Things obviously mattered deeply to her—cars, as well as people. It beat the shallowness he usually encountered all to hell. He leaned toward her. "Mine's Ralph," he whispered confidentially. "Of course, I don't dare call him that in public. I'd be laughed off the racing circuit."

"Then those aren't just publicity photos on the wall. You actually do race that car?"

"I did up until a few months ago."

"You quit?"

"More or less. My father had a heart attack. The doctors told him to lighten up his workload or die within the year. We have ten of these dealerships around the state. So, here I am, making my monthly pilgrimage. Between paperwork, problem solving and trying to keep my father from sneaking into his office, there's not a lot of time left for entering Grand Prix events."

"You're very loyal, too. It must have been hard to give up something you obviously loved."

"I did it grudgingly, sort of the way you bought that car."

"But you did it, just the same. I think what you did is very noble. I never gave up anything."

"Except Hawaii."

"That wasn't noble," she said ruefully. "That was a necessity and I did it kicking and screaming all the way. If I could have managed without a car, I would have."

Brad had a sudden inspiration. "When's your vacation?" he asked.

"There is no vacation."

"I mean the dates. Have you told your boss you're not taking off?"

"Not yet. I think it's called denial."

"Then don't tell him. You're going to have your vacation."

"But I can't afford to go anywhere."

"You can take a vacation right here."

"This isn't a vacation. This is home. I don't want to waste another perfectly good vacation sitting around in my apartment cleaning the closets."

"Who said anything about cleaning closets? Thousands of people come to San Francisco every year. Songs have been written about this place. It's one of the most romantic, exciting cities in the world. If you want a taste of Asia, it's here. A suggestion of the French wine country, it's here. A quaint, cliffside city by the sea like Italy's Portofino, it's across the Bay. Why should you go anywhere else?"

"To get away from my brothers."

"Turn off your phone. Tell them you're leaving town, if that's what it takes. Take a fresh look at this place. Have you ever looked at the Golden Gate Bridge at twilight?" His own enthusiasm was definitely mounting as the impulsive notion took hold. He hadn't felt this carefree and excited in all the months since his father's heart attack. He was talking with the fervor of a tour guide. The chamber of commerce would love him. "Well," he persisted. "Have you?"

"Every night when I'm stuck in traffic."

"But have you ever really seen it?"

"Not really," she murmured.

"Then for one entire, fun-filled week you and I are going on vacation in San Francisco."

She looked thunderstruck. To be perfectly honest, he was feeling a little that way himself.

*"You?"* she whispered.

Brad shrugged. "Why not? I've been noble for the past year myself. Even you said so. I deserve a vacation," he said emphatically.

"But you could go anywhere."

"I could," he admitted readily. "But I can't imagine a better way to spend a vacation than with a woman who just bought her very first, very flashy convertible."

The words rolled off his tongue with all of his prac-
ticed charm, but to his amazement he realized that
somewhere deep inside he'd never meant anything more
in his life. Seeing the world through her fresh, unjaded
eyes just might turn out to be the best investment of time
he'd ever made. Maybe they'd even turn up a few
dragons for him to slay.

# Two

Karyn had never made an impetuous, throw-caution-to-the-winds decision in her life. She'd certainly never had to make one involving a man who was heart-stoppingly handsome, witty, rich and apparently famous enough to know at least half a dozen very sexy actors, if the framed photos and clippings on the wall were any indication. But during twenty-six years of nonstop struggling just to survive, the longing for adventure and storybook romance had flourished. She'd never quite gotten over "Cinderella." From what she'd observed, the man sitting across from her had all the qualifications of a handsome prince.

She studied him closely as she considered his unexpectedly tempting suggestion. She ticked off his attributes with the nervous anticipation of a certified public accountant hoping a column of figures would add up correctly. He had spoken of his father with genuine affection, despite the sacrifices he'd made on his behalf. He was boldly confident without being arrogant. He was impeccably dressed without being flashy. And there was an energy and vitality about him that counterpointed her own quiet personality.

Most important, he seemed to be trustworthy, even if points were deducted for that unnerving glint in his eyes. She had a feeling that glint was exactly the sort of thing her brothers had been worrying about since she'd reached adolescence. She rather liked the champagne-sparkly feelings those eyes set off inside her.

He'd been very kind, very compassionate to her. She had felt an almost instantaneous rapport with him, which was all the more incredible considering the man apparently traveled in celebrity-studded circles. The closest she'd ever come before to anyone famous was when she'd subbed for the executive secretary to the senior partner in her law firm on the day his picture had been in the *Chronicle*.

There was, of course, a negative side to all that fame and obvious sophistication: Brad was probably very experienced at portraying whatever image circumstances called for. Maybe in his circles it was even acceptable for him to pick up and discard women as casually as other people tossed aside old clothes. Since Karyn had never followed auto racing, she had no way of knowing for sure what sort of reputation the Brad Willis of those bold sports page headlines had in the more scandalous tabloids. Just thinking about the possibilities made her doubt her own judgment. She hadn't exactly dated extensively. She hadn't had time. Would she even recognize a rogue before it was too late?

Still, she reminded herself, there were only cars and men in all those pictures on his office wall, no women. She glanced instinctively at his ring finger. It was

tanned, well-manicured and unadorned. That was promising, but hardly conclusive.

"Are you married, Mr. Willis?" she asked with the sort
of bluntness she'd heard her boss use successfully in
taking depositions and cross-examining witnesses in
court.

It didn't seem to rattle him in the slightest. He
grinned, in fact. "It's Brad," he corrected pointedly,
"and obviously some of your brothers' caution has worn
off on you."

The evasive response made her nervous. Though
Karyn kept her tone light, she persisted with a deliber-
ateness that would have done her brothers and her bosses
proud. "Isn't it considered proper to know a little about
the person one plans to spend an entire vacation with?
Even if we aren't going to be sharing hotel rooms, surely
it's important to know if we have anything in common."

"So you want to know if we have my marital status
in common?"

The return of that devilish glint of amusement in his
eyes was plain. Karyn hoped that was a good sign.
"Something like that," she admitted. "Doesn't it matter
to you whether or not I'm married?"

"We wouldn't be having this conversation if you were."

"How do you know, though? You didn't ask."

"No ring."

"Not conclusive."

"No hovering husband on the car lot to poke his head
under the hood."

"Maybe I'm mechanical. After all, I did keep a '68
VW alive."

"Joe did that," he said, his knock-your-socks-off smile emerging again.

"Which still doesn't answer my question."

"Which one? How I knew you weren't married or whether I am?"

"Both, but if I have to make a choice, the latter."

Brad folded his hands on his desk, leaned forward, met her gaze intently and said solemnly, "No, Karyn Chambers, I am not married. There are not even any serious entanglements to speak of, now or ever. I'm afraid I've lived in the fast lane in more ways than one."

There was an intriguing note of regret in the honest admission. "Do you still?" she asked with a mixture of curiosity and trepidation.

"Live in the fast lane? I told you I'd given up racing."

"And women?"

"I'm not a monk, but the times are changing, in case you haven't heard. And I'm older and wiser."

She felt like purring with satisfaction. She doubted her brothers would view the comment the same way. "How much older?"

"I'm thirty-two. Want to see my birth certificate?"

"No. Your driver's license will do."

Never taking his eyes from hers, Brad reached for his wallet. He moved very slowly, obviously expecting her to back down from the impertinent request. Karyn determinedly held out her hand. "I'm not about to let a total stranger drive my new car until I'm sure he has a valid driver's license."

Laughing, Brad handed over his wallet. It had enough credit cards in it to charge the entire stock of clothing at Nordstrom without putting a dent in his credit limit. The license told her far more than his driving status in the state of California, badly minimizing some of his best points and elaborating on a few of her own impressions.

His eyes, which she could see for herself, were a rich, fascinating shade of emerald and were listed simply as green. Obviously the clerk who'd put it down had no imagination. He was six foot two inches tall, one hundred eighty pounds and, by her assessment, all muscle. He lived in Malibu at an address that inspired images of redwood sun decks, which were draped in vibrant pink and purple bougainvillea and opened onto wide expanses of sandy beaches. His birth date, May 15, told her he was a stubborn Taurus, which suggested that she might as well give in now about this vacation.

She'd known for the past fifteen minutes she was going to do it anyway.

Her brothers were going to kill her. Or maybe they'd kill Brad, she conceded, if they ever found out about him.

"What's the itinerary?" she asked before she could start worrying about how Brad would fend off the six angry Chambers men, who made up in sheer numbers and street-fighting savvy what they lacked in health-club fitness.

"You haven't said when your vacation begins."

"Technically, a week from Monday."

"Perfect. That gives me time to get back down to L.A., take care of a few details and free up my own time. You just leave the itinerary to me. I promise you the vacation of a lifetime."

"I'm not sure I can afford anything that dramatic."

"I promise this will be first-class all the way and it won't cost you a dime."

"If you can accomplish that, maybe you should go into the travel business."

"I have more business than I'd like now. I certainly don't want to get into another one."

That statement raised a nagging concern. "Are you really sure you want to do this?" Karyn asked. "Maybe you ought to think about it. I mean, it's a lovely gesture, but you don't even know me."

He stretched a hand across the desk, palm up, and waited for her to put her hand in his. When she did, he folded his long fingers around it in a grip that was warm and strong and reassuring. "I've never wanted to do anything so much in my entire life."

His voice practically throbbed with apparent sincerity. Karyn's unsophisticated pulse skipped several beats and a pleasant warmth stole through her. This was definitely a man with a knack for selling. She was about to take the charm with a grain of salt, until she looked into his eyes.

His green eyes glinted with golden sparks and his gaze never wavered. This was not the cold sheen of a precious metal, but the romantic allure of the moon and the brightness of a thousand stars.

This was the magic she'd been waiting for all her life.

Trying to explain her vacation plans to her brothers, who were sprawled around her tiny studio apartment like so many muscular, intense security guards, went about as well as Karyn had anticipated. They probed. She evaded. If it had been a chess game, they would have played to a draw. If only circumstances hadn't kept her living at home so many years longer than most of her friends, Karyn thought with a sigh. Her brothers had gotten into the habit of watching over her. She'd been so busy trying to manage school and work, she'd had little time for dating, anyway. Their protectiveness had never mattered all that much. Breaking them of it now was going to take either extraordinary tact or dynamite. Judging from their scowling, wary expressions, she should probably start hunting for someplace to buy the dynamite.

"I thought you had to cancel Hawaii to get the car," said Frank, the eldest and the one who'd led all family discussions since her father's death when she was still in elementary school. He had obviously sounded the alarm for the others the instant he'd realized that she was going ahead with her vacation. They had arrived on her doorstep within fifteen minutes of each other. Not one of them had been surprised to find the others there. Unity was a Chambers motto, especially where their baby sister was concerned. Maybe it would have been better if she'd been a gloriously tall, assertive redhead, instead of a barely over five-foot shrimp. Maybe then, they'd understand that she was way past due to take charge of her own social life.

"I did cancel the trip," she admitted.

"Then what are you going to do?" asked Peter.

"Stay right here," she said.

The cheerful tone was obviously a mistake. Jared regarded her suspiciously. "I don't get it. I thought you'd be upset about this."

"She was upset," Daniel confirmed. "When I was here last Saturday, she was moping around."

"Yeah," Kevin agreed. "When I called on Sunday, she sounded real depressed."

Karyn rolled her eyes as they continued to discuss her recent moods as if she'd left the room and they all had degrees in psychology. Eventually, they'd get back to her. They always did. It was Frank who finally turned to her again and said, "Okay, sis, what happened to perk you up?"

She shrugged with exaggerated innocence. "Nothing happened. I'm just resigned to my fate, if you must know. What's wrong with that?" Resignation was so far removed from the tingles that swept through her every time she thought of Brad Willis, it was all Karyn could do to keep a sappy, lovesick grin off her face.

"Nothing," Timothy interceded quickly. If Timothy had had half a chance to go to an Ivy League college, he'd have been a perfect diplomat. He was wasting his skills as a transit worker, handing out transfers and reminding tourists which stop was closest to Ghirardelli Square. By the time he worked his way through college at night, he'd probably be too old to go traipsing around the globe for the State Department.

"I'm sure Karyn can find lots of things to do right here in San Francisco," he said.

"Well, of course, she can," Jared grumbled. "For one thing this apartment needs to be painted. Why don't we all come over tomorrow night and help? I can get the paint on sale."

"No way," Karyn said adamantly. Six startled faces stared at her, stunned by her sharp tone. She backed off at once. She did not want to arouse their suspicions. "I mean, I can paint this place myself. Besides, I do not intend to spend my vacation working around the apartment. That's not a vacation—that's drudgery." At that moment, an untimely recollection of Cinderella flitted through Karyn's head, along with an even clearer image of the prince. He looked so much like Brad, she almost smiled.

"Then what are you going to do?" Frank said, clearly bewildered. His last vacation had been spent taking apart their mother's shuddering, fifteen-year-old washing machine and putting it back together. He'd actually enjoyed it. Their mother had been thrilled. The incident had convinced Karyn it was past time for Frank and his girlfriend of five years to get married. Now was not the time, though, to plague him about it.

"I don't know. Maybe sleep in a little." She came dangerously close to blushing at that one. She raced on, "Go to a couple of museums. I'll just play it by ear. That's what a vacation is all about."

She hoped she sounded noble, self-sacrificing and just sufficiently contented that they'd leave her alone for the next week instead of setting out to keep her company. It would not be the first time that they'd considered it their duty to protect her from boredom.

"I'm off Tuesday," Peter began.

"No, really," Karyn said, patting his knee and trying not to show her alarm. "You should be spending your day off on your own social life, not worrying about mine. Besides, I already have plans for Tuesday." She hadn't talked to Brad since the previous Friday, but she knew in her heart that he would show up on Monday.

"What plans?" asked Frank, his gaze narrowing.

"With a friend."

"What friend?" he persisted.

"Frank, she obviously doesn't want to tell us any more about it," Timothy said.

"Well, I don't care what she wants," her eldest brother blustered with something akin to parental indignation. "If she can't introduce us to her friends, then I have to wonder why not. What's wrong with them?"

"Nothing is wrong with any of my friends," Karyn said, thoroughly exasperated. She was worn-out from the whole exchange. Although she had been prepared for her brothers' objections, the prospect of using dynamite to break them of their habit became more and more appealing. "Will you all please go away. I want to get some sleep."

"It's only eight o'clock," Jared pointed out.

"I think that just means she's tired of arguing with us," Timothy said. "Come on, guys. Let's go and leave her in peace."

She looked over at him gratefully. "Thanks, Timmy."

He winked. He was the youngest of the brothers and had had more than his share of protective custody, as well. He'd been so grateful to have her come along when he was six that he'd come to her rescue more than once through the years.

Still grumbling, the pack finally vacated the premises.

"If you change your mind about the painting," Frank said at the door.

"I won't change my mind."

"But you might. By Wednesday you could be bored to tears."

Another image of Brad popped provocatively to mind. She would not be bored by Wednesday. In fact, if she had her way, by Wednesday her life would be just beginning to reach fairy-tale status.

When the pounding on the door began, Karyn moaned and pulled a pillow over her head. It did not shut out the sound. She lifted the pillow and peeked at the clock. It was exactly five minutes before six.

In the morning.

On the first day of her vacation.

She was going to kill whomever was on the far side of that door, assuming that it wasn't someone who planned to kill her first. Killers, she reassured herself as she dragged on her bedraggled terry-cloth robe, probably did not knock. Her brothers, to her everlasting regret, all had their own keys.

As she stumbled the few feet from the sofa bed to the door, she called out, "Who's there?"

"It's Brad."

The announcement sent her adrenaline surging faster than three cups of straight caffeine. She'd counted on him showing up sometime today, but not before she'd even taken a shower.

"Brad? What are you doing here? It's the middle of the night."

"Wrong attitude. It's the first day of your vacation. You don't want to waste a minute of it."

She sagged against the door. Had it been only ten days ago that she'd actually admired his energy? Why hadn't she suspected that it was not nearly as attractive at 6:00 a.m. as it was twelve hours later in the day? Maybe because she'd never before had a man outside her door at 6:00 a.m.

"Are you going to let me in?"

She glanced down at her faded, baggy T-shirt, her shapeless, beltless robe, her unshaven legs and the chipped polish on her toenails. "Not on your life. Come back in an hour."

"In an hour the sun will be up."

"That's the general idea."

"If the sun's up, it'll ruin my plan."

"We don't know each other well enough for any plan that requires the dark," she said, sliding to the floor in embarrassment as the implication sank into her muddled brain. She drew her knees to her chest and tugged the shapeless shirt over them. Thank heavens the man couldn't see her. What had gotten into her? Sweet, innocent Karyn Chambers did not say daring, dangerous things like that. Brad's low, silky laughter, however, confirmed that she apparently did and that he was enjoying the banter. No wonder her brothers worried about her. At heart, she was obviously capable of becoming a brazen flirt. The idea made her smile.

"I'll be ready in ten minutes," she compromised finally. "Wait for me."

"Out here?"

"Out there."

"I suppose it's what I deserve for not calling ahead."

"Exactly."

"Is this indicative of your overall attitude toward surprises?"

"Pretty much. I haven't had a lot of experience with them."

"We'll have to work on that. Hurry up, now, or your coffee will get cold."

"You have coffee out there?"

"Of course."

Karyn opened the door as far as the chain would allow and poked her hand out. "Please."

"I've always loved women who beg." The bold taunt sent a shiver down her spine.

"In your dreams," she retorted, pleased that her voice didn't waver. She wondered if it was possible to develop a jaunty, sophisticated attitude in a week simply by praying for it.

"Now hand over the coffee," she added forcefully.

He put the take-out cup in her hand. "Want the croissants that go with it?"

She was tempted, but the prospect of eating her breakfast alone on one side of the door while Brad remained locked in the hallway did not appeal to her any more than the idea of letting him see her before she'd pulled herself together. "Hold the croissants. I'll be ready in five minutes."

It actually took her closer to fifteen. She refused to skip shaving her legs. As it was she had four nicks on one knee and a gash on the opposite ankle from hurrying. When she finally opened the door, she almost swooned. It could have been from the loss of blood, but more likely it had to do with the dark-haired rogue who was sitting placidly on the steps waiting for her. In a business suit, he'd been gorgeous. In jeans and a navy blue and lime-green rugby shirt, he was devastatingly sexy.

To his credit, he didn't say a thing about the fact that she was most likely standing there with her mouth hanging open. He merely stood, popped a piece of buttery croissant into her mouth, then brushed a friendly kiss across her cheek. The croissant was melt-on-your-tongue good. The kiss, innocent as it was, was delicious.

"Where are we going?" she asked, when she could finally collect a sufficient vocabulary to form a coherent sentence.

"For a walk."

*A walk?* "You woke me out of a sound sleep at six o'clock in the morning to go for a walk?"

"A very special walk," he confirmed, steering her unresisting form down the steps and through the door before she could rally a strenuous objection.

Karyn stopped dead still in the middle of the sidewalk. She looked up into emerald eyes in search of the remembered warmth, the remembered promise of romance. There was a spark of something in the returning gaze, a responding flutter of awareness in the pit of her stomach.

She nodded in satisfaction, linked her arm through his and muttered in her sweetest tone, "It better be one hell of a walk."

# *Three*

The walk was spectacular! Awesome!

It was the drive that almost killed her.

Brad Willis roared through the predawn streets of San Francisco as if he had a particularly challenging Grand Prix course spread out in front of him. Her VW's aged engine had never permitted speeds this fast, even had Karyn been tempted to try attaining them. Karyn clutched at the edge of the seat with fingers that were rigid with fear. The wind whipped through her short black hair and lashed color into her pale cheeks. Her heart beat wildly. She'd hoped for a few thrills, not this death-defying race around impossible curves.

She wasn't certain of the precise moment when exhilaration replaced panic. Perhaps it was when Brad clasped her hand in his and gave it a reassuring squeeze. Perhaps it was the instant when she caught the glimmer of excitement in his eyes, heard the low rumble of his laughter as they crested an incredibly steep hill.

Most likely, though, the evolution took place when

she learned to trust, when she realized that he knew exactly what he was doing and precisely how far he could push the car. By the time they reached the waterfront, her eyes were sparkling with delight and her pulse raced with the wind. Never had she witnessed such an incredible blending of man and machine. Her car had become an extension of Brad, subject to his whims, mastered by his skill and daring.

"You've just tripled the difficulty of impressing me with this walk," she warned as they got out of the car. Her pulse was finally settling into a more comfortable, sedate rhythm.

Brad smiled with serene confidence as he led her along the street. When she realized where they were headed, she regarded him in amazement.

"The Golden Gate?"

"Can you think of a more appropriate place to begin a San Francisco vacation?"

"Most people simply drive across it or look at it from one of those little tour boats in the Bay."

"You and I are not most people. We are adventurers," he reminded her.

"Right," she said. There was more hope than conviction in her voice as she studied the magnificent span that linked San Francisco and Marin County.

"Did you know that on the day this bridge opened in 1937, two hundred thousand people walked across it and that they paid a nickel for the privilege?"

"It must have been crowded," she observed as she stared up at the art deco towers disappearing into the fog. The steep cliffs of Sausalito weren't yet visible in the dawning daylight.

Brad ignored her unimaginative observation. He took her hand and tugged her along. He rattled off a steady stream of historical tidbits about the bridge. Her favorite was about the Englishman who'd proclaimed himself monarch during the Gold Rush era and declared that such a bridge should be built.

"I thought you were down in L.A. cleaning off your desk. Obviously you spent the past week studying some encyclopedia," she said.

"Travel brochures and guide books," he corrected. "You keep forgetting we're on vacation. Lesson one—a vacation is always enhanced if you do your homework."

"I'll try to remember that," she said solemnly.

"It'll come with practice."

Karyn wondered if she'd ever have enough travel experience to make any trip and its planning seem routine.

As if he'd sensed her discouragement, Brad said, "You'll see. I promise. Now, let's hurry. We don't want to miss this."

As they reached the middle of the bridge, he drew her close to his side and gestured around them. Karyn was so absorbed by the newness of having Brad's arm around her waist, she was hardly aware of their surroundings. As his hand settled lightly on her hip, she found she was holding her breath as her body accustomed itself to the excitement of his touch. Not one of those rare dates she'd permitted herself during the demanding schedules she'd had in high school and college had prepared her for the sensual possibilities of the right man's touch.

"Now wasn't this worth getting up for?" he prodded. She had to force herself to focus her attention on something other than the man beside her. Because he expected it, she glanced dutifully around.

Fire-engine-red cables rose thousands of feet above them, splashed like colorful ribbons across the thick, impenetrable layers of fog. Karyn could hear the pounding of the surf below, but she couldn't see it. Even though she could feel the throb of rush-hour traffic just beginning, it didn't dispel the notion that they were isolated in a world of shadows and imagination. The early-morning air made her shiver, which was apparently incentive enough for Brad to wrap his arms around her. An unexpected burst of fire deep inside warmed her. A feeling of contentment that was at odds with the wild, howling wind and bone-chilling dampness stole through her. It was definitely awesome.

"What do you think?" he murmured against her hair.

Her senses sang with exhilaration. "I think I've died and gone to heaven."

"It is a little like being above the clouds, isn't it? Is it any wonder people have left their hearts here?"

"You realize, of course, that I will probably be late for work every day for the rest of my life," she said, relaxing in the warmth of his embrace.

"Why's that?"

"I'll want to stop and take this walk."

"Then do it."

She sighed with regret. "No. If I did, I suppose it would become old hat after a while. It would lose the sense of enchantment."

"Not if you keep your mind open to the subtleties, a change in the direction of the wind, the shimmer of color when the sun begins to reflect off the metal. The slow lifting of the fog. The threads of sunlight lying in silver pools on the water."

The poetic words spun a web of magic around her heart. "You should stop peddling cars for a living and write guide books."

"You inspire me."

His embrace tightened ever so slightly with the quietly spoken and seemingly heartfelt compliment. Karyn lifted her gaze to his and caught a faint suggestion of wistfulness that tugged at her heart. She turned slightly and, with fingers that trembled, touched his cheek. His skin was warm and smooth from a morning shave, his jawline angular. He was flesh-and-blood male, not a daydream, but she didn't understand him any more than she could capture an illusion. Her experience had been with honest, down-to-earth, hardworking men whose level of gallantry extended no further than opening a car door. Men like that talked about football point spreads and baseball batting averages. They did not wax eloquent about threads of sunlight.

"What makes you tick, Brad Willis?" she wondered aloud.

He refused to take her question seriously, shrugging it off with a laugh and a grin. "I'm driven by demons," he said flippantly, but Karyn heard the odd note in his voice that warned her the description fit in ways she couldn't begin to fathom. Before she could pursue the truth, Brad released her and opened the bag he'd been carrying. He plucked a bottle of champagne from its depths.

"To toast the sunrise," he said, popping the cork.

"Sunrise?" Karyn repeated with a lift of an eyebrow

as she surveyed the endless vista of gray. The sky was lighter now, but no less muted.

"It's out there," he promised. "It's just one of those things in life you have to take on faith."

"That's a dangerous practice. I learned long ago not to count on anything I couldn't see or touch."

The edge of cynicism sobered him. He caressed her jaw with his thumb while gazing deep into her eyes. "You haven't had an easy time of it, have you?"

Now it was her turn to shrug off the serious moment, the unwanted sympathy. "Not easy, no, but far better than some. I've had to work hard for it, but I have an education. I have an interesting job with plenty of opportunity for advancement. Most important, I've always had a family who loved me."

"Those are all the basics, but that's not always enough to take away the hunger."

Karyn tried again to lighten the tone. "Hey, it wasn't that bad. We had food on the table, just not much else in the way of extras."

"People can hunger for more than food, my literal one," Brad said, sounding like a man who knew such hunger firsthand. "Hawaii, for example."

"And Grand Prix victory?" she guessed.

"I had my share." The statement suggested Brad took pride in his accomplishments, but his tone was flat, drained of all emotion.

"That doesn't mean it was enough. People with a craving for pickles, for instance, never seem to get enough."

"Pickles?" he repeated, grinning at the comparison.

She laughed. "It was one of the extras. Like picnics and

vacations. To this day I can't pass up a juicy, fat dill pickle. Thank heavens I didn't develop a craving for diamonds."

Despite her laughter, his grin died. "I'll add pickles to the agenda this week," he promised. "As long as you don't want them for breakfast. I'm not sure I could bear that."

"No, for breakfast, champagne in the middle of the Golden Gate will do very nicely." She watched him closely. "What else do you hunger for, Brad? Besides another race?"

The burning glint in his eyes intensified and Karyn's heart thundered in anticipation. "Until right this minute, I haven't known for sure, but this, I think," he said softly and bent his head, capturing her lips with a hunger that took her breath away.

Karyn had never known such need, never experienced such powerful masculine possession. She gave herself over to it with a passion that very nearly overwhelmed her. Joy burst inside her. It was as though she were discovering springtime after a hard winter. It was the heat of fire after the chill of snow. It was…awesome.

Shaken and vulnerable in the aftermath of that kiss, Karyn couldn't bring herself to meet Brad's eyes. He tilted her chin up until she had no choice. "Don't hide from me, Karyn. Please," he said softly.

Dazed, she shook her head. "I won't."

"I was right, you know."

"About what?"

"You are what I've been hungering for. There is a freshness about you, an innocence, that I haven't known for a very long time."

It wasn't his words or the tone of his voice that

dazzled Karyn. It was the blaze of fire in his eyes. She reached out to touch the icy, bright red metal of the bridge, to ground herself in reality. Even that couldn't rob her of the sensation that the bridge was falling away beneath her, that Brad Willis, a man she'd known for such a short time, held her fate in the palm of his hand.

"You're trembling," he observed, his expression troubled. "Am I going too fast for you?"

"A little," she admitted shakily. Boldly, though, she looked into the depths of eyes the same deep green shade as the churning water below and said, "But don't stop."

With a heavy sigh, he drew her close. "I don't think I could if I wanted to."

Brad tangled his fingers in her hair and rested his chin atop her head. She could hear the steady, thumping rhythm of his heart. The tangy scent of his soap filled her senses. His warmth surrounded her. When he spoke again at last, the words rumbled up from deep in his chest.

"Where would you like to go next on your vacation?" he asked. "Italy? China? France? Take your pick."

Smiling, Karyn lifted her gaze to his and gave herself over to the fantasy. "Italy, I think. Will it take long to get there?"

"Not long at all. In fact, if you look closely enough, you can see it from here."

"Oh, really?"

"Yes, you can," he said, chiding her for her skepticism. He pointed toward the cliffs of Sausalito. "Look there at the flowers tumbling down the hillsides, the little twisty roads. Doesn't that remind you of an Italian seaside village?"

"My imagination must not be as vivid as yours. It looks like Sausalito to me."

"Then I think our first stop should be to buy you some rose-colored glasses. Any true romantic could see what I see."

"I haven't had a lot of time for romance in my life," she said, unable to prevent a wistful note from creeping into her voice.

Brad's fingertips were warm against her cheek as he vowed, "Then that's about to change."

Hand in hand, they returned to the car. With Brad's dangerous promise still ringing in her ears, Karyn sat silently looking out the window as they crossed the bridge. Her world was suddenly spinning like a top, reeling away from reality as she had known it—dull, consistent, unchanging. What was emerging was a way of life colored with vibrant, passionate shades and throbbing with excitement. After a few days of this, would she ever be content with her humdrum existence again?

It didn't matter, she told herself staunchly. The taste of enchantment was worth whatever heartache might follow. Determined to savor it all, Karyn put her hand trustingly into Brad's as they left the car near the ferry dock and began the walk through the winding streets of the quaint village.

With the total enthusiasm of a dedicated shopper, Brad dragged her in and out of one boutique after another, watching her closely as she tentatively touched the unique jewelry, studied the paintings or ran her fingers over the fabric of handcrafted woolens or delicately screened silks. She fell in love with a scarf in shades of gold and red, but Brad shook his head and reached instead for one in bright blues and boldest turquoise. When he held it close to her cheek, she could see at once that he was right. It brought out the warm peach tones in her skin and emphasized the unfamiliar sparkle in her eyes.

Astonished by the difference, she teased, "You have quite a knack at that, Mr. Willis. Have you spent a lot of time picking out women's clothes?"

"Some," he murmured and Karyn's heart fell. "But never as successfully as this." He turned to the salesclerk. "We'll take it."

"Brad, no," she protested, glancing at the exorbitant price tag. "It's far too expensive and impractical."

He shook his head. "What am I going to do with you? Vacations are meant for frivolous purchases. Now pay attention and repeat after me—for the next week, if I see something I really, really want, I'll buy it. That's lesson two."

Karyn laughed at his serious expression. "And who will pay the bill for all these extravagances?"

He waved aside the practicalities. "That's something you worry about over the long months between vacations. Besides, this is a gift from me to you."

"I can't accept it. It's one thing for you to be entertaining me all week long. This is too much."

"Don't you want me to enjoy this vacation as much as you do?"

"Of course."

"Then you'll have to accept the gift. It makes me happy to give it to you, to see your eyes light up when you look at it and at me."

The rich colors and cool silk of the scarf tempted, but not nearly as much as the hopeful gleam in Brad's eyes. For a fraction of a second, Karyn could almost believe it really mattered to him whether she accepted the present. "Thank you," she said finally.

"You're welcome," Brad replied, his eyes locked with hers as he wound the scarf loosely around her neck. His fingers brushed her nape, then trailed along the neckline of her sweater. Against her bare flesh, his touch blazed a path of fire and new, unfamiliar emotions burst forth deep inside her.

Karyn had never experienced such tenderness before, such attentiveness to her needs. It wasn't so much Brad's gift that mattered as the fact that he'd caught the longing in her eyes, that he'd cared enough to recognize how rare such treasures were for her. She reached up and touched the delicate fabric. The emotions born this morning were just as fragile, just as unique.

Was there any way, she wondered, to tell how long either would last?

# Four

The sun burned away the last wisps of fog and like more magic, San Francisco emerged across the Bay as Karyn and Brad lingered over coffee in one of the cafés that dotted the Sausalito waterfront. Though Brad kept her entertained with innocuous stories of past travels with his family and on the racing circuit, she was not unaware of the speculative looks constantly cast in their direction. The reminder of Brad's celebrity status was disconcerting at best to someone used to remaining quietly in the background.

It was one thing when a boy of about twelve asked hesitantly for an autograph. It was quite another to have a flashy redhead in a skintight miniskirt wiggle over, drape herself around Brad's neck with obvious familiarity and kiss his suddenly flaming cheek. Karyn couldn't quite tell whether Brad's blush was caused by embarrassment or outrage. Her own reaction was even more confusing. Not only did she feel uncomfortable in the presence of such intimacy, she discovered that she was also capable of gut-wrenching jealousy.

"Brad, honey," the woman whispered in a throaty, all-too-sexy purr. "It's been too long."

Brad shot an apologetic look at Karyn as he tried to disengage the woman's fingers, which were threaded through his hair. Quickly, he stood, threw some cash on the table for the bill and reached for Karyn's hand. "Nice to see you," he mumbled to the woman, then headed for the door at a determined pace that could have earned him first place in a marathon.

"Sorry about that," he said when they were finally alone and a full block from the restaurant.

"The run or the interruption?" Karyn asked, drawing in a ragged breath.

"The interruption."

"Who was she?"

"Beats me."

"You didn't know her?"

"Let's just say I don't remember her."

Karyn stiffened at his cold, dismissive tone. "It's not particularly gallant of you to say so. She certainly seemed to know you."

He stopped and turned her around to face him, his hands on her shoulders. "There are a lot of women who follow professional sports, including racing. They show up at parties. They claim an intimacy that may or may not be real. I probably have seen that woman before. I may even have had a conversation with her, but I guarantee you that it's never gone any further than that. I may have had some wild moments during my years on the circuit, but I remember all of them."

At Karyn's doubtful look, he repeated, "All of them, sweetheart."

Karyn felt the knot that had formed in her stomach finally begin to dissipate. She supposed what Brad said was entirely possible, but the woman had spoken in such a familiar way. Such brazen public behavior was beyond her experience. It emphasized once more the wide chasm between her level of sophistication and Brad's. He might not like what had just happened, but he was apparently used to it.

"Does that sort of thing happen to you a lot?" she asked as they started to walk again, his arm settled comfortably across her shoulders. She liked the way it felt there, liked the hint of possessiveness.

"Not as much as it used to. I've been away for a while now. People start to forget. New faces have taken my place."

"Did you enjoy all the attention?"

"I enjoyed winning. The rest was unavoidable. To be perfectly truthful, there were times I took advantage of it. It can be very lonely, if you don't. Women like you don't want to get involved with a man who's always on the run. The glamour wears thin very quickly. They want someone they can count on when the kids get sick or when the washer breaks down."

"Someone like Frank," Karyn said, unable to restrain a grin.

"Frank?"

"My oldest brother. He's very handy. He turns positively rapturous at the sight of something broken."

"Just the kind of man I meant," Brad concurred, laughing at the description.

"I want more," Karyn countered, warming to the subject. "I mean, I know there's a lot to be said for stability and responsibility, but I'm perfectly willing to rely on myself for those. They weren't traits that did my mother any good. My father was as responsible as they come, but he died when he was barely fifty and she was left on her own with little education and no marketable skills. It's not smart for a woman to count on anyone other than herself."

"That's a pretty cynical attitude."

"Not cynical," she contradicted. "Realistic. I'm not dismissing the value of love, mind you. I'm all for romance and storybook endings, but not solely for the purpose of providing a safe, secure future."

"Ah," he said. "I think I'm beginning to catch the distinction. I think it puts you somewhere between feminism and fairy tales."

"You're laughing at me," she said indignantly.

"No, sweetheart. I'm envying you. You're so certain about what you want out of life."

"Is that how I seem to you?"

"Absolutely. I've never known anyone more confident in herself and her goals. All that self-reliance is a little intimidating to a man who's going through a midlife crisis that's not of his own choosing."

"Only if you think the only way to maintain a relationship is for the man to control the purse strings. Are you that insecure, Brad? Can't you conceive of a relationship with a woman that's a full partnership in every sense of the word?"

"I've never thought about it before," he said. "I guess

we'll just have to wait and see how deep my macho chauvinism runs, won't we?"

"When do you anticipate knowing?"

"Oh, I'd say I should have a better idea by the end of the week. Now why don't we talk about your insecurities for a minute."

"Mine? I thought you just said I was intimidatingly confident."

"With one exception that I've discovered so far. You turned practically green with jealousy when that woman came up to our table. Why?"

"She seemed like exactly the kind of woman who knows how to go after everything she wants and get it." *Including you,* she thought to herself.

He shook his head. "I guess I'll just have to spend the rest of this week proving to you that you have absolutely nothing to worry about from a woman like that." His fingers combed back through the short curls of her hair until his palm rested against the curve of her cheek. "You are a beautiful, vital, exciting woman. No man who's out with you would ever turn his attention to someone else unless he's a damn fool."

The attempt to still her self-doubt was sweet, but Karyn wasn't crazy enough to believe she could compete with the full-figured, flamboyant redheads of the world. "It's very nice of you—"

He pressed his finger against her lips. "No doubts."

"Brad, how can I not have doubts?" she said, trying desperately to cling to reality when he was leading her toward fantasy at a dizzying pace. "I'm not glamorous."

"So what?"

"I'm not sophisticated."

"Thank God."

"There are so many things I've never experienced."

"Which will make it all the more fun for us to do them together. Now are you quite through denigrating yourself?"

"I am not putting myself down," she argued. "I don't believe in self-pity. I'm just trying to make you see my limitations. I am what I am. I'm proud of what I've accomplished. It just may not be enough for someone like you."

"Sweetheart, those things you mentioned are only limitations to you, definitely not to me. Do you want to know what I see when I look at you? I see spirit and determination. I see the innocent delight that makes your eyes sparkle. I see someone who's not afraid to laugh, who still takes pleasure in little things like pickles or a scarf. I see excitement at the prospect of discovering new things."

All the things he mentioned were traits that Karyn thought of as merely an irritating lack of experience. "You really mean that, don't you?" she said, searching his expression and seeing nothing but heartfelt sincerity.

He nodded. "I really do. Now let's go. We have an entire city to explore and only a week to see it. Think you can keep up with me?"

After the tiniest hesitation, she smiled and a weight lifted from her heart. If Brad Willis was content with her company, who was she to suggest that he would soon grow bored? "Absolutely," Karyn said with renewed confidence. "What's next?"

"Fisherman's Wharf. We began the day as tourists. I think we should end it the same way."

The honky-tonk atmosphere of the famed waterfront area, along with the Cannery and Ghirardelli Square, was exactly what Karyn needed. The sidewalk entertainment, the diverse shops and outdoor cafés set against the backdrop of the Bay gave them a chance for more leisurely, hand-in-hand strolling in an environment that defied depressing thoughts.

She discovered that while Brad was knowledgeable about the offerings of the exclusive boutiques in Sausalito, he was just as enthusiastic about inexpensive tourist trinkets. He insisted that she have a San Francisco T-shirt and was endlessly patient while she chose one. When the purchase was made, he promptly tugged the shirt over her head, his hands lingering for just a moment beneath her breasts. The light, casual brush of his fingertips set off waves of shivering delight. It was a sensation Karyn knew she'd remember weeks from now when Brad was gone and she was alone in her bed, wearing the oversize shirt.

"You're trembling," he noted, his gaze locked with hers.

Her throat too dry to respond, Karyn nodded, terrified he could tell how his touch aroused her.

"I think that calls for some Irish coffee," he decided, apparently misreading the cause of the shudders sweeping through her. She was relieved at first, until she caught the knowing glint in his eyes and realized that he had deliberately taken her response lightly to set her at ease. Karyn realized then what she should have known all along: Brad knew all about seductive pacing, just as he did about negotiating the curves and hills of a Grand Prix course. It should have made her cautious. Instead, it filled her with anticipation.

They walked to the Buena Vista Café on Hyde Street,

where they were finally able to find a table for two squeezed into a corner of the crowded restaurant famous for its Irish coffee. When the steaming coffee was in front of them, Karyn clung to the cup and searched for something witty to say. Her range of repartee seemed all too limited. She doubted he would want to hear about her class in interrogatories or her struggle with taking depositions. For the first time in her life, she regretted not taking more time away from her classes and work to develop the social skills that were second nature to most women her age.

"You're retreating again," Brad accused gently.

"You're right," she admitted. "I don't have a lot of practice making small talk."

"Small talk is between strangers. Surely we're more than that by now."

"Not really."

He settled back, crossed his legs at the ankles and grinned. "Okay, fire away. What would you like to know?"

She seized the opening with enthusiasm. Leaning forward, Karyn propped her chin in her hand and said, "Tell me about your family."

"You already know about my father. My mother is a bit of a socialite in her own right. Her parents had money. They thought she married beneath her when she married my dad. I think that's probably why he became such a workaholic. I think he's always been trying to prove himself. Ironically, he never needed to prove anything to my mother. She adores him and she stopped caring what her parents thought the day she walked down the aisle."

"Any brothers or sisters?"

"A younger brother."

"Does he show any inclination to take over the family business? Couldn't he relieve you of some of the responsibility, so you could race again?"

"Unfortunately, Brian is only interested in making sure that he gets his share of our father's estate. If he had his way, I'm sure it would be sooner, rather than later."

"That's awful," she said, genuinely appalled. "Don't they get along?"

"It's not that. Brian is a gambler, a real high roller. It's an addiction, but he doesn't see it that way. Dad gave up on him a long time ago. He put money in a trust fund for him so that he'd never have grounds to challenge his will, but he won't allow him access to the business. He's afraid he'd lose it in a high-stakes poker game or use it for collateral to bankroll a bet on the races at Santa Anita. Brian gets a healthy amount from the interest on the trust, but it's never enough. He's always borrowing from Mom or me or our grandparents. He only dares to turn to Dad when he's desperate."

Karyn listened carefully for some evidence of anger. She heard none. "You don't sound bitter. Why? He's keeping you from your dream."

"I feel sorry for him. Gambling is a sickness for him, but until he realizes it, he'll never change. As for me, Brian's not keeping me from anything. I made a choice about how I wanted to handle my life and my relationship with Dad. I owe him a lot. Without him, I'd never have been on the race circuit in the first place. I'm going through a rough period of adjustment now, but I know what I'm doing is right."

"I saw that picture of the two of you that's hanging in your office. He looked very proud."

"He was. I think he feels tremendous guilt about what's happened. I've tried not to let him see the frustration I feel, but sometimes I'm sure he does. Fortunately, for all of us, it's getting better."

Brad took her hand in his and rubbed his thumb across the knuckles before raising it slowly to his lips. That sense of shivery anticipation raced through Karyn again as he lingered over the tender caress. "I'm finding more and more to like about this more stable lifestyle," he said in a low voice that skimmed across her senses with the fire of whiskey.

"Brad." With the roaring of her blood in her ears, she was barely able to choke out his name.

"Um?"

"Maybe…I'd better go home. It's been a long day and it's getting late."

He smiled ruefully. "Why am I so certain that you mean to go alone?"

"I'm sorry."

"You needn't be. It's part of what makes you special. Come on, then. I'll walk you to your car."

"I'll give you a lift," she offered, suddenly reluctant to put an end to the day, fearful the joyous feelings she'd been discovering would vanish like a wisp of fog in sunlight.

"No. If I get into that car with you, I may not want to get out. It's better if I walk back to my hotel."

She felt oddly hesitant. What if sending him home alone proved to him just how silly and unsophisticated she was? "I will see you in the morning, won't I?" Though her tone was light, she knew there was no mistaking her doubts. She regretted it, but she couldn't stop it.

"Maybe not at dawn again, but I will be there," Brad promised. "Count on it."

His arms slid around her then and his lips found the sensitive spot on her neck before claiming her lips one last time. "It's been a special day, Karyn. One I'll never forget."

"Do you really mean that?" she asked, anxiously searching his eyes.

"Every word, sweetheart."

With his words warming her heart, Karyn got in the car, turned on the ignition and started to back up. A bus pulled part of the way past and stopped, blocking her way. She hit the brakes and waited. The bus didn't move. Finally growing increasingly irritated, she turned and glared toward the driver.

It was Timmy—and the expression on his face as he scowled down at her and Brad, who was still waiting nearby, was not filled with brotherly love. She had no doubts at all that the only thing keeping him from climbing out of the bus and pummeling Brad right then and there was the fact that the bus was filled with passengers. Even so, he appeared torn between expressing his indignation and his professional responsibility.

"Brad, I think you'd better go on," she whispered urgently.

Brad heard the odd nervousness in her voice, but more than that he saw a quick flicker of panic in her eyes. It shook him. He reached out to touch her cheek reassuringly, but she moved away. Puzzled, he asked, "Karyn, what's wrong?"

She again glanced anxiously toward the bus that was

blocking her car. "The man driving that bus," she whispered, "the one with murder in his eyes…"

"Yes?"

"He's my brother Timmy."

Brad turned around slowly and looked toward the bus. He studied the driver and caught the hint of brotherly outrage on his face. For the first time he fully understood just how protective her family was. A part of him appreciated such deep loyalty and concern and liked the fact that someone had been looking after Karyn as he himself would have done. What worried him was the effect it seemed to have on her. One minute she had been all woman in his arms. The next she had been as skittish as a kitten.

In an attempt to disarm Timmy and relieve Karyn's nervousness, Brad waved. As Brad had intended, the friendly gesture obviously disconcerted her brother. Timmy gave him a halfhearted wave then, with obvious reluctance, responded to the noisy, irritated rebukes from his passengers. He pulled into traffic and drove on.

With his departure, Brad could see Karyn's tension visibly abate, though she continued to shiver. He realized then that he couldn't possibly let her go home alone, when it was obvious she was going to spend the night worrying herself sick over the prospect of a confrontation with her brother. Before she could put the convertible back into gear, he leaped over the door and settled into the passenger seat.

Clearly startled, she stared over at him. "Brad, what do you think you're doing?"

"Going home with you."

"You can't," she protested.

"Why not?"

"Because—"

"Because your brother is going to show up with a thousand and one questions, right?"

"If I'm lucky," she said with a sigh of resignation.

"And if you're not?"

"He'll also have the *rest* of the family in tow."

"That's exactly why I'm coming along. We've done nothing wrong. The fact that he saw me kiss you goodnight is hardly grounds for hysteria."

"You've obviously never encountered anyone like my brothers. They plopped me on a pedestal at birth and I can't seem to get down. They definitely don't want anyone up there with me."

"Very Victorian," he said, and laughed at her grimace. "I'm looking forward to meeting them."

She turned and stared at him in apparent astonishment.

"I am," he repeated emphatically.

She looked glum. "You don't have to do this, you know."

"I know."

"Then why are you?"

"Because you and I are going to continue seeing each other and your brothers and I might as well get that straight right now."

A bright spark of hope lit her eyes. It was almost as bright as the desire he'd seen there earlier. The combination was too much for a mere mortal like him. Brad felt himself falling wildly, crazily in love. Karyn had presented him with one more dragon to slay and judging from the expression on her face, he'd done just fine.

# *Five*

Karyn awoke with a crick in her neck and a pain in her back. It was just after 7:00 a.m. and once more someone was pounding on her door. Obviously any opportunity to sleep late during her vacation was doomed. Still groggy, she stumbled halfway across the room before she remembered that Brad was sprawled on her sofa, where he'd fallen asleep sometime shortly before dawn. Since the pounding didn't seem to be fazing him at all, she doubted that there was anything she could do to get him up and out a window before the person on the other side of that door barged in.

She swung open the door. "Keep it down, please. My head hurts," she grumbled.

"More than your head is going to hurt by the time we finish talking," Tim growled right back as he stalked into the living room.

He was halfway to the kitchen when he caught sight of Brad, who was just beginning to stir. Tim's expression went from shocked to outraged to thoughtful in a matter of seconds as he watched Brad kick the quilt to the floor. Fortunately, he was fully clothed beneath it.

Tim locked his hand around her elbow and propelled her into the kitchen. "Okay, sis, who the hell is he and what is he doing here at this hour?"

"We were waiting for you," Karyn said, plugging in the automatic coffeepot and dumping in an extra scoop of coffee. She had a feeling they were going to need the strongest brew she could make. "When I saw you last night, I figured you were upset about seeing Brad and me, well, you know." She gazed at him beseechingly.

"Kissing? Right in the middle of the street? Were you out of your mind?"

She figured the question was rhetorical. "Anyway," she went on, "Brad came back here with me so I wouldn't have to face the music alone. Not that there should have been any music to face, mind you." She gazed at him pointedly. He scowled. "By the time it dawned on me that you were working the night shift, we were both too exhausted to move. Before you ask, he slept on the sofa. When he offered to sleep there, I didn't have the heart to tell him that was actually my bed. I guess he figured there had to be a bedroom somewhere. Most people do have them, you know." She couldn't seem to stop rattling on.

Tim nodded. "Okay, so far. What I'm more concerned about is where *you* slept."

Something inside Karyn snapped at the inquisition. In the past she'd simply shrugged them off. She'd certainly had nothing to hide. Now, however, it was definitely time to put a firm stop to these ridiculous intrusions into her personal life once and for all.

"Not that it's any of your business," she began well enough. Her resolution wavered under Tim's penetrating gaze. "Okay, I slept on the floor, which is why every bone and muscle in my body is protesting this morning. If you're going to act brotherly, do it in a hurry and get out, so I can stand in a hot shower for an hour or two."

"Alone?" Timmy inquired.

"Yes, dammit, alone. I hardly know Brad Willis, but I might add, if I were not going into that shower alone, that, too, would be none of your business." She faced him with hands on hips. "What is wrong with you? I thought you were the one brother I could count on not to behave like an overly protective jerk."

"Call me anything you like, sis. I can take it. Just tell me this, why haven't we met this guy?" Tim was still scowling in the direction of the living room, where Brad was finally sitting upright and looking as though he might be able to get his cramped body on its feet any minute now.

"Because I just met him a week ago," she admitted reluctantly.

"A week ago? Are you out of your mind letting a total stranger into your apartment in the middle of the night?" Tim scrutinized Brad from head to toe. No suspect in a criminal investigation had ever been studied more closely. Karyn didn't have a doubt in the world that Tim now felt competent to identify him should he walk off with the family silver or, to be more precise in her case, the stainless steel.

"He looks familiar," he said finally.

"He used to be a race car driver."

"A race car driver!" His tone made the profession

seem comparable to ax murdering. "Where the hell would you meet a race car driver?"

"Thanks for the vote of confidence in my appeal."

"That wasn't what I meant and you know it. Stop evading and answer me."

"We met when I bought my car."

"You bought a convertible, not some souped-up hot rod."

"I don't think Brad drove souped-up hot rods in Grand Prix events."

"Brad Willis?" Tim said with dawning understanding. "Of course. I've seen his picture in the paper. Sis, he's not your type."

"What is her type?" Brad inquired curiously, pulling a stool up to the bar that separated the kitchen and living room and reaching for a cup of coffee. He looked perfectly at home.

Tim wasn't the least bit taken aback by being overheard. "Someone less...I don't know, less..."

"Experienced?"

"Yeah. That's exactly it."

"Your sister is twenty-six years old. Most of the men she's likely to meet are going to be experienced."

"I wasn't referring just to sex," Timmy said bluntly.

Karyn put her head down on her arms and groaned.

"Neither was I," Brad countered.

A very tense silence ensued. When Karyn could stand it no longer she got up, put bread into the toaster, then coated it with butter and slammed it down in front of the two men. They continued to study each other as if they were prospective sparring partners.

Brad dumped sugar and cream into his coffee, then

stirred it slowly. He ignored the toast and looked directly into Tim's suspicious eyes.

"I'm glad you've always taken such good care of your sister," he told him, then added gently, "But it's time to let her go."

This time Tim *did* look thrown by the blunt pronouncement. His gaze narrowed. "Exactly what are your intentions toward her?"

"Timmy!" Karyn protested, moaning inwardly. Embarrassing moments were piling up so rapidly this morning, she'd never live them down.

"Keep quiet, sis. I want to know how this man feels about you."

"This man doesn't even know me!"

"He knows you well enough to sleep on your sofa."

"On my sofa," she reiterated. "Not in my bed."

"Your sofa is your bed," Timmy reminded her.

"It is?" Brad said, staring at her. "Where did you sleep?"

"On the floor and that's not the point. There is a difference, Timothy Michael Chambers, between having a man fall asleep on the sofa and inviting him into my bed!"

After another moment of tense silence, her brother nodded sheepishly. "You're right. I apologize."

"Maybe you should go home and get some sleep," Karyn suggested. She wanted him out of there before he began cross-examining Brad about his career prospects and bank balance.

"Are you sure?"

"I'm sure."

Tim directed another measuring glance at Brad. He

seemed to visibly relax finally, though that didn't keep him from warning, "If you hurt her, Willis, the world won't be big enough for you to hide in."

Brad gave him a faint smile. "I wouldn't have it any other way."

Karyn's heart tumbled at the tenderness in his voice. It was almost impossible for her to draw her gaze away, but finally she was forced to walk Tim to the door, since he didn't seem inclined to get there on his own.

"You're not going to say anything to the others, are you?" she pleaded.

He glanced over her shoulder at Brad, who was watching the two of them with interest. "I don't think it would do any good. Just be careful, sis. You could be playing out of your league."

"I thought so, too, at first."

"Not anymore?"

She felt herself smiling. "No. I think I'm right where I belong."

"I'm happy for you, then."

"Thanks."

She closed the door behind him and leaned back against it with a sigh of relief. Brad came over and pulled her into his arms. She nestled against him, awed by how right it felt for her to be there.

"That wasn't so awful, was it?" he whispered.

"It could have been worse," she admitted. "Frank would have slugged first and asked questions later."

"Then I'm glad Tim was the brother who showed up. Did you mean what you told him? Are you feeling comfortable with what's happening between us?"

"More and more every minute."

She could feel his sigh. "I'm glad, sweetheart." Brad
tilted her chin up and touched his lips to hers in the lightest
of caresses. But the passion that had been kept at bay all
night flared into full flame, the heat swirling through
them. Karyn lost herself in the enveloping warmth.

It was Brad who pulled away eventually. "We'd best
slow down or those brothers of yours will really have
grounds to take me apart."

Karyn's knees felt so weak without Brad's arms
around her that she sank down on the sofa. "I don't
understand what you do to me." She cast a look of
appeal in his direction. "I've always been in control of
myself, but when you touch me, it's like I just float off
to some incredible place."

"And you see that as bad?"

"I see that as terrifying."

He sat down next to her. "I promise you that you have
nothing to fear from me. I meant what I told your
brother. I won't hurt you."

The comment was reassuring, but hardly realistic.
"You can't possibly guarantee that."

"There you go again. You've obviously had too much
legal training. Let me correct myself, then. I will do my
very best never to hurt you."

"I think I liked it better when you were making more
adamant claims."

"You can't have it both ways, sweetheart. Now, how
about getting out of here? We're wasting our vacation."

"Just let me take a quick shower and change."

"I don't suppose," he began, but his voice trailed off at
one quelling look from her. He grinned. "I didn't think so."

Still shaken by the intensity of the feelings that Brad

had aroused in her in such a short time, Karyn lingered in the shower far longer than she should have. She dressed slowly and emerged from the bathroom with her hair curling damply about her face.

"You had a call," Brad told her. "Your office. Someone named Mary Lee wants you to call back right away."

She didn't waste time worrying about what impression Brad's answering her phone might have made on her boss's secretary. She dutifully picked up the phone and dialed.

"Mary Lee, it's Karyn. Did Mr. Wetherington need me for something?"

"Hi, hon. Yeah, he wondered if you could work this afternoon. He knows it's your vacation and all, but since you're in town, he thought maybe you wouldn't mind. He said he'd make up the time later."

Karyn looked at Brad. Clutching the receiver more tightly, she said, "I'm sorry. I can't make it. I have plans for this afternoon."

It was the bravest thing she'd ever done. Conscientious Karyn Chambers did not turn down requests from her boss. She waited for Mary Lee to announce that she was to get to the office at once or else face immediate firing.

"Okay, no problem," the secretary said instead. "See you next week, hon. Enjoy the rest of your vacation."

The breath she'd been holding escaped on a sigh as she hung up.

"Saying no was really tough for you, wasn't it?" Brad said.

She nodded. "In my family taking risks did not extend to career matters. We've always needed the money too badly."

"You don't anymore, Karyn. Don't ever let yourself feel that someone has that kind of power over you. There are other jobs."

"Rationally, I know that. And I know I have a little savings now to fall back on. It's difficult, though, to break old habits. I keep seeing the worried expression on Mama's face when payday would come and the money wouldn't quite add up to cover the bills. If one of us got sick, it threw the budget into turmoil for months."

"But the world didn't come to an end when you said no just now, did it?"

She shook her head.

"Most bosses respect people who have their priorities straight and who stand up for their own needs. Remember that. Your time is every bit as important as your boss's."

She grinned. "Then why are we wasting it on this silly discussion?"

"Because every once in a while, you obviously need to be reminded how important you are and that you deserve to be taken care of."

"Yes," she said more seriously. "I suppose I do." For the first time in her life she was actually beginning to feel that way. She felt as if she were Cinderella at the ball, but like the fairy-tale heroine who'd finally savored magic, she felt as though she were watching the clock tick away the final seconds of her dream. A part of her wanted to cling to the excitement she was discovering with Brad, but another part knew when the time came, she would have to let it go.

As if he'd caught her melancholy mood, Brad planned a day designed to touch the romance in her soul. He took her on the spectacular Seventeen Mile Drive along the rugged coast of the Monterey peninsula. Each setting they passed was more breathtaking than the one before. Finally, he pulled into a parking lot designated as a lookout point. It was crowded with tourists snapping pictures of the glorious scenery. Thrilled by the view, Karyn leaned back against the convertible's seat and sighed.

"It's beautiful," she declared softly.

"I'm glad you like it. I wasn't sure if you'd been here before, but it was the closest I could come to Hawaii on short notice. It's not exactly the same, but you do have beaches and endless vistas of deep blue water."

Tears filled her eyes at the sentimental thought. "You really brought me here because you wanted me to experience Hawaii?"

He brushed a strand of hair back from her face, his fingertips caressing her jaw. "I want you to experience everything. Will this do for a start?"

"It's almost perfect."

"Almost?"

She grinned at his indignant tone. "The only thing missing is the scent of frangipani," she confessed wistfully. On rare special occasions she indulged in scented bath salts that filled the steamy bathroom with the fragrance. Then she'd lie back in the tub and soak, imagining herself on an island beach surrounded by the soft, sweet scent of plumeria blossoms. She looked at Brad and caught a flicker of satisfaction in his eyes.

"That's where you're wrong," he said, clearly gloating as he reached into the backseat for a box that he'd hidden from view.

Karyn's eyes widened when she saw the name and address of a Waikiki florist embossed on the side. "But when? How?"

He laughed at her astonishment. "You were in that shower long enough for me to fly to Hawaii and back," he teased.

"Seriously, where did you get it?"

"I called first thing yesterday and had it flown in. It really did arrive while you were in the shower. I ran down and tucked it into the car while you were dressing."

With trembling fingers, Karyn awkwardly opened the box. The remembered scent of the waxy, fragile blossoms wafted up. She lifted the lei gently from the box and held it to her face, breathing deeply.

"Oh, Brad, it's the nicest present anyone's ever given me," she whispered. "They're just the way I'd always imagined." She turned eyes that were misty with tears toward him. "Thank you."

"You don't have to thank me, sweetheart. The look in your eyes is thanks enough. Let me put it on for you."

Brad settled the lei around her neck, then kissed her on each cheek. Then, while staring deep into her eyes, he must have seen her longing or perhaps what he saw there merely mirrored his own desires, because slowly, he bent his head and his lips deliberately covered hers. Instead of satisfying the yearning, though, the kiss merely fueled the keen awareness of the textures of his skin, the silky moistness of his lips, the faint stubble on his cheeks. A sweet, insistent ache spread through her and she moved closer still, seeking the fulfillment that her body somehow knew Brad and only Brad could provide.

Lost in the building passion, Karyn was unaware that the fragile blossoms were being crushed. When Brad reluctantly pulled away, his body taut, the touch of his fingertips still lingering against the sensitive peak of her breast, only then did she see that the petals of her extravagant gift were damaged.

But nothing—nothing, Karyn thought with a sense of wonder and conviction—could harm the love that was flowering between them.

# Six

Karyn had a good, long, heart-to-heart talk with herself before Brad picked her up for the next-to-last day of their vacation. She reminded herself that when it was over, he would go back to his life and she would return to hers. She was merely a diversion for a man used to a more sophisticated woman. Even those who dined regularly on caviar and beef Wellington occasionally yearned for fish and chips—and vice versa. Happily ever after only happened in storybooks.

There were to be no regrets. She had indulged in a once-in-a-lifetime dream. She had savored each moment of delight stirred by his kisses, but that's where it had to end. Even Brad seemed to understand that and had not pushed for a deeper intimacy. The day before he had even chosen activities that had kept them safely amidst people—from the vast displays of Asian art at the De Young Museum to the twisting, jumbled streets of Chinatown. If their other adventures had touched her heart and soul, yesterday's had reached out to fulfill her thirst for knowledge.

In front of each intricately carved jade figure, as they had looked at each delicate painting on silk, Karyn had questioned Brad endlessly about Asia. He had answered tirelessly. Worlds that she had only known through books came alive through his eyes. They had settled for a time into the comfortable roles of tutor and student. She had been grateful, not only for his enthusiastic teaching, but for the chance to regain her equilibrium, to forget the delightfully enticing way it felt to have his arms around her, his breath whispering against her cheek.

Once more today, sleeping late had been ruled out. Brad had insisted that the day begin with a hot-air-balloon ride over the Napa Valley. Flights lifted off just after dawn, which meant that the night had been all-too-short. Drowsy and still flushed from sleep, Karyn was waiting in the lobby when Brad arrived with a picnic basket.

*"Comment allez-vous?"* he asked, his eyes lighting up at the sight of her.

She blinked sleepily at the unfamiliar language. He grinned. "How are you?" he translated. "I was just trying to get you ready for our trip to France."

"Let me know when we get there," she mumbled unappreciatively and climbed gratefully into the car. "This vacation stuff is wearing me out. You may be used to burning the candle at both ends, but I'm not used to late nights and early mornings."

"Believe it or not, neither am I anymore."

"At least you look alive." Actually, he looked quite a bit better than that. With a teal-blue sweater over a bright yellow polo shirt and hip-hugging jeans, he looked as devastatingly handsome and virile as ever.

"You'll feel that way, too," he promised, pulling her into his arms and raining gentle kisses on her forehead, eyelids, cheeks and finally her waiting lips. Her pulse quickened at once and her senses were instantly alert. It was better than any alarm clock she'd ever owned and twice as addictive as caffeine.

"Amazing," she whispered, linking her hands behind his neck.

A faint smile curved his lips and a quizzical look flitted through his eyes. "Isn't it, though?" he murmured. "Karyn…" he began, then shook his head. "No. Not now."

"What?"

"Nothing. We'll talk later. Right now we need to get on the road."

They drove through the darkened streets at Brad's usual breakneck pace, crossing the Golden Gate and heading north on U.S. Highway 101. As they came to the narrow, two-lane roads that took them into the heart of the Napa Valley, he finally slowed down.

"Have you ever been ballooning before?" Karyn asked.

"Once, over France. It's a gloriously free feeling to be soaring just above the earth."

"Not like being in a plane?"

"No. For one thing you're not nearly as high up. Nor are you going anywhere near as fast. And it's just you and maybe a few other people up there all alone. You can feel the air rushing past. You feel as though you could touch the clouds. The weather has to be just right, the clouds no more than wisps. I think we're going to be okay today. It looks as though it's starting out to be a perfect day."

When they arrived at the site, several balloons were stretched out on the ground being slowly filled with air. Couples and families were sipping coffee and waiting for the last streaks of a pink and golden sunrise to give way to endless blue. Fascinated by everything that was happening, Karyn plied Brad with more questions. When he ran out of answers technical enough to suit her, he laughingly introduced her to the pilot of the balloon he'd hired for the morning.

Moments later Brad lifted her into the gondola and followed her in. Filled with anticipation, Karyn held on to the side and peered down, then up into the vast interior of the cloth balloon. The tethers were removed, flames shot up heating the air and they were off. Theirs was the second balloon to rise slowly from the ground. More cumbersome than she'd anticipated, it quivered and jostled them until it was fully aloft. Then it floated, drifting through the morning sky like a colorful cloud.

Karyn's breath caught in her throat as the earth fell away. Eyes wide, she clung to Brad's hand. It was only when they'd been in the air for several minutes that she shifted her gaze from the panorama below to Brad's face. He was watching her intensely, his eyes mirroring her excitement.

"Happy?" he asked quietly.

"I'll never forget it," she said, touching a fingertip to his cheek. It was morning-shave smooth and warmed at once beneath her touch. "Thank you. No one has ever had such a special vacation."

"It's been special for me, too. Seeing things through your eyes has reminded me how important it is to stop and find the joy in living again."

"I'm glad, if I've given you that," she said. Their gazes met and held, unblinking, searching. Yet another timeless moment was captured forever in her memory. Then she remembered that she'd brought along her camera. She could fill her scrapbook with images of Brad and years from now, when life seemed tedious and mundane, she could look at the photos and remember magic.

As Karyn tried to break away, Brad held her hand more tightly. "Up here, you can't run away," he teased lightly, though there was an intensity underlying the words that she didn't fully understand.

"I'm not going anywhere," she said, sidestepping wherever he was heading with the pointed remark. "I just wanted to get my camera from my purse."

With an indulgent amused expression, he watched as she took the inexpensive camera out and aimed at the distant fields below, then at the magnificent balloon above.

"Now you," she said, positioning him where she could capture his dimpled smile.

"Now one of us together," he insisted, turning the camera over to the pilot. He pulled her back against his chest and they faced the camera. Just before the shutter clicked, he tickled her so that the snap captured her gasp of surprised laughter.

"I think that's the one I'll carry with me always," he said. "Maybe I'll have it blown up and put on the wall in every one of my offices."

"First you have to get the negative away from me," she reminded him.

"No problem." He reached over and with no effort whatsoever plucked the camera out of her unsuspecting grip and tucked it into his pocket.

She lunged after it before she realized the precarious balance of the gondola. When it dipped and swayed, she fell against the solid wall of Brad's chest.

"Yet another way to get you into my arms," he said delightedly, holding her tightly against him. "I'll have to remember it."

Little did he know that he could get her into his arms with just the slightest hint that he wanted her there. He would never know the power he had gained over her in just a few short days. She would walk away from him with dignity, her pride intact, even if her heart was in pieces.

The whole day was a collage of such moments, a sudden burst of melancholy counteracted by carefree laughter, heart-stopping embraces followed by breathless chases that always ended in yet another embrace, another fiery memory.

After the balloon ride they toured half a dozen vineyards and ate their picnic lunch with the warmth of the sun beating down on their shoulders and the warmth of the wine curling seductively inside.

Karyn stretched out lazily on the blanket Brad had brought, her face turned toward the sun. "What a rare treat this is," she said, and sighed with pleasure.

"And this?" Slowly, Brad lowered his mouth to hers. She could taste the burgundy they'd had with lunch, the full-bodied flavor almost as intoxicating as the caress of his lips.

"Definitely a treat," she murmured, though the words were lost in yet another stolen kiss, this one deeper and far more urgent. His fingers slid beneath her shirt, lingering against bare flesh before seeking the tautness of her breasts. Her breath caught as his insistent strokes stirred wonder deep inside her.

Aching with a need more profound than any she had ever known, she turned sideways until her body was aligned with his, her hand resting against his chest where she could feel the heat of his skin and the quickening beat of his heart.

"I want to make love to you," he said quietly, searching her expression for a response. She tried desperately to cling to reason in the face of his entreaty, but the heartfelt plea in his eyes matched the yearning that was growing inside her.

"It would be a mistake," she said, trying one last time to make him see what was so very clear to her.

"Why?"

"Because after tomorrow you'll be gone. I don't want that much of my heart to go with you."

"I will only be gone if that's the way you want it."

She shook her head. "It's not what I want. It's just the way it has to be."

"How can I convince you that's not true?"

"You can't," she said sadly, wishing she were wrong.

He levered himself away from her with a sigh, but his touch lingered at her breast. He squeezed gently, watching the darkening of her eyes, witnessing the power he had over her. Karyn could almost hate him for that, hate him for proving to himself and to her that he could overcome her resistance easily, if that's what he chose to do.

She brushed his hand away angrily and straightened her shirt. "You can make me want you," she admitted. "So what?"

"I think that says quite a bit about where we stand."

"Passion's easy. Even animals experience lust."

"And you think that's what it is between us? Nothing more than lust?"

"Of course. You come charging into my life like a white knight and sweep me off my feet. It's no surprise that I respond to you physically."

"So you see this as just part of the vacation package. Join Brad Willis on his tour of the San Francisco area, complete with a quick tumble in the hay. Satisfaction guaranteed or your money back."

Karyn was startled by the bitterness in his voice. Before she could respond he said angrily, "Let me make one thing perfectly clear. If that's all that was going on, we would have been in bed together that very first night. I've held back because I knew you felt some uncertainties. I wanted you to have time to get used to the idea of the two of us together, but I'll be damned if I'll let you go on thinking that we're just a couple of animals in heat. You may not know it, but I do. What we have is special. I will not let you throw it away because of some misguided notion that we're from such different worlds that we couldn't make a go of it."

"Make a go of what? An affair? We could probably manage that, but how long would it last? A few weeks, maybe a couple of months, until you got bored."

He shook his head. "I'm not sure which makes me angrier, your lack of faith in me or your own insecurities."

Tears filled her eyes as he lashed out furiously. This wasn't the way she wanted it to end between them. "Brad, I'm sorry."

"Sorry for what?"

"Because…" She realized then that she wasn't at all sure what she was apologizing for. She'd only been trying to be honest with him. "Maybe I'm not sorry," she said quietly. "I only wanted you to know how I felt. I think your response just proves my point. We are worlds apart on the things that count."

His body taut with anger, Brad got to his feet and began gathering their things. "Let's go."

Suddenly cold inside, Karyn shivered, but she stood and followed him to the car. The long ride back to San Francisco was made in tense, angry silence. It seemed somehow fitting that as they reached the outskirts of the city, a cold, damp fog began to roll in, turning the beautiful day to a gloomy gray. It reminded her all too closely of the very first day her Hawaiian vacation plans had been dashed.

Feeling alone and miserable, Karyn paid little attention to the road, looking out only when the car had stopped. Brad was parked on a hill in front of his small hotel in Pacific Heights. Staring straight ahead, his white-knuckled grip still tight on the steering wheel, he said, "I'm sure you can find your way home from here."

She nodded. Then she looked again at the angled line of his tense jaw, at the stubborn set of his shoulders. The thought of never being held in his arms again stirred an aching emptiness so overwhelming that she nearly gasped aloud in dismay.

"Brad…" she began hesitantly.

Only a slight tic in his jaw indicated that he'd heard her whisper his name.

"Don't you think we could talk about this?"

He sighed heavily. "We're past talking."

"I don't think so. I'd like to try."

After the longest sixty seconds of her life—she heard them ticking away on the car clock—he said simply, "Where?"

She took a deep breath, recognizing the risk she was taking, not only with the suggestion, but with her future emotional well-being. "Here. Now."

Brad turned a startled gaze on her. "In my room?"

"I trust you," she said simply. There was no need to say that she didn't trust herself nearly as much.

"You shouldn't," he retorted bluntly. "My body is aching for you right now. I can't make any promises about what will happen once we get inside."

"You would never hurt me."

"Not intentionally."

"Then there's no reason to be concerned. We need to talk. We're here. It seems like the logical place."

"And you're very big on logic," he said with a touch of wry humor. "I hate to tell you, sweetheart, but this time I think you may have outsmarted yourself."

Nerves alive with anticipation, Karyn nodded. "Maybe so," she admitted. It didn't keep her from being the first to open the door and head up the walk into Brad's hotel.

# *Seven*

Karyn was charmed by the small hotel, which had once been an old Victorian house. The staff was welcoming, greeting Brad by name when they went inside. He and Karyn climbed the steep, curving staircase to his room, her heart pounding harder with each step. She knew exertion wasn't responsible for her breathlessness. The fluttery feeling in the pit of her stomach warned her that she was entering dangerous territory. Her resolution was wavering. Like shifting sand, the arguments pro and con slid in and out of her mind. Desire and sensation were easily winning over caution.

Brad opened the door to his room. She stepped inside, holding her breath as the door shut quietly behind her. The click of the lock jangled her nerves and she shot an anxious look at Brad before looking hurriedly away and studying the intimate, unique surroundings.

Old-fashioned lamps cast a romantic glow in the dusky light. Soft music played from an old radio. The setting was perfect for seduction. A window was open to the damp breeze and the air practically throbbed with their mutual hunger. She realized at once that there was no question of talking first, of resolving differences. There was only this white-hot flame that melted the very core of her. She began one last, halfhearted protest and then she was in his arms.

The minute he held her, Karyn knew this was the right choice. No matter what happened between them after this week, she wanted the magic of the vacation to be completed. Brad's touches had been so tender up until now, his kisses as alluring as springtime. She wanted to know the power of his caresses in passion, the wild intoxication of his deep, hot kisses at the height of loving. She would never forgive herself if he left and she never knew.

Brad backed a step away, stood facing her and waited.

"There's still time to change your mind," he said, his voice gentle, though his eyes blazed with desire.

Karyn shook her head. The decision had been made before the door to the room had closed behind them. "Not a chance."

The defiant lift of her chin seemed to amuse him. "Are you absolutely sure you're here because you want to be?" he said. "Only a little while ago, you were so sure this wasn't what you wanted, that this was the last place you wanted to come with me."

She met his gaze evenly. "I have to know," she said helplessly.

"Know what?"

"What it's like to make love with you. I realized

driving here that I didn't want to go through life not knowing."

"How will your family feel about this?"

The question irritated her all the more because it was fair. She had put her family between them. "My family has nothing to do with it," she snapped, then sighed. "I'm not trying to defy them, if that's what you're afraid of. This is just between you and me. I swear it, Brad." She heard his breath catch, saw the tension begin to ease. Her voice dropped to a whisper as she moved into his embrace. "Just you and me."

"I hope so." With a touch that trembled against her cheek, he brushed a strand of hair from her face. "I've discovered this week just how selfish I can be," he said in a voice that was raw with emotion. "I don't want to share you, Karyn, not even with your family."

The words seduced as effectively as his caress. No one had ever wanted her so much. No man had ever treasured her above all others. That this man did—even for this timeless moment only—staggered her. Karyn felt herself melting, the last lingering doubts swept away.

"Kiss me," she pleaded, gazing into his eyes. "Show me how much you want me."

The request seemed to shatter the last of his powerful restraint. His arms tightened around her waist as he captured her lips on a sigh of pure pleasure. The hot, moist invasion of his tongue was as sweet as honey, the heat of his body as warm as a January fire. When his strong hands slid beneath her sweater to span the bare flesh beneath, the sensation was as wicked as a million midnight dreams. Her body hummed with the unfamiliar music of his touch, quickly in tune, delightfully in sync.

Karyn was so absorbed by the soaring sensations that captivated and teased, she was hardly aware of the precise moment when her clothes were stripped away. Only the sudden chill of the air against burning skin shocked her into awareness and then she was lost again, clinging to Brad as he led her into a sensory world she'd only dared to imagine.

The sweet throb of tension low in her abdomen grew until it was her only reality. As glorious as it was, she knew there was more, knew that until Brad's body was united with hers, she would remain incomplete. Burning with fire and too shy to say the words, she used her body with some shockingly instinctive expertise to tell him how badly she needed him, how desperately she wanted him.

Brad heard her frantic, unspoken plea and with one powerful thrust he moved inside her, causing the tiniest instant of pain, then filling her, carrying her to the edge of wonder and then beyond. Their exultant cries came together, born someplace deep within each of them, unifying them for all time...no matter what the future held.

Joy spread through her as she collapsed at last against the pillows, Brad heavy on top of her. When he started to shift his weight, she held him tight. She'd waited a lifetime for this sense of absolute harmony and completion, and she didn't want it to end.

"Don't move," she begged. "Not yet."

"I'm too heavy."

"No. You're perfect. Holding you like this makes

everything more real. I want this moment to last forever."

"Maybe that's something we could arrange," he said, his tone so serious that Karyn's breath snagged in her throat.

"Brad, don't…"

He interrupted the whispered plea. "Listen to me. I think it's time I met the rest of your family, time we talked about the future."

"No!"

At the single, harsh exclamation, he did roll away, leaving her feeling bereft. She dragged at the sheets to fight the sudden chill, but it was bone-deep.

"Dammit, Karyn. Don't tell me even after this that you think what we've shared isn't lasting."

"It can't be," she insisted adamantly. "And I won't have you dragging my family into it. It would only upset them, if they knew I was having a wild, impossible fling—"

Brad's harsh, muttered oath cut her short. "Impossible! It is not impossible."

"It is." She met his furious gaze without flinching. "I will not…" She tried again to make him see reason, but the phone rang before she could complete the warning. She didn't want promises. Despite what she'd said, she wasn't expecting forever. She couldn't involve her family in something as tenuous as what she and Brad had. She had hoped for a little more time—just this one tender, romantically sensual night—before reality intruded. The insistent phone already precluded that.

Brad swore again as he reached across her to answer it. Scowling down at her, he was clearly every bit as angry with her as he was at the interruption. "Yes," he barked at the hapless caller.

As he listened to Tim Chambers's urgent warning, Brad's impatience gave way to wariness. He glanced at Karyn, who was still regarding him with indignation. "She's here," he admitted tersely. "Do you want to talk to her?"

"No. Just get her out of there. You haven't got much time. Frank and Jared are on their way over. I tried to stop them, but Frank wasn't inclined to listen to reason. If he owned a shotgun, he'd have it with him."

"Don't worry. I'll handle it."

"Look, Willis, I'm not too crazy about this situation myself, but I'm warning you. Get Karyn out of there. She doesn't deserve to be embroiled in some messy scandal."

"What the hell makes you think I'd let that happen?"

"Because some sleazy tabloid guy is hot on your trail. That's how Frank found out in the first place. The guy called here looking for dirt. I don't know exactly what he said, but it was enough to send Frank rampaging out of here. I've never seen him so furious."

"Thanks for the warning. I'll take care of it on this end."

"Don't thank me yet. I have a few questions about all of this, too. I'd just rather ask them when everyone's calm and rational."

Another dragon to slay, Brad thought as he hung up the phone. The timing, however, was lousy.

"Who was it?" Karyn asked.

"It wasn't anything for you to worry about."

"But you said something about my being here."

"It was just the concierge," he improvised quickly. "He wanted to know about breakfast."

She regarded him skeptically. "If that's all it was, why are you pulling on your clothes as if the demons of hell are snapping at the door?"

Brad leaned down and kissed her. "Stop worrying. I'll be back in a minute."

"You have to go downstairs to discuss breakfast? It's not even dinnertime."

He cursed himself for not being more inventive. He should have known she'd have a million questions about any excuse that flimsy. He tried another deep, drugging kiss. "Back in a minute," he said when she was breathless. He was out the door before she could react.

Puzzled, Karyn stared after him. Something very odd was going on, something Brad clearly didn't want her to know about. It wasn't until she heard the sound of raised voices that she figured out exactly what it was. Her brothers! Dear God, how had they found out? More important, why hadn't Brad told her? She had every right to know that her family was on the warpath. The very last thing she needed or wanted was another man intent on taking care of her. She had just barely gained her independence.

Not waiting for the battle to escalate into the crashing sound of flying furniture, she jumped out of the bed and began yanking on her clothes. She was still hopping on one foot, trying to get her other leg into her jeans, when Brad returned. He was wearing a very self-satisfied masculine smirk. If she'd had any strength left after their lovemaking, she'd have smacked it off his face. Instead, she gave one final tug on her jeans, slid the zipper up and faced him squarely. In her bare feet, she barely reached his chin. She had to look up to glare at him properly.

"My, my," Karyn began scathingly, "that was some argument. Couldn't you agree on whether or not to poach the eggs?"

She caught a first flicker of doubt on Brad's face. "You heard?"

"Not everything, but enough to guess that my brothers were here. I'm amazed you're in one piece."

"They're not unreasonable men, Karyn."

"Are you sure you're talking about *my* brothers?" she said incredulously.

"That's who they said they were. Frank and Jared."

"Oh, God," she moaned. Even though she'd known it, she'd been hoping against hope that she'd been wrong. "Then they were here?"

"Oh, yes. They were definitely here. Actually, Jerry had held them at bay for five or ten minutes before I even came downstairs. The man's so discreet, I doubt if he'd admit to a fire if he thought the arrival of the firemen would compromise a guest's privacy."

"Then why on earth didn't you just come back upstairs and let him handle them?"

"Because they were not buying Jerry's story for one second. Frank already had one foot on the first-floor landing and Jared was holding Jerry three inches off the floor. I figured there wasn't a door in the place that was safe until they found their baby sister."

"So, what did you tell them?"

"That I was in love with you."

Even as her pulse leaped, her common sense

kicked in. "How dare you tell them something like that?" she shouted. "Don't you get it? Now they'll expect you to marry me."

"No problem. I told them we were working out the details."

Karyn buried her face in her hands. "I will never hear the end of this. They'll track you, Brad. They'll make you go through with it. They'll camp outside your office door at the car dealership. You'll never be able to show your face there again."

He grinned. There still wasn't the slightest evidence of anxiety. "Then you'll just have to make an honest man of me, won't you? What would you think of an August wedding? For that matter, we could fly to Las Vegas tonight. How about it?"

Something snapped inside her at his presumption. Not only had he marched off to fight her family war for her, now he'd backed her into a corner. "What kind of proposal is that?" she raged.

"I was *trying* to propose when Timmy called," he reminded her calmly.

"That's not the point. Dammit all, Brad Willis, can't you see that you're just as bad as my brothers? You haven't once given me credit for being able to make up my own mind about things. I've spent my whole life letting other people fight my battles for me, make the decisions about what's best. Not this time. I'll be damned if I'll jump from the proverbial frying pan into the fire."

She picked up her purse and with one final, furious scowl in Brad's direction, she yanked open the door.

"Karyn," he said quietly. She turned back and saw that he had stretched out on the bed, his back propped against the stack of pillows, his hands behind his head. "I wouldn't go down there quite yet, if I were you," he warned with lazy nonchalance.

Karyn regarded him warily, trying to decide if he was honestly warning her or attempting to trick her into staying. He sure as hell didn't seem to be taking her seriously. "Why not?"

"Because unless I miss my guess Frank and Jared are still planted in the parlor like a couple of giant redwoods."

With a heartfelt sigh, she closed the door slowly. "They're still down there?"

Brad nodded. "I don't think they trust me entirely." He didn't exactly sound broken up about it. He sounded more like a man who was confident of the eventual outcome of this mess.

Karyn wanted very badly to walk out on him, but if he was right about Frank and Jared—and he probably was—she needed to buy herself some time. She looked around for a place to sit. There was only the bed and Brad was occupying a rather intimidating portion of that. She perched on the side as far from him as she could.

"Are you staying?"

"Only until the coast is clear."

He shifted his body until he was sitting next to her, thighs touching. "How about we put the time to good use?"

Every nerve in her body leaped to life at the contact and at the seductive tone of his voice, but she wasn't giving in. Not about this. "No, Brad," she said. Her voice was firm, but she didn't dare meet his gaze. Those green eyes of his could be her undoing. "I am waiting here just long enough to avoid some sort of public scene with my brothers. Then I am going and you and I will never see each other again."

"You don't mean that," he said, but there was the tiniest hint of uncertainty in his voice.

"I do mean it. I do not need somebody to fight my battles for me, Brad. I do not need somebody to support me or take care of me. All I ever wanted was someone who'd love me."

"But I do love you."

"That's not love, Brad. That's smothering. I ought to know. I've lived with it all my life."

Because she couldn't bear the confused, hurt expression in his eyes one single second more, she got up and walked away. Whatever the consequences might be of encountering her brothers downstairs, they couldn't be any worse than sitting here with a man she loved after discovering that he didn't know the meaning of the word.

Karyn had thought her pain couldn't possibly get any worse, but it did. Her brothers had left the lobby of the hotel, but as she emerged, she ran smack into the man who'd gotten her into this mess in the first place. A rumpled but extraordinarily persistent photographer was waiting at curbside. Lazing against the fender of a car, he was instantly alert at the sight of her. He snapped several shots before Karyn realized what was happening.

It was the final straw. She slung her purse as hard as she could, hitting the man upside the head, then took off down the hill toward Fillmore at a run. She was almost at the bottom when she heard a familiar shout.

"Karyn," Frank yelled from his car. "Get in here!"

She whirled on him. "I think I've been rescued quite enough for one day. Just go home!"

She began walking again, the car creeping alongside. "Come on, sis," Jared pleaded. "I know you're upset, but we were just trying to protect you."

"You have no right to interfere in my life. None. I am twenty-six years old. If you all would get on with the business of living your own lives, maybe I could live mine. Now go away. I want to be by myself."

"What about Willis?"

"You don't have to worry about him anymore. He's as bad as the rest of you. I just finished telling him off, too. I trust that makes you happy. You've done your duty. The relationship is over."

She glanced sideways just long enough to see an exchange of guilty looks flash between her brothers. It gave her a fleeting instant of satisfaction before she dashed across the street behind them and caught a bus going in the opposite direction. She didn't really care where it was going. Just about anyplace today was going to feel like hell.

# *Eight*

How in the name of everything holy were you supposed to prove your love to a maddening woman like Karyn Chambers? The question had reverberated through Brad's head so often since his return to Los Angeles, he thought he was going nuts. What had he done that was so terrible? He'd tried to protect her from her brothers' wrath, tried to shield her from embarrassment. She'd reacted as if he'd committed a crime.

For days he paced through the L.A. car dealership, in and out of his office and around his house muttering under his breath about women who didn't know the first thing about accepting love. Then he finally tried putting himself in her shoes. While Karyn struck him as being an innocent in need of protection, she saw herself as a woman in desperate need of asserting her independence. She was still trying to prove to herself— and her brothers—that she could stand on her own two feet. His actions, well-intentioned as they'd been, had knocked her feet right back out from under her.

Brad was used to fighting fiercely for what he wanted, charging after it with everything that was in him. He hadn't won races by being cautious. He'd won them by taking chances, by wanting them so badly that no risk seemed too great. He wanted Karyn Chambers. He needed every stubborn, feisty inch of her. She'd snagged a part of his heart that had been lonely and untouched for a very long time. Every fiber of his being wanted to roar back up the California coast and claim her.

But some gut instinct told him that would be exactly the wrong thing to do with Karyn. She didn't need to be pressured right now. She needed to work through what had happened between them and reach her own conclusions about the depth of their love. He vowed to wait, to maintain his distance, while she did exactly that.

He had no doubts, none at all, about the eventual outcome. He only hoped he wouldn't go mad in the interim.

The clear, color picture on the front page of the tabloid showed a startled, wide-eyed woman emerging from a familiar San Francisco hotel. A second photo was a close-up of Brad's face. As she stood in the checkout line, Karyn felt a moment of sick uncertainty before she realized that she was the woman who appeared above the headline: Hot Driver Brad Willis Races Toward New Love.

The story below added the lurid details, including Brad's complete and seemingly endless list of romantic conquests, her name and occupation and the recent discovery of their love nest at the Pacific Heights hotel. "Is this the lady who finally lured Brad Willis away from fast cars?" the newspaper asked. "Karyn Chambers might be beautiful, but can she compete with his Porsche? Others have tried, but none have succeeded."

They made it sound like some tawdry competition. *Love nest!* The very phrase left her trembling and feeling sick to her stomach. It was bad enough that she'd made a fool of herself over the domineering jerk, but now the whole world knew about it.

After putting the paper back on the rack, Karyn turned and walked out of the store, leaving behind a shopping cart filled with frozen low-cal meals and three pints of chocolate-crunch ice cream. The dinners had been for her conscience. The ice cream had been a futile attempt to fill the void that Brad's departure had left in her life.

He'd only been gone for a few days and already she was lonelier than she'd ever been in her entire life. He hadn't called, not even once. Though she'd been the one to break things off, she regretted it hourly as the minutes dragged by and she missed hearing the sound of his voice. Maybe if she'd been wiser in the ways of love, she'd have recognized what they had sooner. Maybe she'd have fought harder to work things out, rather than running at the first hint of trouble. Brad's actions might have been wrong, but she was a coward.

For one fleeting second she was almost tempted to go back for that awful newspaper just so she could stare at Brad's picture. Though her memory was good, it didn't capture him as vividly as that sleazy photographer had. Even she was able to recognize the irony in that. As for her own pictures, they had remained in the camera that Brad had nabbed from her while they were on their balloon ride.

Still dazed by the discovery that love didn't vanish immediately upon the arrival of disillusionment, Karyn was even more confused at finding herself a media celebrity. She walked slowly home, her thoughts in turmoil. At her apartment she was greeted by the sound of the phone ringing and the sight of the light on her answering machine blinking insistently. Incapable of dealing with either until she'd sorted out her thoughts, she ignored both and sank down on the sofa.

"Now what?" she murmured. How was she going to live down this latest fallout from her brief affair with Brad? The law firm had been supportive and lenient during her long struggle to complete the training to become a paralegal, but it was a staid, old organization. Seeing her picture by every grocery-store checkout stand was not something her bosses would condone. The partners didn't even like to take divorce cases in which they expected a lot of dirty laundry would be aired publicly.

As for her brothers, she had no doubt at all that once one of them had spotted the report, they'd begin pestering her all over again about moving back home. She wouldn't be surprised if they personally packed her bags for her or at the very least permanently locked the hinges on her foldout bed.

One thing was certain, she wasn't going home again. If she had to find another job, so be it. Nothing was going to make her regret her week with Brad. He had opened new worlds and no matter who tried to turn that into something dirty and capricious, she knew better. She believed in her heart that what they had shared was a kind of love, fleeting perhaps, but love nonetheless. If only he hadn't been so overly protective. If only she'd listened to his explanations. If only he'd fought harder to overcome her doubts.

There were those two sad words again—*if only*.

The rattling of the doorknob warned her that the family onslaught was about to begin. There was no place to run, so she sat right where she was and waited. She refused to help by getting up and opening the door.

Fortunately, it was Tim who came in holding a copy of the paper.

"Hi," she said in a flat tone.

"I take it you've seen this," he said.

"I've seen it."

"Frank is going to blow a fuse."

"I don't doubt it."

"And Mom. What is she going to think?"

At that moment the doorknob twisted again and Karyn's mother came in. If she'd worked to learn her cue, she couldn't have timed the entrance any more effectively. Only the worried furrow between her brows indicated that she was troubled. Her smile was as bright as ever as she sat next to Karyn and wrapped her arms around her.

"Are you okay, Karyn Marie?" she said, studying her intently.

"Fine, Mom. I assume you didn't just drop in. You've seen the paper."

"Mrs. Murtaugh brought it by."

"I'm sorry."

"Don't you be sorry, baby. That old woman's nothing but a busybody. I'm not one bit concerned about what she thinks. I'm just worried about you. Timmy, go make a pot of coffee while your sister and I talk."

"But—"

"Go. And make it a big one. I expect the others will be here before long."

When Tim had gone into the kitchen area, Karyn's mother laid a work-roughened hand against her cheek. "You in love with this man?"

"Yes," she admitted, relieved to have it out in the open at last. "It doesn't make much sense, though, does it?"

"Whoever said anything about love making sense? The one thing I do know is that those special feelings aren't something you turn your back on."

"But he's *exactly* like Frank and the others. He thinks I need looking after."

"And that's so bad?"

"I want to be on my own, be my own woman, make my own decisions."

"Don't you think he'd let you do that? There's a big difference between caring what happens to you and taking over your life. A man who cares too much, why, he might make a mistake every now and then and push too hard, but it's usually in the name of love. That's not control, Karyn Marie. Not by a long shot. Maybe the very first decision you ought to make to prove you're all grown-up is whether you really want this man enough to fight for him. Now why don't you tell me about him."

Despite herself, Karyn found that she was eager to talk about Brad, anxious to say his name aloud, to pour out everything to a sympathetic ear. "Actually, we just met," she began.

"When?"

"A couple of weeks ago," she admitted sheepishly.

"Oh, my."

"Exactly."

She patted Karyn's hand. "Well, never you mind about that. Where is this Brad Willis now?"

"Back in Los Angeles, I guess."

"Is he coming back?"

"I don't know. I haven't talked to him."

"Oh, my."

"No, it's not what you think. I told him I didn't want to talk to him. I told him I couldn't love a man who wanted to run my life the way my brothers always have."

As if on cue again, the entire Chambers part of the world descended en masse, led by a scowling Frank. Before he could say a word, though, Tim asked, "Coffee, everyone?"

"Beer," Frank corrected tersely, sitting down and eyeing Karyn as if she'd grown two heads.

"Don't you dare sit in judgment on me, Frank Chambers," Karyn snapped. "Did I interfere in your life when you got involved with that two-timing little tramp from Oakland? Have I said one word about the fact that it's taken you five years to get around to proposing to Megan, even though she's head over heels in love with you and actually thinks you're the smartest, handsomest man on the face of the earth? Have I? And what about you, Jared? Do I tell you how to live your life?"

"It's not the same," Frank grumbled.

"No, it's not," Jared agreed. "You're our—"

"Don't you dare finish that," she ordered. "I am no longer your *baby* sister. I am no longer a baby. I am a woman and I may make a few mistakes now and then, but they're mine to make."

"You have to admit, sis, this one's a doozy," Tim said gently as he handed her a cup.

*"Et tu, Brute?"* she said, flashing him a hurt look.

"Sorry, but it's the truth. Maybe if I hadn't warned Brad—"

Shocked eyes turned on him. "*You* warned him?" Frank said, aghast.

"Warned him about what?" her mother asked.

"Yes," Timmy said defiantly to Frank. "I told him you were playing outraged father of the year. I didn't see any need for Karyn to be embarrassed."

"Well, maybe if she'd been a little more embarrassed last weekend, her picture wouldn't have been right up there beside Cher's today." Frank looked ready to explode. "Good God, Timmy, what were you thinking of?"

"Will one of you explain?" their mother ordered.

Karyn shrugged. "They found out I was with Brad last weekend and they came charging over to rescue me. Only, Timmy called and warned us and Brad went down to meet them without telling me they were coming, which is why I got mad and left him."

"He *lied* to us," Jared interjected indignantly. "Let's not forget that the man told us a bald-faced lie. You were obviously upstairs when we were there. It wasn't an hour later when we found you running down the street."

"I think whatever Brad told you was justified under the circumstances," Karyn countered, just as the door opened and the man in question walked through. Her heart did an untimely somersault in her chest. Despite everything, she was very glad to see him. She figured if she showed it, though, Brad would be lynched before he could cross the room to kiss her. That was really too bad, too. She could have used one of his kisses about now. They still had a lot of talking to do, a lot to work out, but this time she wasn't going to run away from it. This time she was going to behave like a woman who knew exactly what she wanted from life.

Frank and Jared were already on their feet. Her mother looked slightly dazed by the tall, handsome man who was regarding her daughter with a passionate gleam in his eyes. Timmy took a protective step closer to her.

"What do you want, Willis?" Frank demanded.

Brad met his gaze evenly. "To see your sister. We need to talk."

"She doesn't want to see you," Jared said.

"I can speak for myself," Karyn interrupted firmly.

"Well, you don't want to see him, do you?" Daniel said, speaking out for the first time and taking a defiant step toward Brad. He balled his hands into fists at his sides.

"Yes, I do want to see him," Karyn said. As she looked at the shocked faces turned toward her, her stomach rolled over, but she insisted, "Privately, please."

Her mother regarded her intently, then nodded in satisfaction. Apparently she saw something that no one else in the room saw, including her daughter. Karyn just wanted to be alone with the man behind the chaos in her life.

"Come on, everyone," her mother insisted. "It's time we get out and leave these two alone. They have things to talk about that are none of our concern."

"I am not leaving her alone with him," Frank said.

Her mother reached over and grabbed him by the ear, oblivious to the ridiculous picture it presented. "Out! Now!" she ordered. "The rest of you, too."

"Thanks, Mom," Karyn said, giving her a hug.

"Just remember what we talked about. Don't worry about what makes sense. Just worry about doing what feels right."

"You can't be serious," Jared blustered, just as his mother latched onto his arm and yanked him toward the door.

"Nice to meet you, young man," Mrs. Chambers said politely. "Don't mind this troupe. Sometimes they just don't have sense enough to know when to butt out."

"I appreciate your help," Brad said.

"Don't be fooled," she retorted. "Right now, I'm on your side. Hurt my girl, and I'll be the first one to load a shotgun."

Brad grinned. "I'll keep that in mind."

While everyone was getting out, Karyn went into the kitchen area and poured herself another cup of coffee. She held up the pot and gestured toward Brad.

"Please," he said, then took the cup she held out for him. "Are you coming back in here or are you going to hide behind the counter?"

"I think I'll stay right here," she said, refusing to be taunted.

"Coward."

"I think I have every right to be a little cautious with a man who apparently changes women more often than he changes shirts."

"That's overstating things a bit, don't you think?"

"I wouldn't know. All I know is what I read in the papers."

"I may be a great defender of freedom of the press, but that doesn't mean those particular rags have much interest in accuracy. Besides, I never pretended to be a saint prior to our meeting."

"But now you've gone and sprouted the wings of an angel?"

"No, sweetheart, I'm only a man. There have been a lot of times in my life when I've been a very lonely man. Relationships have helped to fill the empty hours."

"And is that what I was doing, filling the empty hours? You had a few days off and didn't want to spend them alone?"

"You know better than that. I had to turn a few things upside down and backward to get that time off. I thought it was worth it to get to know you."

"Was it?"

He smiled for the first time since he'd walked into the apartment and Karyn felt something shift inside her, making way for the first ray of hope that he wanted to work things out as badly as she did.

"You know it was," he said. "I fell in love with you. I thought I was going to teach you a lesson, that I was going to bring a new perspective on living into your life. Instead, you're the one who taught me. I learned something about loyalty and loving that will make all the difference in the rest of my life."

"Glad to be of service," she said dryly. "Should I charge for this lesson?"

"You won't be giving it again, except to me. Marry me, Karyn. I swore I wasn't going to come back here and pressure you, but I couldn't stand being apart another day."

"If you hadn't come, I would have come after you," she admitted.

"You would have?"

"I finally realized what I was thinking of giving up. I couldn't do it. Not without talking things out, at least."

"You want to talk now?"

She nodded, never taking her eyes from his.

"Okay. I understand why you blew up at me for taking over and trying to handle things with your brothers. I promise it will never happen again. It's just that you're so much more innocent, so much less jaded than other women I've known, it brings out a protective streak in me. I guess I've always wanted to be a dragon slayer for someone."

"I can slay my own dragons," she said quietly. "And even when I can't, that doesn't mean I want you to step in and do it for me."

"I'll try to remember that. I really will, but I don't know if I'll ever be able to sit by and let you be hurt, not if there's anything in my power that I can do to stop it."

In a way Brad's promise seemed only to bring them to a stalemate. "I'm not sure I'll be able to recognize the difference," Karyn admitted. "I'm so scared of becoming dependent on you for my happiness, of taking the easy way out and letting you do things for me."

"I have a feeling you'll never hesitate to tell me when I'm getting out of line. You're stronger than you think. You walked out on me, didn't you? Even though you wanted to stay."

The hint of masculine self-confidence grated. "You're awfully sure of yourself."

"I'm sure of what we feel," he corrected. "Even your mother could see it. That's the only reason she left you here alone with me."

Karyn sighed. "Despite everything she's been through, my mother appears to be an incurable romantic."

"So am I," Brad said. "I believe with all my heart that we have the makings of a forever love. That's why I came back." He grinned ruefully. "That and the fact that my father swore he'd wind up having another heart attack if he had to watch me pacing around the office much longer."

"Your father's back at work?"

"Part-time. Long enough for us to go on a honeymoon, in fact."

"But we've just had a vacation." As soon as she uttered the mild protest, Karyn knew that what she'd really said was *yes*…to their love, to working on their problems together, to marriage, to a honeymoon filled with long, lazy hours in Brad's arms.

"Consider that practice," he said, stepping closer until she could feel the whisper of his breath on her cheek. "This time we'll do it for real."

"You could take me to Paris or Greece or Tahiti, but you will never give me a more romantic vacation than the one we just had," she murmured as she found herself back in his arms, her head resting against his chest.

"Then we'll stay home for our honeymoon. I'm not choosy. As long as you marry me. Will you?"

"I will," Karyn said with absolute certainty.

Her acceptance was captured and stolen by Brad's

kiss. As their breath mingled and their hearts pounded, Karyn had second thoughts.

"Maybe I spoke too soon," she murmured against his marauding mouth.

"Oh?"

"I think Paris would be a fine idea."

"No problem," Brad said, nibbling on her lower lip.

"And maybe Greece."

"Whatever you want."

"And I've always wanted to see the place where Gauguin painted all those wonderful pictures."

"Tahiti. Absolutely, if that's what you want."

Karyn sighed happily. "Let's not leave just yet, though."

"Okay, when?"

"I ought to be ready to leave this bed right here in another five or ten years."

\* \* \* \* \*

# SISTER OF THE BRIDE
## Susan Mallery

# *One*

"Katie, honey, you need a date for your sister's wedding."

"I had a date, Mom. He's marrying the bride."

"All right, fine. Your sister stole your boyfriend," Janis McCormick said with a sigh. "And it was wrong. But that was nearly a year ago. It's water under the bridge. They're getting married. The whole family is flying in and we have two hundred other guests. We're going to have a long weekend of all kinds of events and, trust me, you'll feel better if you have a date. The extended family will torture you if you don't, and that will make us both crazy." Her mother finally paused for a breath. "For me, Katie? Please?"

At times like this Katie really hated the whole concept of growing up and acting mature. There were situations where a good temper tantrum seemed like the exactly right solution to a problem. Like this one. But she'd never been into drama—that was her sister's thing. And it was difficult to refuse her mother. Mostly because Janis didn't ask for very much. She was one of those warm, loving parents who worried and slipped Katie an extra fifty dollars every time they had lunch, despite the fact that Katie had been on her own since college and had a great job that she adored.

"Mom," she said, "I love you. You know that."

"Don't say 'but.' I'm on the edge as it is. Your sister is driving me nuts. I didn't have to start coloring my hair until she got engaged. I swear, the second she brought over bride magazines and started talking tulle, I began going gray."

Katie leaned forward in the booth of the restaurant. She and her mother were having a quick lunch to talk about the latest changes Courtney had made to her wedding. The fact that it was only two weeks away didn't seem to worry Courtney.

Nor had stealing Katie's boyfriend.

She wasn't going to be bitter, Katie reminded herself. She was going to rise above petty emotion. Courtney was her sister and the sisterly bond was powerful and lasting. And if Courtney woke up with a zit the size of Cleveland on her wedding day, well, that would be fun, too.

Katie cleared her throat. "However, as much as I would love to bring a guy to the wedding festivities, there isn't anyone. We're talking Fool's Gold. You know there aren't a lot of single guys hanging around. I can't come up with anyone I would trust to pretend to be involved with me."

"Are you telling me you haven't dated since you and Alex broke up?"

Technically, they hadn't broken up. Katie had brought Alex home for one of their usual Sunday-night dinners with Katie's parents. Something she and Alex had been doing regularly for months. The only thing that had been different about that night was the feeling Katie had that Alex was going to pop the question. Mostly because she'd accidentally found a receipt for a diamond ring in his coat pocket when he'd loaned it to her at a football game.

Katie hadn't been sure Alex was the guy she wanted to spend the rest of her life with, but she'd figured being unsure was normal. After all, how could anyone *know* any particular guy was the one? Only, he hadn't proposed. Their friendly dinner had been interrupted by Courtney's unexpected arrival. Alex and Courtney had taken one look at each other and Katie had ceased to exist.

"Katie?" her mother asked. "You're not seeing anyone?"

"No. I've been busy with work and not in the mood."

Her mother sighed. "It's four days of family and stress. I know I don't want to have to field questions about your lack of love life and you have to want it even less. You have to bring a man."

"Sorry, no."

"What about Howie?"

*Dear God, no.*

Katie thought about banging her head against the table, because honestly, the pain would be less. "Mom, no."

"Why not? He's smart and rich and very funny."

And his name was Howie. He was the son of her mother's best friend. The two women had been doing their best to fix up their kids for years. Katie had resisted with all her might. The last time she'd seen Howie, he and his mom had been visiting Fool's Gold. He'd been maybe sixteen and smart enough that he was already in college. Tall, skinny, with too-short pants, thick black-rimmed glasses and a way of peering at her as if she were an uninteresting form of bug. They'd had nothing to say to each other.

"Most of the time I'm willing to take one for the team. But I'm not interested in Howie," she said firmly. "I'd rather deal with the awkward questions." No one was desperate enough for Howie—certainly not her.

"Katie, don't make me use my bad-mom voice."

Katie smiled. "Mom, I'm twenty-seven. The bad-mom voice doesn't work on me."

"Want to bet?" Her mother sighed again. Worry darkened her eyes. "Please? I'll beg. Do you want that? I'm desperate. I want you to have a good time." She paused. "Well, as good a time as you can have at this. And I don't want you to worry about what everyone else might be thinking. It's four days. You'll barely have to see each other."

It was four days trapped in a hotel with her family at the top of a mountain. Where was she supposed to go to avoid them—and Howie?

"He's doing some big project at work," her mother added. "I'm sure he'll be busy most of the time."

Katie hesitated, not just because she adored her mother but also because the questions from family about why she wasn't married had begun to border on brutal. There she was—the older sister—still not married, no prospect of a boyfriend. Courtney could barely go fifteen minutes without falling in love.

"Fine," Katie conceded at last. "Just for the wedding, though. Nothing more. Ever."

Her mother beamed. "Wonderful. I'll let him know. This is going to be wonderful. You'll see."

*Wonderful?* Katie could think of a lot of words but that wasn't one of them. She was already knee-deep in regrets. Four days with Howie? Fourteen years ago, they'd barely lasted an hour in each other's presence.

The only bright spot in the whole thing was that back then he'd disliked her as much as she'd disliked him. Maybe he would do a better job at telling his mother no and then none of this would be an issue.

"Mother, I won't," Howard Jackson Kent said firmly. "I see."

Two simple words. They didn't matter in and of themselves, it was the tone that was going to come back and bite him in the ass. He could already feel the teeth.

"We'll ignore the fact that Janis McCormick is my best friend," his mother said, staring at him from across his desk.

They were in his office, his mother having dropped by unexpectedly between his meetings. There was only one way she would have known he was free, which meant later he would be having a little chat with his personal assistant.

"We'll ignore the fact that Janis has asked for my help."

*If only that were true,* he thought, leaning back in his chair and rubbing his temple.

"You could do it for Katie," his mother said. "She's such a nice girl."

Never words to make a single man's heart beat faster, he thought grimly. "Katie and I don't get along."

Granted, it had been a lot of years ago, but he remembered that summer afternoon clearly. His mother had insisted he come along with her while Tina met with her best friend. He'd agreed and had regretted the decision the second Katie had looked at him, then sighed with obvious disappointment.

Katie had been opinionated, only interested in sports and obviously contemptuous of him. Sure, he'd been a nerd and awkward and he'd never communicated well with others. But she'd been difficult and unfriendly. She'd also threatened to beat him up. At the time, she probably could have.

"Things could be different now," his mother said. "She's lovely."

"Uh-huh."

His mother straightened in her chair. Tina Kent was small, but he knew better than to judge her by her size.

"Do you remember ten years ago when I had breast cancer?" she asked.

He held in a groan and nodded. *Not this,* he thought. *Anything but this.*

"You were in college. I didn't want you to know how bad it was because I wanted you to focus on getting your masters."

It was in that program he'd developed the software that had launched his company and turned him into a multimillionaire in three short years.

"Mom—" he began.

She held up a hand. "When you came home, you

were worried. I promised you I would get better." She paused expectantly.

"I said I would do anything if you would," he said dutifully.

"I kept my promise. Now it's time for you to keep yours. You're going to be Katie's date for the wedding. You'll spend four days at the resort in Fool's Gold, and you'll do everything you can to make Katie feel like a princess."

*Dammit all to hell.* Why couldn't he be like some of his friends and never talk to his parents? Why did he and his mother have to get along? Except for this obsession with Katie McCormick, his mom was a great woman to have around. They'd always been able to talk and he respected her opinion. But right now he would give anything for a brief but meaningful estrangement.

"Mom," he began, then shook his head. It was four days. Surely he could survive that. "Fine. You win."

She smiled broadly. "Good. Janis was there for me every day when I was sick. I'm so happy to finally be able to repay her, at least a little."

"You're selling out your only son. What will the neighbors think?"

"That it's about time you found yourself a woman."

# *Two*

**K**atie waited nervously at the entrance to the Gold Rush Ski Lodge and Resort. The name misled those who didn't know the history of the place, or the luxury of the rooms.

The hotel nestled in the mountains above Fool's Gold—a grand old place with an architectural style somewhere between Victorian and chalet. What should have looked awkward or busy was instead welcoming. The views were impressive, the restaurant five-star and the service unmatched. There were world-class boutiques in the lobby and a spa that tempted celebrities from all over the world. If this had been Katie's wedding, she would have chosen to have the ceremony on the shore of the lake in town, with the reception in one of the local restaurants. But her sister had always wanted something grander and more expensive. So a four-day extravaganza at the Gold Rush Ski Lodge and Resort it was.

Katie had already checked in, as had the rest of her

immediate family. Those traveling from out of town would be arriving any second and she had to find Howie before anyone else did. Getting their stories straight was essential. Otherwise, there was no point in having him stick around for the long weekend.

For a brief second, she weighed the idea of exposing the sham. She would be free of Howie, but reduced to spinster status. Yes, it was a new century. Yes, women could do anything. Yet in the world of the McCormicks, being single and within three years of thirty was both a disaster and a source of shame.

"But you're a sports writer," her aunt Tully would say yet again. "Can't you catch a rich husband from all those sports you watch?"

If only it were that simple. The problem was while she loved sports—the competition, the quest for greatness, the odd quirks that made every game interesting—she was less thrilled by athletes. Maybe because she'd seen them at their worst—one of the perks of her job. It was sort of like working in the kitchen of a restaurant. Dining out would never be the same again.

A tall, dark-haired man entered the lobby. He was good-looking enough to turn heads, with a body to match. Broad shoulders and long legs, all dressed neatly in a soft-looking blue-striped shirt tucked into jeans. If only, she thought regretfully, looking past the hunky guy and hoping to see the bumbling nerd who was on the verge of being late.

He was into computers. Maybe she should have sent Howie an e-mail reminder.

"Katie?"

The tall, dark stranger stopped next to her. She stared

at his firm mouth, his strong jaw and the gorgeous green eyes barely concealed behind steel-rimmed glasses.

Her mouth opened. She felt it, then had to consciously close it. No way. Not possible. On what planet could this be happening?

"H-Howie?"

The man smiled. It was one of those sexy, self-deprecating smiles that made every woman in the room want to purr.

"Jackson," he corrected. "I go by Jackson now. My middle name."

Or eye candy. That name would work, too, she thought, her brain stuttering as she attempted to take in the changes. He was taller, more muscular, even his hair was perfect.

"H-Howie?" she repeated.

The smile turned into a low chuckle. "I'm not that different."

Au contraire.

"You've, ah, grown up," she managed, hoping she didn't look as stupid as she felt.

"So have you."

She wrinkled her nose. *Up* wasn't exactly the right word. She was about the same height she'd been at thirteen—a very average five foot five. The difference was she'd lost about forty pounds since then. And figured out how to play up her equally average features. She wasn't complaining—not exactly. But in a family of very tall, thin, attractive people, she was a throwback to the short, curvy lineage that everyone thought had been bred out.

"Yes, well, I've at least lost the baby fat," she said, figuring there was no point in ignoring the obvious.

Jackson studied her. "Your eyes are the same. Pretty. I remember the color."

"Because I was glaring at you?" she asked.

"Uh-huh. I was terrified you were going to beat me up."

"You treated me like I was an idiot."

"I was overcompensating for feeling like I didn't belong." He shrugged. "Don't take it personally. I acted that way everywhere."

"One of the downsides of being the smartest guy in the room?"

"You held your own."

She laughed. "I was reduced to threatening physical violence. Not exactly the definition of holding my own."

"You did fine. Now I hear you're a famous sports writer."

If Katie had been drinking, she would have choked. "Not exactly. Is that what your mom told you?"

He nodded.

"I work for the local paper. The *Fool's Gold Daily Republic.* I write the sports page, the occasional op-ed and I've done an emergency feature story when they were desperate. No one's definition of fame."

"You like what you do. I can hear it in your voice."

"I do like it." She found herself staring into his green eyes and wishing she'd listened to her mother sooner. Howie…ah, Jackson…was all that and more. "I've heard you're some kind of impressive computer guy."

She winced, thinking maybe she should have done a little homework. "You created a program about, um, something business-y."

The slow, sexy smile returned. "Inventory control. Trust me, you don't want to know the details."

"Probably not, but it's good someone keeps track of all that inventory stuff. It's wily."

He raised his eyebrows. "Wily?"

"I studied sports communications, not business. *Wily* is the best I could come up with, under the circumstances. Give me a deadline and I can be much more impressive."

"Maybe I'm already impressed."

She wasn't sure if it was the words or the way he said them, but for the first time in a long time, she felt positively girly. If her hair had been a couple of inches longer, she would have been tempted to flip it. As it was, she was grateful her mother had made her wear a sundress instead of jeans and a T-shirt, and that she'd taken the time to brush on mascara and lip gloss.

"You're not what I was expecting," he continued.

"I know," she admitted, trying not to flutter her lashes, although the need was powerful. "When my mother suggested you as my emergency date, I wasn't exactly grateful. But I do appreciate you showing up and taking time to help with this."

"Not a problem."

"You say that now, but you have no idea what you're in for." She smiled. "Maybe I should confiscate your car keys before I say any more. So you can't run screaming into the night."

"That bad?"

"Let's just put it this way, my sister is only happy when there's drama surrounding her and I have an aunt who has a habit of seducing other women's boyfriends and husbands. As I'm sure your mother told you, the groom is my ex-boyfriend. And that's just for starters."

"Sounds like fun."

"You have no idea. Want to make a run for it?"

"I can handle it. Do you doubt me?"

Not when he looked at her as if she were something delicious to eat. Which he couldn't possibly be, so it had to be a trick of light. Maybe a problem with his glasses.

"We should, ah, check you into the hotel," she said. "Have you been to Fool's Gold much in the past few years?"

"Not since our last meeting."

"But you grew up in Sacramento," she said. "It's so close."

"I went the other way after college. Toward the coast." He glanced around at the lobby. "The resort has a reputation for good skiing in winter."

"You ski?"

"Some. I like it more than I'm good at it."

"Me, too," she said. "It's easier than snowboarding, at least for me. I love trying different sports, but so far I haven't found one I'm very good at."

She led the way toward the front desk. "There are several excellent runs here during the winter. This time of year, the draw is more hiking and camping. The hotel keeps busy with things like weddings and various theme weekends. They fly in five-star chefs or art experts. That sort of thing. Then people come in from all over to hear lectures or go to demonstrations."

"You work in travel in your spare time?"

Katie laughed. "I live in town. It's not hard to keep track of what's going on."

"You grew up here and never wanted to leave?"

She tilted her head, considering. "Not really. I

went to Ashland College and while I loved it, I couldn't wait to get back. Fool's Gold is home for me."

Katie spoke with certainty, as if her belief was unshakeable. Jackson had been comfortable growing up in Sacramento, and later at MIT. He'd lived on the East Coast for a while, but when he'd been ready to start his software company, he'd gravitated west. There was something about California.

Now he lived in Los Angeles and while he liked the city, he couldn't say it was home with Katie's obvious passion.

She was nothing he'd expected. There was an energy about her, as if she enjoyed everything she did. Her blue eyes sparkled with intelligence and humor. She was curvy to the point of being a walking, breathing temptation just by standing in the room. There was something about the way she moved—purposeful, with a subtle sexiness that made parts of him grumble hungrily.

At thirteen, she'd terrified him. Fourteen years later, she tempted him, not that he would do anything about it. The daughter of his mother's best friend was completely off-limits. Not only would both mothers want to monitor any potential relationship, he could only imagine what *his* mother would say if she suspected he was about to break the heart of her best friend's daughter.

Too bad, he thought with more than a little regret.

"The family is in a block of rooms," Katie was saying as they approached the front desk. "However, I made sure you weren't close to them. We don't want Aunt

Tully sneaking into your room at night." Her smile turned impish. "You're still young enough that the thrill of Aunt Tully might do lasting damage."

"I don't know if I'm looking forward to meeting her or ready to bolt."

"I'll protect you."

He checked in quickly and was handed an old-fashioned key.

"You're through here," Katie said, pointing to the elevators on the far wall. "Brace yourself because it all starts tonight. There's a party." She paused and gazed up at him.

"Parties are fine."

"A fifties-style theme party. A costume has already been delivered to your room."

A costume party? He could see his mother had left out more than a few details. "Sounds great," he lied.

She laughed and touched his arm. "Don't worry. It's only a short-sleeved white T-shirt for the guys. Jeans are fine and if you have loafers, all the better."

"With white socks?"

"That would complete the look."

Her fingers were warm against his skin. He liked that she was a toucher. It made him want to touch back—to take control of the situation.

His gaze dropped to her mouth and lingered there. Her lips were as curvy and full as the rest of her. Katie defined lushness.

"I'm stuck wearing a poodle skirt," she continued. "With a twinset, if you can believe it."

An interesting image, he thought, still looking at her mouth. He'd never been turned on by anything retro before, but he had a feeling Katie would make a believer out of him.

"We should probably get our stories straight," she said, her voice slightly strained.

Reluctantly he raised his gaze to her eyes. Her pupils were slightly dilated and she seemed to be a little breathless.

"About how we met," she added.

"We could stick with the truth. Our mothers set us up."

"Um, right. That's good." She cleared her throat. "Say six months ago?"

"Works for me. We've been together ever since." He grinned. "I was a little surprised when you offered to sleep with me on the first date, but being a gentleman, I didn't refuse the invitation."

Her eyes widened, then narrowed as she drew her brows together. "Excuse me? You're the one who was completely crazy about me within five minutes of us meeting. You practically stalked me. I only went out with you because I felt guilty about turning your life upside down."

He chuckled. "Or we could settle in the middle. Mutual attraction and a growing interest."

"Fine. But I really like the idea of you being desperate."

She had no idea how little it would take to get him to that state, he thought, wanting to touch her skin again to see if all of it was as soft as her hands had felt before.

They walked toward the elevators. Before they got there, an attractive fiftysomething woman hurried up to them. Jackson recognized his mother's best friend.

"Hello, Janis," he said. "Good to see you again."

"Howie," she said absently.

He did his best not to wince at the name. His mother had refused to call him anything else, so it made sense her best friend wouldn't know about the change to something less pathetic than "Howie."

"We have a crisis," Janis told her daughter.

"Only one? I was sure there would be more."

"Don't tempt fate. It's plenty early." Janis drew in a breath. "It's the cake. Actually it's the cake decorator. Apparently the decorations are made in advance and then there's a cake and they come together and it's beautiful. I'm not sure of the details."

"Okay. So what's the problem?"

"The decorator was in a car accident. She's going to be fine…in eight weeks after her broken arm heals. I don't mean to sound unsympathetic, but did that have to happen today? The cake was in the car. So we have decorations. They were delivered yesterday, but no cake."

Janis clutched Katie's arm. "I can't do this. Your sister is hysterical, your father is hiding because he sees the panic on my face. Your relatives are arriving and Aunt Tully has already made a pass at the bellboy. You have to help me."

"Why are they *my* relatives?" Katie asked. "*My* sister. *My* father. You're related to them, too."

"You're not helping," Janis said, her voice getting more shrill with each word.

"Sorry. We'll find another cake decorator."

"How? It's prime wedding season. They're all busy. This is a sign. This wedding is going to be a disaster, I can feel it."

"Mom, calm down."

"I can't."

Jackson pulled out his cell phone. "Maybe I can help. I have a friend who runs a catering business. She used to decorate cakes. I'm sure I could persuade her to help out."

Janis turned to him. "Don't play with my emotions, Howie. I'm right on the edge."

"I'll call her right now."

He scrolled through his list of contacts until he found Ariel's cell. Seconds later she answered.

He greeted her and explained the problem.

"This isn't your wedding, is it?" she asked warily.

"No. A friend's. I'm here for the weekend, then heading home."

She hesitated. "Normally I wouldn't have time, but I had an unexpected cancellation. I'll be there in the morning. I'll need access to the kitchen to get the cake made." She named a price that made him wince, but Janis simply nodded.

"Great," she said. "I'm looking forward to seeing you."

"Thanks. See you soon."

When he hung up, Janis hugged him. "You've saved us all."

"It's a cake, not a rescue from a burning building."

"Close enough." She put a hand on her chest. "I can breathe again, at least until the next crisis. Now go to your rooms and get ready for the party. I'm off to get drunk."

She walked toward the bar. He pressed the up button on the elevator, then glanced at Katie.

She raised her eyebrows. "So…Ariel's an ex."

"How did you know?"

"The average guy doesn't have a former cake decorator on speed dial."

"She's on my contact list. That's different."

"Close enough."

The doors opened and they stepped inside. Katie pushed the button for the fourth floor.

"Bad breakup?" she asked.

"Actually an easy one. She left me. I thought I'd be bro-kenhearted and I wasn't." He'd gotten over her fast enough to make him realize that they'd be better off as friends.

"I guess that beats pining for months."

He looked at her. "Are you the type to pine?"

"I've had a sulk or two in my life, but not an actual full-on pine."

The elevator stopped and they stepped out. Katie led the way to his room.

"I'm across the hall," she said.

He moved his gaze from the door to her. "Can I trust you?" he asked.

She smiled. "If you'd been this fun fourteen years ago, I wouldn't have threatened to beat you up."

"If I'd been like this fourteen years ago, I would have wanted you to try."

They stared at each other. Katie blinked first, then glanced at her watch.

"The craziness starts in an hour," she said. "Brace yourself."

"I don't scare that easily. Besides, I'll have you to protect me."

"Just pray Aunt Tully doesn't take a liking to you."

"I can handle Aunt Tully."

"You say that now," Katie called over her shoulder as she left.

# Three

There was something oddly fun about wearing a poodle skirt, Katie thought as she looked at herself in the mirror. Sure, the poofy style did nothing to make her legs look longer—always a challenge for someone from a long-legged family—but the layers of petticoats also made her waist look tiny. She twirled a couple of times for effect, then smoothed her skirts.

She'd pulled her shoulder-length hair back into a ponytail, tied it with a chiffon scarf, fluffed her bangs and added a string of fake pearls to complete the costume.

A knock on the door sent her hurrying across the hotel room.

She pulled it open and nearly swooned at the sight of Jackson in a very fitted white T-shirt and jeans. He'd slicked back his hair and rolled up the sleeves of the T-shirt. He looked both sexy and dangerous—a very tempting combination.

"*West Side Story* is one of my mom's favorite movies," she said with a laugh. "You're the perfect Jet."

He looked her over slowly enough for her toes to curl in her thrift-store oxfords. "Very nice. Like the skirt."

She twirled. "I've never worn a petticoat before."

"You look…"

"Wholesome?" she offered. "Virginal?"

"Like the kind of girl you give a class ring to."

His words gave her a little jolt in her belly. She did her best to hide her reaction. "That's me."

She slipped her lip gloss and her room key into her pocket and motioned for him to lead the way out.

As they waited for the elevator, he leaned against the wall and watched her.

"Touching?" he asked. "No touching? How do we show the world, or at least your family, that we're a couple?"

Sex, she thought unexpectedly. They could have sex. That would certainly do it for her. "Um, some touching. Courtney and Alex are all over each other, but at some point that just gets tacky."

"Agreed."

There was something about the way he was looking at her. As if trying to figure something out. His steady gaze made her nervous. She glanced at the floor, then forced herself to look at him. Was it just her or did it seem like the elevator was taking forever?

The seconds ticked past. Jackson straightened, moved toward her, cupped her face in his hands, then leaned in and brushed his mouth against hers.

The brief contact was soft, hungry and unexpected. Heat exploded inside her, making her strain toward him. He stepped back long before she was ready for him to, but kept his large hands on her skin, his thumbs caressing her cheeks.

"For practice," he said, his eyes bright with amusement and something she could only pray was interest. "So we get it right, if anyone asks."

She didn't think there would be a required kissing demonstration, but it *was* good to be prepared.

Just as she was about to suggest another practice session, the elevator doors opened. Unfortunately, Aunt Tully was the only occupant.

"Katie!" the older woman exclaimed happily and threw herself out of the elevator. "I've been looking all over for you." Tully shifted her attention to Jackson and raised her eyebrows. "Hello, gorgeous. Katie is very fond of me and likes to share."

Jackson immediately dropped his hands to his sides and took a step back. If the situation hadn't been potentially hazardous in more ways than Katie could count, she would have found it funny. Sort of.

Tully was her father's sister. A round, short, blond dynamo who dressed like she was twenty…or maybe sixteen. Except for the jewelry. It was all flash and proof that she'd married well. Several times. Tully was currently looking for husband number six.

Married or not, Tully loved men. All men—even those who were married or involved with other women. She was the life of the party, a charming drunk and completely lacking in boundaries. Katie both loved and feared her.

Jackson seemed to recover. He held out his hand. "You must be Aunt Tully. Nice to meet you."

"Come now," Tully said, holding out her arms. "We're family. We need to do more than shake hands."

He moved in warily and leaned toward her, as if to give her a nonromantic A-frame hug. It was like one of those twisted reality shows on TV. As much as Katie wanted to look away, she couldn't.

Tully waited until Jackson was close and slightly off balance, then grabbed him and pulled hard. He crashed into her ample chest, tried to right himself, and found the natural place his hands needed for leverage was her breasts. Obviously determined not to touch them, he flailed for a few seconds before managing to step away. But not before Tully planted a kiss on his mouth.

Tully smiled with satisfaction. "Any good?" she asked Katie.

Katie moved toward the slightly stunned Jackson and slipped her arm through his. "He's mine. You can't have him."

Tully pouted, her blue eyes thoughtful. "Are you sure? I'll buy you a car. The new Lexus hybrid."

"Thanks, but no."

"Cash?"

Jackson cleared his throat. "Ms. McCormick, while I'm flattered by—"

Tully dismissed him with a wave. "You don't get to negotiate. Katie?"

"Sorry. No."

"Fine. I'll have to see who else is available. Does the groom have a brother?"

"No," Katie said, proud of herself for not suggesting Alex instead. While there would be karmic justice in having the man Courtney had stolen taken from her, it would create too much trouble for everyone else.

Besides, there was a slight possibility that Courtney really did love Alex.

The elevator returned to their floor. Tully got on it.

"We'll take the next one," Katie said, thinking Jackson would need a moment.

"See you at the party."

The door closed.

Jackson leaned against the wall. "That was Aunt Tully."

"I tried to warn you."

"She wanted to buy me."

"I know."

"For cash."

"She likes men."

"She's old enough to be my mother."

"Technically she might be old enough to be your very young grandmother, but try not to think about it."

He shook his head and straightened. "Now I know why you needed a date for the wedding."

"My family isn't all bad. My parents are great. Courtney is very pretty." Katie wanted to add that it would be nice if Jackson didn't fall for her sister, but what was the point? He either would or wouldn't.

"Tully's the worst of it, right?" he asked.

Katie laughed. "Yes. I promise. The rest of my family will only ask pointed questions. Things like how long have we been going out and what are your intentions."

"They want you married, huh?"

"It's an ongoing goal. You'd think having a great career and lots of friends would be enough, but it's not. You, being a man, don't get the same kind of pressure."

"My mother makes not-so-subtle statements about wanting grandchildren, but I ignore her."

If only she could do the same, she thought. She tried, but every now and then, the volume got to her.

She pushed the down button to call the elevator. "Which begs the question—why aren't you married? Or are you one of those men who doesn't want to be tied down?"

"I like the idea of a wife and family," he said, moving next to her. "When I was younger, I couldn't get the girl."

She glanced at his broad shoulders, the sexy green eyes and the shape of his mouth. "At the risk of feeding your ego, I don't think that's a problem anymore."

"No. Now the problem is finding the right girl."

"What are you looking for?"

His gaze settled on her. There was something knowing in his expression. As if he thought maybe—

The elevator doors opened.

"Katie, darling. There you are." Katie's mother swayed slightly on her feet.

Katie got on the elevator and turned to her dad. "She's drunk."

"You think?" Her father held out his hand to Jackson. "Mike McCormick."

"Jackson Kent. I'm Tina's son."

"Of course." He kept his arm around his wife. "Your mother had two martinis."

Katie winced. "One usually puts her on her butt. While she's a charming drunk, I doubt this is the time or the place."

Janis patted her husband's cheek. "Don't be mad. You know you like me drunk. It's when you get lucky."

"Mo-om!" Katie covered her ears. "Please, stop. I don't want to hear this."

Janis smiled at her daughter. "You should be happy your parents are still having sex. It means we have a good marriage. You don't want us getting a divorce, do you?"

"Should I hum loudly?" Jackson asked with a grin.

"You think this is funny?" she snapped. "Want to talk about your parents doing it?" Katie faced her mother, while trying to avoid looking at her father. "This is Courtney's wedding. You have to focus."

"I will. I'm just saying, the sex really does get better as one gets older. Back in the day, we always had to worry about you and your sister interrupting us. All those afternoon showers, when we were just trying to get in a quickie. But did you cooperate? Of course not. It was always Mom this and Mom that. You startled me so much once, I nearly bit off your father's—"

The doors opened and Katie bolted out onto the lower level, where the party would be held. She walked fast, as if she could outrun the hideous image in her head.

"Kittens and puppies and ice cream," she murmured as she moved. "London. I'll think about London." She came to a stop and covered her face.

Then strong arms were around her, pulling her close. The supportive gesture was mitigated by the shaking chest as Jackson laughed.

"If it makes you feel any better," he said, "your father is mortified."

"It doesn't. How could she say that stuff?"

"There was alcohol involved."

"Still." She shuddered, her face still pressed into his shoulder. "It's gross. Not the happy-marriage part. I want them to be happy, not just for me but for them, too. But parental sex shouldn't be discussed in front of children."

"You need a distraction."

"Or some kind of mind meld."

"Katie?"

Instinctively she looked up. As soon as she did, he kissed her.

His warm, teasing mouth claimed hers. Skin against skin, the sensual movement making her blissfully incapable of doing much more than feel.

He held her firmly, carefully, but with a confidence that made her willing to surrender. One hand was below the other on her back, angled so his fingertips lightly grazed the curve of her rear. Even through the layers of skirt and petticoat, she felt the heat of him, the pressure.

He touched her lower lip with his tongue and she parted. He swept inside, claiming her with his mouth. She angled her head to deepen the kiss, wrapped her arms around his neck and gave herself up to the moment.

Wanting swept through her. Need and hunger. It had been a long time since she'd been swept away. Too long. She'd forgotten how good it felt to be held. To have the solid strength of a man's body right against hers.

In the distance, she heard the sound of conversation but ignored it. Nothing mattered but kissing Jackson. As far as she was concerned, she could do this forever.

Apparently he didn't read minds as well as he kissed because after a few minutes, he drew back.

"Better?" he asked.

She blinked at the question. "You did that to distract me?"

"Partly."

Great. So she'd been having an out-of-body, take-me-now experience and he'd been doing the sexual equivalent of patting her on the head.

His mouth curved into a sexy, promising smile. "I also did it because I wanted to."

# *Four*

The next morning Katie forced herself out of bed long before she was ready to leave, pulled on her workout clothes and made her sleepy way down to the hotel gym. She'd barely brushed her teeth, hadn't done a thing with her hair and was pleased she'd remembered to bring a bottle of water. She was also expecting to find the room empty, except for a rabid business person or two.

Instead she found Jackson already sweating on one of the two elliptical machines.

He looked good in sweat, she thought as she stared at him. Tall and lean, but with enough muscle to make life interesting. He had on a headset and was watching the early-morning national news. So far he hadn't noticed her.

After her mother's sexual confessions and the mind-numbing kiss, the rest of the evening had been calm by comparison. Aunt Tully had kept her distance from Jackson, although she continued to eye him with interest. No one had gotten too drunk. But the weekend was young, Katie thought as she made her way to the second elliptical.

Not working out wasn't an option. Not with her weight history and gene pool. If she didn't watch what she ate and exercise regularly, she porked right up. Sad, but true. If she had to face Jackson while looking like a cross between a "before" picture and cat gack, so be it.

She got on the machine and studied the console. She used one just like it at the gym, so she knew what she was in for. After punching in her favorite program and only lying about her weight by seven pounds, she hit the start button and braced herself for pain.

Next to her, Jackson removed his headset. "Morning," he said with a smile.

The man hadn't showered pre-exercise, either. Had done nothing with his hair, hadn't bothered shaving. So why did he get to look like a model advertising naughty sex first thing in the morning?

"Hi."

"You're up early."

"It's necessary to keep my BMI in the two-digit range."

Jackson looked her up and down before shaking his head. "No way. You look great."

She flushed with pleasure. As she was already red-faced from exercise, she had the comfort of knowing he wouldn't notice. "Thanks, but it's true. You saw me at my chunky best. I'm one uncontrolled corn dog away from that happening again."

What Jackson remembered most about Katie as a teenager was how pretty she'd been, even when she'd threatened to beat him up. He hadn't wanted to waste his afternoon with a kid, but the second he'd seen her, he'd been…intrigued. As much as a repressed, nerdish sixteen-year-old boy could be.

He wasn't repressed anymore, he thought, doing his best not to stare at her breasts bouncing along in time with her movements. Not only didn't he want to get caught looking, his workout shorts wouldn't hide the inevitable reaction to his interest and wouldn't that make for an awkward moment.

"You worry too much," he told her.

"You weren't ever fat," she told him, her blue eyes bright with amusement. "But it's okay. I've been exercising regularly for nearly twelve years and I'm to the point where I almost like it."

He chuckled. "Is that the goal? To enjoy it?"

"Everyone deserves a fantasy life."

"Is that when you got interested in sports? You were exercising?"

She reached for her water bottle and took a long drink. "No. I've always loved sports. I think it's my dad's influence. My mom says instead of reading me fairy stories at night, he would read the sports page. I grew up interested in football and baseball."

"Do you play any?"

She shook her head. "I wish. I've tried them all. The best I can say for myself is I wasn't hideously bad at soccer. I wasn't close to good, but that's okay. I'm just not coordinated. Or fast. Or athletic. You met Aunt Tully. Physically, I take after her. So it's that old saying—those who can do. Those who can't write about it. I went to Ashland College to learn how."

"Where you studied sports communications."

Something flashed in her blue eyes. "You remembered."

He'd remembered nearly everything she'd said, he thought. She was the kind of woman a man would have trouble forgetting.

"You're my first sports communications major," he said lightly. "A guy remembers his first time."

She laughed. "You're good. Seriously. Have you been back to your high school reunion?"

He shuddered. "No, thanks. I'd rather face the fires of hell."

"You should think about it. You're the guy who will cause quite the reaction. All those girls who blew you off will be all over you."

"Maybe I don't want them all over me."

"You're not into revenge?"

"No. I don't need their approval to enjoy my life." He studied her. "Are you into revenge? If you are, this is the weekend for it."

She wiped her face with a towel. Even sweaty and hot, she looked good, he thought. Her hair stood in spikes, her breasts continued to bounce. This was his idea of a great morning.

"To quote you from a second ago, no, thanks. I'm not interested in Alex. He had his chance with me and he blew it."

"The man's an idiot."

Katie smiled. He felt the heat of if all the way down to his groin.

"You say the nicest things," she told him. "Courtney can be a pain. But you have to understand the context.

She was sick when she was a kid. Cancer. Everyone spoiled her and when she got better, we all kept treating her like she could die any second. She got used to the attention, and then she grew up gorgeous and guys kept falling for her. She'll grow up someday, and when she does, she'll be a good person. For what it's worth, I think Alex really does love her. This is their weekend. I want everything to go well for them."

Although his workout was over, he kept going until she was done. They walked out of the gym together and headed for the stairs. On the main floor, he was about to ask her to breakfast, when someone touched his arm.

"Jackson? Hi."

He turned and saw Ariel standing in the lobby. She was still tall and beautiful, with golden-red hair and eyes the color of spring grass. Pretty enough, but not anyone he'd missed after she'd left.

"Ariel," he said, then shifted his attention to Katie. "Katie, this is Ariel, cake decorator extraordinaire."

Katie glanced between them, then gave a smile that didn't seem happy. "Great. We're thrilled you're here. Have you had a chance to see the kitchen yet? We spoke to the staff and they've set up a work area for you. The pastry chef made the cakes last night, so they should be cooled and ready for you to work on. We all really appreciate you helping us out."

Ariel focused on him instead of Katie. "No problem. This gives me a chance to take care of a few things myself." She gazed into his eyes for another second, as if willing him to understand something, then looked at Katie. "I haven't been to the kitchen."

"Why don't you two take care of that now," he said,

wondering why Ariel was acting strange. Was she pissed because he'd called her about the job? If she hadn't wanted it, she could have refused.

"Sure," Katie said. "The kitchen is right this way."

Ariel was one of those women who entranced men and intimidated women without breaking a sweat. Katie, on the other hand, had been sweating for the past forty minutes. She was not at her best as she showed the tall, gorgeous redhead back to the kitchen. Fortunately, Katie didn't seem to register on Ariel's radar, so she hadn't appeared the least bit critical.

Katie showed the other woman the freshly baked cake, the decorations and introduced her to Andre, who was their "kitchen liaison." Then she headed for the coffee station in the lobby.

After taking her first sip, she closed her eyes and inhaled the aroma. It wasn't that she needed the caffeine to feel awake—it was that the ritual would ground her in a world where goddesslike women weren't ex-girlfriends and former nerds like Jackson didn't make her heart beat faster with just a kiss…or a smile.

Just when she'd been thinking about possibilities, she thought grimly. She'd been so sure they'd had great chemistry, that he really liked her. That he'd been interested. Maybe he had been, but there was no way she could compete with someone like Ariel. Not that it was a competition, but still. Couldn't Jackson have dated someone slightly more…ordinary?

She refilled her cup and headed for the elevators. When they opened, her sister, Courtney, stepped out. It might be early, but Courtney was charmingly dressed in a flirty little skirt and formfitting top. Her long hair gleamed, her makeup was perfect.

"Katie." Courtney looked and sounded shocked. "What happened to you?"

"I worked out."

"You look awful." Her gaze narrowed. "Are you sure you're okay? Your face is really red."

"That's what happens when I exercise," Katie said cheerfully, trying to maneuver around her, only to have the elevator doors close. Sighing, she pushed the up button again.

"I know you have to work out because of your weight, but you really shouldn't be out like this in public. Alex always said—" Courtney paused and smiled tightly. "Did you sleep well?"

Katie could have pushed and discovered what Alex always said. That she wasn't at her best in the morning? That she didn't wake up looking radiant and tall? Then she decided it didn't matter.

"Fine," she said. "And you?"

Instead of answering the question, her sister put a hand on her arm. "I know this is hard for you."

Sleeping? Not so much. Most nights it was amazingly easy. "What is hard for me?"

"Seeing me with Alex."

"I've had nearly a year to get used to it."

"I know, but this is different. We're getting married. I know you thought *you'd* marry him."

"Not anymore," Katie assured her, silently begging the elevator to return and rescue her. "I'm fine."

"Mom had to buy you a date."

Katie sucked in a breath. "Jackson isn't an escort. No

one paid for him." At least she didn't think so. "He's a friend of the family." Sort of.

"Still." Courtney looked both sympathetic and pitying. It wasn't a combination designed to make Katie feel better. "It's just so sad that more guys don't see beyond appearances. I couldn't stand it. You must be lonely."

*Kill me now,* Katie thought. Or maybe just Courtney. Before she could make a decision, the elevator arrived and she practically threw herself into it.

As the doors closed, Katie promised herself she was having wine with lunch.

# *Five*

Katie fluffed her curls and sprayed them for the third time since using the curling iron. As long as she avoided open flames, she would be fine.

Tonight's dinner was to officially welcome the rest of the family members who had arrived that day and to serve as a celebration for the happy couple. The event was somewhat formal, so she'd chosen a cocktail dress that fit her perfectly. She'd paid extra for tailoring, but it had been worth it, she thought as she put down the hair spray and turned so she could see herself from the back. In the right light, and wearing her three-inch heels, she could almost pass for tall. Given how her day had begun, she deserved a little sass in her evening.

Although to be honest, after a hideous start, her day had gone reasonably well. She'd spent the morning welcoming the rest of the family members as they'd arrived. Jackson had been a friendly and handsome escort for lunch. They'd been seated at a table that didn't include Courtney and the willowy Ariel hadn't been seen. Katie was willing to call that a win.

She left the bathroom and walked toward her purse. As she reached it, someone knocked on the door.

Jackson, she thought, her heart beating a little faster than it should. Right on time.

Sure enough, her date for the weekend stood in the doorway, looking handsome and sexy in a dark suit, white shirt and gray tie.

"Is this formal enough?" he asked. "I brought a tux."

"You look great," she said honestly, thinking it didn't get much better than a good-looking man who was prompt *and* owned his own tux. "I'm going to have to provide a physical barrier between you and Aunt Tully."

"I'd appreciate that. Although I noticed at lunch she seemed more interested in the groom's father."

"Well, wouldn't that cause some fireworks." Katie made a mental note to pass on the info to her mother. Not that she'd forgiven the other woman for the sexual outburst in the elevator. Knowing about parental sex was one thing, but having to hear about the details was just plain wrong.

"How are you holding up?" he asked.

She checked that her room key was in her small beaded evening bag, then pulled the door shut. "I'm fine. Counting down the days until it's all over. What about you?"

"It's not my family," he pointed out. "Although I have decided that when I get married, I want a simple ceremony. And everything done in a day."

"I agree. This is like a special kind of hell—it never ends."

As the party had grown larger, their dinner was to take place in one section of the small ballroom. The ceremony would be held there on Saturday, with the reception to follow in the bigger ballroom.

As they got closer to the party, Katie heard the sound of laughter and the clink of ice in glasses. She mentally braced herself for a whole night with her extended family. When she would have entered the room, he drew her back into the hallway.

"I want you to know you look amazing," he said, staring into her eyes.

She could see his thick lashes, the light of appreciation in his gaze. Even though she'd always wished to be taller, she had to admit there was something to be said for having a man tower over her. At least this man.

"Thank you," she murmured. "You're nice."

His dark brows pulled into a frown. "Excuse me?"

"You're really nice."

The frowned deepened. "I tell you that you look great and you insult me?"

Although he looked fierce, she saw the slight tug at the corner of his mouth. As if he were trying not to smile.

"Who does that?" he asked sternly. "I'm leaving."

She fought back the urge to giggle. "Jackson, wait. I'm sorry. You're not nice."

The frown didn't budge.

"You're actually…" She hesitated, then lowered her voice. "Bad. Very bad. You're the guy my mom warned me about."

"Better." His tone was grudging. "Just remember that."

He leaned in to kiss her. Her muscles tensed in anticipation of a really good time, her breath caught and the nerve endings in her trembling lips did a fair imitation of yearning.

"There you are." A shrill, quavering voice jerked Katie from anticipation all the way into nightmare. "Katie, darling. Come give me a kiss."

Katie stepped back from Jackson and smiled at the tiny old lady teetering toward her. "Nana," she said and moved toward the woman.

Sucking in a breath—for reasons no one could explain, Nana Marie always smelled like fish—Katie leaned in and kissed her papery cheek.

"There's a good girl. Let me look at you."

Katie stood still, then turned when she was directed.

"Very good. I see you're keeping off the weight. We were all so worried you'd stay fat. But you've proved us wrong." Nana Marie glanced at Jackson. "Who are you?"

"Jackson Kent."

"Jackson, this is Nana Marie," Katie told him. "She's…" Katie shook her head. "Nana, how are we related?"

"We're not. I was a friend of your grandmother's." Nana smiled at Jackson. "Aren't you handsome? We're all so happy that Katie finally has a man in her life. That Alex—leading her on and then falling for Courtney. That girl is about as emotionally deep as a potato chip. Not like our Katie."

Nana squeezed Katie's chin hard enough to make her eyes water. "You have a man now. That's what counts. Now I have to excuse myself and go make water."

Katie watched her head toward the restrooms, then wondered if pounding her head against the wall was an option. Sure, it would leave a bruise, but at least that would give people something to talk about that wasn't her weight or her love life.

"I'm sorry," she said miserably. "This is so much worse than I ever imagined."

Jackson moved close and lightly stroked her cheek. "Hey, I signed up for this. Besides, I like her."

"Wait until she pinches your cheek."

He chuckled, then grew serious. "Don't take this wrong, but your family really needs to stop judging you. You have a great job, you're beautiful and sexy. When you're ready, you'll get married. Any man would be lucky to have you. Alex is an idiot for picking Courtney over you."

Katie blinked at him. There were so many wonderful places to start—she couldn't pick just one.

"Thanks," she whispered.

"You're welcome." He put his arm around her and led her toward the party. "We'll circle by Alex and Courtney and the poor guy can get a look at what he's missing."

Nana Marie turned out to be one of the easier relatives to deal with, Jackson thought three hours later as he and Katie moved together during a slow dance. The McCormick family was large, loving and way too focused on their perception of Katie's flaws. If someone wasn't mentioning her weight—again—he or she was exclaiming over the fact that she had a date. As if that was a surprise.

He didn't get it. Granted, he was a guy and maybe not the most insightful male in the room, but what was the big deal? Katie was gorgeous. She had beautiful eyes, great skin, shiny blond hair and those were just the average parts. Right now, holding her as they moved together to the music, he could feel her breasts nestling against his chest and rested his hand on the curve of her hip. There was nothing wrong with her shape. On the contrary, his body was telling him it was exactly right.

People were strange and families were the worst. At least he was here and could protect her.

A sweet, slightly floral fragrance drifted to him. The appealing scent made him think of dark bedrooms and tangled sheets. Without thinking, he guided her over to a large pillar at the edge of the dance floor. When they were out of view of everyone else, he bent down and kissed her.

Her mouth welcomed his with a soft pressure that made every part of him ache. Her lips parted and he moved his tongue against hers. She tasted of chocolate and wine and temptation. In a matter of seconds, he was hard.

Trying to be a gentleman, he kept some slight distance between them. At least he tried. She wrapped her arms around his neck and leaned into him. When her belly came in contact with his erection, she made a sound that was part groan, part purr. He felt the vibration all the way down to his groin.

"We can't," she murmured against his mouth, then nipped his lower lip. "It would be a seriously bad idea. Dangerous even."

He dropped his head and kissed his way down her neck. As he licked that sensitive spot below her ear, he felt her shudder.

"Bad idea for who?" he asked.

"Me. Us. It's just a weekend, Jackson. I don't do one-night stands."

He straightened and stared into her beautiful blue eyes. "Why does it have to stop at one night?"

She was flushed and looked thoroughly kissed. Through the thin fabric of her dress, he saw her nipples were hard. Angling around, so he was between her and anyone who might see them, he touched the tight tips with his fingers. Her breath caught.

Wanting burned in her eyes. "You are every kind of temptation."

He kissed her again, this time sucking gently on her tongue. Need grew, pulsing inside him. There was something about Katie.

He sensed more than heard someone approaching and stepped back. Seconds later, her parents rounded the pillar.

"There you are," her mother said. "Well, this went well. We're at the halfway point. Two evenings down, two to go. I wanted to tell you that you can leave anytime you want. Everyone is turning in. Tully went up an hour ago. Alone, thank goodness, although she was eyeing one of the waiters."

"We're tired, too," Katie said quickly, not meeting his eyes. "We'll come with you."

They rode the elevator together. He and Katie got out on the same floor and walked toward her door.

"Jackson, I—" she began.

"It's okay," he said, kissing her lightly.

"What's okay?"

"This isn't the time or place. There's too much of your family around for one thing. When the weekend is over, I'll call. We'll go out." He smiled. "In a more normal setting."

"You're not mad?"

"Katie, I'm not seventeen. I can wait." He kissed her again. "You're worth that."

He took the key she'd pulled out of her purse and opened her door. After handing it back to her, he pushed her inside. "I'll see you tomorrow."

"Okay. Night."

Katie floated into her room more than walked. This couldn't be happening, she thought, practically dizzy with delight. It wasn't possible that Jackson really was funny and smart and handsome and interested in her. Was it?

All the signs were there. Only, she'd been fooled by signs before. But there was a very big part of her—okay, all—that wanted to believe he really was one of the good guys.

She'd barely stepped out of her heels when someone tapped lightly on her door and spoke her name in a low, muffled tone.

Excitement and worry battled in her stomach. While she liked a good seduction as much as the next girl, she really wasn't sure she was comfortable climbing into bed with Jackson right now.

She pulled open the door, prepared to tell him that when she saw the man waiting for her wasn't her date. He was her ex-fiancé.

"Alex?"

"Katie, hi."

Alex took a step into her room, tripping as he crossed the threshold.

"You're drunk."

"Maybe." He stood in front of her, his expression hopeful. Kind of like a puppy. "Maybe we only tell the truth when we're drunk."

Uh-oh. She didn't like the sound of that. "Alex, whatever you have going on, you need to take it up with Courtney. You two are getting married in less than forty-eight hours." She turned him and gave him a push toward the still-open door. "Out you go."

He stood immovable as stone. "Katie, what if it's a mistake? What if I don't love Courtney?"

Alarms went off inside her head. "You're just nervous about getting married." And a jerk for acting like this less than forty-eight hours before the wedding, but that was a conversation for later. "That's all this is."

He reached for her. "Remember how it was with us? How great?"

"No. I don't."

He gave her a lopsided, sloppy smile. "You miss me. You know you do."

Hadn't she just been mature-girl, not two minutes ago with Jackson? Hadn't she done the right thing? And what? This was her reward? On what planet was that fair?

"Okay," she said, giving him a smile. "I need to take care of a couple of things." She pointed to the bathroom. "Just stay right there."

"I could take my clothes off."

She held in a shriek, but instead tried to look seductive. "Oh, Alex. Leave that for me."

He plopped down on the bed. "Okay. I will."

She ducked into the bathroom and pulled her cell phone out of her evening bag. Grateful her mother had given her Jackson's number and she'd put it in her phone, she dialed it and waited.

"Katie?"

"Alex is here. He's drunk and thinks he wants to have sex with me."

"There's a lot of that going around."

"Very funny. I need help."

"Be right there."

He was as good as his word, arriving before she'd walked out of the bathroom. Jackson looked at Alex, then shook his head.

"I don't think so," he said. "You had your chance and you walked away. Now, she's mine."

Confusion clouded Alex's eyes. "You're Katie's new boyfriend?"

"That's me."

"Damn."

Alex stood, leaned a little too far to the right, then straightened himself. He managed to make it to the still-open door and paused.

"Sorry, man."

"Don't let it happen again," Jackson said.

Alex waved and carefully closed the door behind him.

"Impressive," she told Jackson. "Thanks for saving me. If he'd tried anything, it would have been a disaster."

"A scandal, at the very least."

He wanted her. She felt it in his gaze, saw it in the set of his body. But being the kind of guy he was, he would respect her refusal and not even make a second attempt. As she'd thought before…nice.

The smart thing would be to let him walk away. They barely knew each other. This was an overly emotional situation and she wasn't thinking straight. Giving in to sex with a stranger was a big mistake. Huge. She would hate herself in the morning.

All very reasonable arguments, Katie thought as she walked over to Jackson and touched his glasses.

"How well do you see without those?" she asked.

"I see great close up."

"Good."

Sometime between their goodbye and his return to her room, he'd taken off his suit jacket and tie. Her work was nearly done for her. It would be a shame to let that effort go to waste.

"You want to take off your glasses?" she asked.

"What will you give me if I do?"

She laughed. "Whatever you want."

# Six

Jackson put his glasses on the table by the door and turned to her. Katie saw the deep green of his eyes, the thick lashes, the perfect lines of his face.

"You're really a very—"

She didn't get any further. Instead of letting her speak, he pulled her against him, wrapped his arms around her and kissed her deeply.

There was no easing into position, no slight brush of mouth on mouth. Instead he pressed his lips to hers as if he meant to have her, and nothing was going to stop him.

The power of his mouth, the heat, nearly had her swooning. Even as she parted for him and met him stroke for stroke, she felt a tightness in her chest. As if she couldn't catch her breath.

His hands were everywhere—up and down her back, along her hips, cupping her rear, then squeezing. She arched against him, bringing her midsection in contact with his arousal. He was hard and thick, she thought desperately. Deep inside, she felt a liquid warmth easing through her.

She hung on, as much to feel his strength as to stay standing. Wanting grew to desperation. Hunger burned like fire, licking through her body, making her whimper.

With an ease that was impressive, he found and lowered the zipper on the back of her dress. He broke the kiss long enough to slip the fabric down her arms, before returning his mouth to hers. He slid his hands from her back to her waist, then up to the black bra covering her breasts.

"God, you feel good," he breathed as he cupped the curves in his hands.

His fingers found her tight nipples and brushed them. Erotic delight wove through her, settling between her legs and making her squirm. He made quick work of her bra, tossed it aside, then bent his head to her breasts.

He took first one nipple, then the other, in his mouth. He didn't just lick and suck—he feasted on her skin, tasting, teasing, arousing. She trembled, her insides melting, that place between her thighs swelling until it ached. He used his tongue, his lips, his teeth until she was incoherent. When he started backing her toward the bed, she couldn't move fast enough.

They reached the mattress. As she stepped out of her sandals, he toed off his shoes. Her dress hit the floor, as did his shirt and socks. She stood in bikini panties, aware that she was fifteen…okay, twenty…pounds over her ideal weight, but instead of feeling self-conscious, she felt lush. Desirable.

Jackson hid nothing. Not the hunger burning in his eyes or the throbbing of his erection. He let his pants drop, then pushed down his briefs and reached for her hand and brought it to him.

"You're driving me to the edge," he whispered before he kissed her.

She touched his smooth hardness, felt the velvety tip and once again shuddered. But when she would have moved faster, steadier, he pushed her hand away and smiled.

"Let's just say my control isn't what it should be."

Because of her? It was the reason that made the most sense and she was going to enjoy believing it. But there wasn't much time to revel. Not with him tugging at her panties, then lowering them.

She stepped out of the scrap of fabric. He eased her onto the bed, then slid in next to her. They came together in a rush of arms and legs and hot, arousing kisses.

He slipped one hand between her legs and groaned as his fingers sank into the swollen, ready flesh. A finger slipped inside her as he used his thumb to circle her center. The combination, done in perfect rhythm, drove her from very interested to panting in about two seconds.

There was something about the way he touched her. As if he knew exactly what she would like. The finger inside her moved more deeply, then curved up toward her belly, finding an internal fun switch that made her open her legs wide and beg for more.

He eased her onto her back. Her eyes were closed as she lost herself in the sensations washing through her. There was too much, she thought desperately. She couldn't come this fast. But she also seemed to have lost control of everything. There was his thumb going around and around, barely grazing her swollen and hungry center. His other finger matched the movement, but from the inside, touching her in a way that made her want to scream. Her skin was hot, her legs shaking. Muscles clenched in anticipation. It was a runaway train of sexual need and she could only hold on.

Without warning, he licked her right nipple. The unexpected contact made her shudder. Then he drew the tip into his mouth and sucked deeply. A second later, her orgasm burst to life, vibrating through her, making her writhe and cry out.

She rode the pleasure, pressing down on his finger. He replaced it with two, filling her more, letting her grind against him. Waves and waves of pleasure crashed into her, taking her along for the ride of a lifetime.

The sensations slowed, then gentled before fading. Katie felt at one with the universe and a little embarrassed by her out-of-control reaction. What would he think of her? That she was some sex-starved crazy woman? Self-doubt, her least favorite personal companion, slid into bed with them.

But before it could get comfortable, Jackson shifted so that he was kneeling between her legs. He parted her, pushed his way inside, and braced himself above her. It was only then she noticed his arms were shaking.

"What the hell were you thinking?" he asked as he filled her. "You could kill a man like that."

She stared up at him. Her first thought was that he was beautiful. Her second was to ask, "What are you talking about?"

He swore again, even as he pushed into her, then withdrew. "You were incredible. So sexy. I could feel you getting close, and then you were coming and I couldn't get enough of it. I don't know how long I can hold back."

He spoke with wonder, but there was also a guttural need. She felt it *and* saw it. Any lingering doubt faded. She absorbed the feel of him filling her over and over, shifted so she could wrap her legs around his hips and keep him in place.

"You don't have to hold back," she whispered, reveling in his urgency. "I want you."

She moved her hips in time with him, drawing him in deeper. She noticed his gaze kept dropping to her full breasts, moving with every thrust. Acting on instinct, she cupped them in her hands and ran her fingers across the nipples. Instantly he shuddered inside her and groaned out his release.

Later, when they were under the covers in her bed, tangled up together, he kissed the top of her head.

"I'm an idiot," he murmured.

"Why?"

"My mother has been trying to get me to ask you out for years. If I'd listened, we could have been doing this for a whole lot longer."

"I've resisted, too," she admitted, looking at him and smiling. "So we're both stupid. We could send small but tasteful gifts."

"Then they'd know we had sex."

"Based on what I know about my parents' sex life, I don't think that's a problem," she told him.

He laughed, then shifted so she was on her back and he was leaning over her. "Katie," he whispered, right before his mouth claimed hers.

\* \* \*

They spent the night together, then woke early, showered and discovered a whole new level of fun with hot water and soap. Katie found herself leaning forward, arms braced against the tile walls, the water pounding on her back, while Jackson knelt between her thighs and used his lips and tongue to reduce her to a quivery mass. She returned the favor. By the time they stepped out of the steamy bathroom, she was hungry, achy and feeling better than she had in years. Maybe ever.

A quick glance at the bedside clock showed her that it was already past nine.

"Much as I would like to play with you all day, I have to get dressed," she told Jackson. "I have family stuff to take care of. The rehearsal is this afternoon and the dinner is tonight."

He kissed her nose. "I'll come with you."

She blinked at him. "To the family stuff?"

"Sure. I'll distract them with my wit and charm."

She touched his bare chest. "Or you could just take your shirt off. That will distract the women."

"I don't want Aunt Tully getting any ideas."

She pressed her mouth to his shoulder. "Me, either. I suspect a man is never the same after knowing Aunt Tully."

They were both still laughing when someone knocked on her door.

"Katie? Are you still in there?"

Katie winced. "My mom."

He grabbed his clothes and ducked into the bathroom. "I'll be quiet," he promised.

"Thanks."

Katie tossed her towel on the bed and slipped into her robe, then crossed the room.

"Hi, Mom," she said as she opened the door.

Her mother frowned. "You're still not dressed?"

"I, ah, didn't get a lot of sleep last night."

"Me, either. All this stress. Swear to me you won't have a huge four-day event like this when you get married."

"I promise. It's not my style."

Her mother collapsed onto the chair in the corner and rubbed her temples. "It's a nightmare. In no particular order, Aunt Tully made a pass at Bruce and no one is sure if he took her up on it or not, Alex is missing and Courtney is having second thoughts. I've never been someone who medicates her way through life, but I'm thinking this is a good day to start."

Katie stared at her mother. Bruce was Alex's dad. And married. "You think Aunt Tully slept with the groom's father?"

"Honestly, I'm trying not to think about it."

"His wife can't be happy."

"She's not. Let's just say I asked the kitchen staff to inventory the knives until this is all cleared up. There was quite the shouting match this morning over breakfast. You should have been there."

Katie thought about what she and Jackson had been doing instead. "Yes, it's a shame," she murmured, trying not to smile at the memory. Just remembering was enough to get her body tingling. The aching parts of her might be sore but they sure weren't done.

She shook off the memories and focused on the problems at hand. "Is Alex really missing?"

"No one has seen him since the party. Apparently he was drunk."

Katie remembered his visit to her room. "Um, Mom?"

"What?"

"He came by here. He said he loved Courtney but he wanted to have sex with me."

Katie expected shrieking, but her mother only closed her eyes and leaned her head back against the chair.

"Mom?"

"I'm imagining myself in another place. A quiet place with running water and the sounds of happy birds. I am one with the universe."

"Can you be one with the universe and look for the groom?"

Her mother opened her eyes. "No, but you're right. Wedding first, breakdown second." She drew in a breath. "I know those two really care about each other. I've seen it and heard it and believe it. It's just they're both so dramatic. His car is still here, so he has to be somewhere. Maybe he went into the woods to sleep it off."

"Or be eaten by a bear. Didn't you say Courtney was having second thoughts? The untimely death of the groom would give her all the attention without the wedding."

Janis's mouth twitched. "Don't be mean."

"I'm just saying."

Her mother stood. "All right. I'll deal with Aunt Tully and Bruce. We'll leave Courtney to pout in her room. She always loved a good sulk when she was little and that hasn't changed. You go looking for Alex." Her eyes narrowed. "You're not still in love with him are you? If so, I'm not throwing you two together."

Katie thought about the delicious man hovering in her bathroom. How he made her feel when he was around. Jackson listened and appreciated her. He was magic in bed. Smart, funny, charming.

"It's not possible for me to be more over Alex than I am. He is complete history. Has been for months now."

"Good. Then find him and talk some sense into him. Use force if you have to. There *will* be a wedding tomorrow. I swear there will be."

"You go, Mom."

"Don't mock me. I'm a woman on the edge." Her mother gave her a brief hug, then kissed her cheek. "Thank you for being normal."

"You're welcome."

When her mother had left, Jackson came out of the bathroom. He'd already dressed.

"Looks like you're safe from Aunt Tully," Katie told him. "She's replaced you."

"So it seems. Do you really think she's sleeping with the father of the groom?"

"With her, it's not hard to believe anything."

He winced. "There are going to be some wild fireworks."

"There always are."

He grabbed her hand. "Want some help looking for Alex? Divide and conquer?"

"That would be great. I'll take the kitchen and the lower floors."

He nodded. "I'll change into jeans and check the grounds."

"Watch out for bears. You're pretty enough that they'll want you."

"No guy wants to be pretty."

She smiled. "It looks good on you."

"You look good on me."

He kissed her, then left. Katie stood there, wearing nothing but a robe, thinking this was probably the best wedding ever.

# *Seven*

Divide and conquer might make sense, Katie thought a half hour later, when she'd dressed and made her way to the kitchens. But there was a flaw in the plan. A tall, red-headed flaw with long legs, a perfect pouty mouth and an ability to only think about one thing.

"You're with the wedding, right?" Ariel asked as Katie entered the kitchen.

Jackson's ex stood by a counter, carefully assembling a four-tiered wedding cake. Smooth, white fondant covered all the layers. Stacked trays contained already-made flowers in pale pink and yellow. Silver dots lined paper sheets.

"Yes. My sister is getting married."

"Good, so what do you know about Jackson? I saw you with him. You guys are friends?"

Katie thought about Jackson's intimate kiss that morning, in the shower. The way he'd pressed his open mouth on the most sensitive part of her. There wasn't an inch of skin he hadn't touched or tasted. He'd made her come in ways that were borderline illegal.

"We're friends," she said, hoping she sounded calm and slightly disinterested. Her instinct was to rip off Ariel's face, something the other woman might resist. And there was the cake to consider.

"Is he..." Ariel sucked in a breath. "Is he with anyone? We used to go out. I left him because I was stupid. Now I see we were great together. He's amazing, and I totally blew it. I made a mistake. I want him back."

Tears filled her perfect, almond-shaped eyes. No red nose and blotchy skin for Ariel when she cried, Katie thought bitterly.

What Katie wanted to say was that she and Jackson were together. Practically in love. Because they—

The world stood still. She'd heard the phrase, read the phrase, but this was the first time in her life she'd felt it. Everything stopped moving. There was total silence. Even her heart was quiet.

Practically in love? She couldn't be in love. She barely knew Jackson. Okay, yes, he was everything she'd ever wanted and nice and funny and kind. The man had agreed to be her date for the weekend because his mother had asked him. How many guys did that without being scarily attached to the mother in question?

If he was everything she'd been looking for *and* they had amazing chemistry in bed and he made her feel like a goddess, was it unreasonable to assume that there was the tiniest possibility that she was falling in love with him? Crazy, maybe, but possible?

The world lurched into place again.

"Are you okay?" Ariel asked.

"Fine," Katie murmured, feeling more than a little dazed. "I, uh, don't know anything about his love life." She was speaking the truth. Well, excluding his relationship with her.

While she was sure he wasn't seeing anyone seriously—his mother wouldn't have asked him to do the wedding weekend if he was—she didn't know about casual relationships. For all she knew he had a string of women lined up, waiting for their turn. If last night was only a sampling of his talents, then it made sense there would be plenty of takers.

Ariel sighed. "I want to talk to him. Explain. I want him back. I can't believe how stupid I was. A guy like Jackson doesn't come along very often."

"No, he doesn't," Katie said, backing toward the door. "You haven't seen the groom, have you?"

"No. Only your mom. She's really nice."

"We all think so. Thanks."

"Wish me luck with Jackson."

Katie waved instead, and left the kitchen. Dazed, she walked into the lobby, then out into the bright morning light.

She was falling in love with the man her mother had tried to set her up with a thousand times. Talk about ironic. Even more confusing was the fact that she couldn't begin to have any idea about how Jackson felt. Asking him was out of the question. She refused to be one of those scary, needy girls who wanted to talk marriage on a second date. She was used to hiding her feelings from the world. Why should this time be any different?

She glanced toward the hotel. Maybe because Jackson was different, she thought. Or maybe he wasn't. Maybe she was making too big a deal out of a great smile and even better sex.

Jackson didn't have to go very far to find the missing groom. He was passed out on a bench in an outbuilding probably used to store skis in the winter.

Jackson shook Alex's shoulder a couple of times. The other man groaned, rolled over and blinked sleepily up at him.

"Hey," Alex said, his voice hoarse. "I know you. You're here for my wedding. I miss Courtney. She's great. Have you noticed how great she is?"

"Courtney's amazing," Jackson told him. "And you're going to marry her tomorrow."

Alex slowly pushed into a sitting position. "I know. She's beautiful and stuff, but she can be selfish and it makes me crazy. Then I think about not being with her and it hurts to breathe. What do you think that means?"

"You're nervous about getting married," Jackson said firmly. "It happens. You need to focus on what you love about Courtney, how you felt when you proposed. Back then you knew you'd be happy together forever. Remember that now."

Alex blinked several times. "That's deep, man."

"I'm a trained professional," Jackson said, comfortable with the lie. "You need to get up and go back to the hotel. Shower, shave and have a lot of coffee. Then you're going to find Courtney and tell her how much you love her. After that, you'll have to deal with your mother. It's possible that your father slept with Aunt Tully."

Alex's stare turned glassy. "My father what?"

Jackson helped Alex to his feet. "Your mother will fill in the details. Now do you remember what you're supposed to do?"

"Shower, shave, coffee, Courtney, Mom. Got it."

"Excellent."

"So you're a shrink?" Alex asked, leading the way out of the small building.

"Something like that."

"Katie's lucky to have you. She deserves someone really great."

"I know."

"It wasn't me."

"Apparently not."

Alex sighed. "I miss her, too."

"She's not on your list."

"I know."

Jackson watched Alex trudge toward the hotel. When the other man disappeared inside, Jackson stayed where he was and wondered how big a disaster this wedding was going to be.

# *Eight*

"**W**hy does Alex think you're a psychiatrist?" Katie asked later that afternoon as she and Jackson walked toward the room where the rehearsal would be held.

"I gave him advice and he assumed."

"Makes sense." She smiled. "He's not going to be happy when he finds out the truth."

"If the wedding goes as planned, it shouldn't matter one way or the other."

Jackson sounded confident and he looked yummy. Or maybe it was the fact that due to all the stress and trauma, she'd missed lunch.

She eyed him, taking in the tailored pants, the long-sleeved shirt and sports jacket. He looked good. Good enough to make her forget the growling in her stomach. *Danger,* she reminded herself. Falling for Jackson wasn't smart. Not until she knew a little more about him. But they hadn't had much time alone and now that they were by themselves, she couldn't think of a single normal opening line. "So tell me about yourself" didn't exactly meet the subtle requirement.

"Did you get any sleep?" Jackson whispered in her ear, his hand at the small of her back.

Something warm and liquid flowed through her. "I tried, but there were too many interruptions."

"Should I apologize?"

"You weren't the one interrupting me."

He grinned at her. "You know what I mean."

Their gazes locked. She felt the crackle of awareness, of need. "No," she whispered. "Don't apologize."

"Good."

They'd stopped just outside the open door. Katie could hear conversation and knew they should take that last couple of steps and go inside. But staring into Jackson's eyes was the best part of her day. Well, kissing him was better and when he touched her…

"I read science fiction," he blurted.

"What?"

"I read science fiction. I like spy movies and thrillers. I can sit through a romantic comedy if it's important to you. I like relaxed vacations, preferably by the beach, but I can do the mountain thing, too."

He cupped her face. "Tell me what you like."

"Um, I read romances and mysteries. I like most movies, as long as they're not too violent or gory. I can't remember the last vacation I took, but a beach would be nice."

"I fell out of a tree when I was eight and broke my arm."

"I have a tattoo on my butt that says Buddy."

He dropped his hands and stared at her. "Buddy."

She laughed and kissed him. "Kidding. No tattoo."

"I didn't think so. I would have seen it last night." He grabbed her in his arms and spun her around. "We wasted way too much time, Katie. My mom's going to love hearing that."

Her heart pounded hard and fast. What exactly was he saying? Could she hope that he was as crazy about her as she was about him? Was it possible that she was going to get that lucky?

She opened her mouth, prepared to ask, when a soft voice spoke his name.

"Jackson, do you have a second?"

He put her down and they both turned to find a very beautiful, worried-looking Ariel standing behind them.

"I have to go to the wedding rehearsal," he said, his hand still on Katie's waist.

"This shouldn't take long. Please?"

Katie thought about how much Jackson had come to mean to her and how, when compared with the tall, leggy beauty, she was perfectly average. Before falling for him, she would have instantly gone to the bad place. While she was flirting with heading in that direction, there was a part of her that felt strong.

"You should talk to her," she told him.

"Why? I know the rehearsal won't be fun."

"I'll survive, and you won't be that long."

At least she hoped he wouldn't be. Besides, if he was the kind of guy to sleep with her and then want to get back together with an ex, better she know that now. When there was still a chance of getting out with her heart intact. Or at the very least only slightly shattered.

"I'll be right back," he promised, then walked toward Ariel.

Katie didn't want to see the two beautiful people together, so she hurried into the rehearsal room.

She would be fine, she told herself as she raised her chin and strode forward purposefully. Then promptly fell over a handbag, stumbled, twisted, felt an ugly pop and crumpled to the floor.

Katie really wanted to stay where she was. If she could lie on the floor and have everyone pretend they couldn't see her, she would be perfectly happy. Instead, they all gathered around, hovering, asking questions and offering advice.

Alex reached her first and helped her into a chair. "Where does it hurt?" he asked, rubbing his hands up and down her legs.

She pushed him away. "I'm fine. It's nothing."

Her mother reached her next. "Are you all right?"

"I think I pulled something. I'm sure I'll be okay in a second."

Her mother squeezed her hand. "If you're going to try and get out of the wedding, you'll have to do better than this," she whispered.

Katie managed a smile through the growing pain in her knee. "The window was too far."

Her father knelt in front of her and cupped her knee. "It's swelling, kid. I'm guessing a sprain. Let's go have a look."

He helped her hobble to the room next door. She pulled off her sandals and white jeans, then winced when she saw her knee. It was nearly double in size.

"That's attractive," she murmured.

Her dad, a family doctor, probed and squeezed. "You're the sports nut in the family. Want to guess?"

She'd seen enough knee strains to recite from memory. "Ice, elevation, rest, ibuprofen and wrap it when I'm standing."

"That's my girl. If it's not better in the next couple of days, we'll do an X-ray, but my guess is you'll be fine." He stood. "Trying to get out of walking down the aisle?"

"If only." She poked at her knee, then winced. "Talk about graceful."

He supported her as she stood, then helped her back into her clothes. "We love you anyway."

"I appreciate the lack of conditions on your affection," she said and hugged him.

He held her for a second. "This wedding is a disaster. You hear about Tully and Bruce?"

"It beats thinking about you and mom having sex."

"Don't go there."

"Believe me, I'm trying not to."

Her father straightened, then looked at her. "I know Alex hurt you when he dumped you for Courtney, but I was relieved. He was never the right one for you. I hope you know that."

"I do."

"Good."

The door opened and Jackson burst in. "I was gone fifteen minutes. What the hell happened?" He saw Katie's father and stopped. "Uh, sir," he added.

Bad enough that everyone in the wedding party had witnessed her clumsiness, but now she had to tell Jackson about it.

"This is why I only write about sports rather than

actually participate in them," she said with a shrug. "I tripped."

"Are you hurt? I hear you broke something."

"A knee strain," her father said cheerfully. "She'll be fine." He hesitated, then glanced between them. "Should I let you lean on him?"

Katie nodded, and her father left. She turned to Jackson. "How's Ariel?"

"Fine. What happened?"

"Ariel first."

"You first."

She huffed out a breath. "I fell over a purse and twisted my knee."

"She thinks we should get back together. I told her no."

Katie had already known what he was going to say, but it was still a punch in the gut to hear the words.

"Can you be more specific?" she asked cautiously.

He crossed to her. "Do you need ice or something?"

"Ice, elevation, rest and ibuprofen."

"In that order?"

"All at once is better."

"That's what I thought."

Before she could figure out what he was doing, he bent over, gathered her in his arms and picked her up. She shrieked as she left the ground.

"What do you think you're doing?"

"Taking you to your room."

The door her father had closed opened again and her mother stood there, wide-eyed. "I heard screaming and…" She took in her daughter in Jackson's arms, then sighed. "That's so romantic."

"It's not," Katie insisted, hanging on to his neck. "I'm not a cat. Put me down."

"I'm taking you to your room. You need to take care of your knee." He walked easily, as if she wasn't solidly built. "Janis, if you could get Katie's purse?"

"Of course."

They moved through the rehearsal room where everyone gathered around. Everyone except Courtney, who stared at Katie with unconcealed anger in her eyes. Katie buried her face in Jackson's shoulder.

"Don't worry about the rehearsal," her mother was saying. "You walk down the aisle and wait for the bride. How hard could it be? Jackson, you take good care of my girl."

"I will," he promised and stepped onto the waiting elevator.

# Nine

"Better?" Jackson asked an hour later.

Katie lay on the bed, her leg propped up on a couple of pillows, ice held in place with one of his T-shirts.

"I'm dealing more with a sense of the ridiculous rather than pain," she admitted. "I can't believe I did that."

Talk about embarrassing. So far nearly everyone in the wedding party had been by to check on her. Not Courtney, but her sister would assume Katie had tripped on purpose—to ruin Courtney's day.

"I was distracted," she admitted, looking at Jackson, who was stretched out next to her.

He rolled onto his side, his head resting on his hand. "Ariel?" he asked.

She shrugged. "Maybe."

"We're not together. We haven't been for a long time."

"She wants to change that."

"I want to cover you in champagne and lick you dry, but that's not going to happen." He grinned. "At least not tonight."

He leaned toward her and kissed her. "I'm not interested in Ariel."

"She's beautiful."

He shrugged. "I'm over her. I was ten minutes after she left."

Which was both reassuring and concerning. "You don't believe in second chances?"

"Sure, but why would I want her when you're around?"

She felt her mouth drop open. That seemed to happen a lot around Jackson. She closed it. "Nice answer."

"Any more questions?" he asked.

"Not really."

"Good." He kissed her again, this time more slowly. "Think your family is done checking up on you?"

She wrapped her arms around his neck. "I hope so."

"Me, too."


The next morning, Jackson eased himself out of Katie's bed. She was still asleep, her short blond hair spiky against the pillowcase.

She'd spent most of the night on her back, her leg draped over a pillow, to elevate her knee. Now, he saw the swelling had gone down. She would be stiff when she got up, but would heal quickly. His gaze lingered on the painted toenails. Something he'd never cared about one way or the other, but on Katie, they were oddly erotic.

Her skin was soft, he thought as he pulled on clothes. Her body warm, her responses irresistible. There was something about her—something special and unique. Something that drew him in and made him want to stay.

Instead he crossed the room and quietly let himself

out into the hall. He would shower in his own room. Today was the wedding. Katie would need to be rested.

But before he could pull the door shut, Courtney stepped out of the elevator and headed for him.

"Is she up?" the bride-to-be demanded. "I have to talk to her."

"She's still—"

Courtney didn't bother to listen to the rest of it. She pushed past him and burst into the room.

"You're not up? You have to get up. There's something going on with Alex. He doesn't love m-me."

The last word was accompanied by wild sobbing.

Jackson hesitated, not sure if he wanted to go back inside and be supportive or run for the hills. As the mountains were mere feet away, the latter was tempting. Still, he sucked it up and went into Katie's room.

She'd sat up in bed, drawing the sheets up to her shoulders. Their eyes met and she smiled at him.

"Morning," she said, her voice low and sexy.

"Morning."

"Are you listening to me?" Courtney demanded loudly. "Alex isn't sure he wants to marry me."

That got Katie's attention. She stared at her sister. "You said he loves you before. Which is it?"

"Does it matter? I'm miserable."

Katie did her best not to roll her eyes. "Why? You're marrying a really great guy who adores you. This is going to be a great day."

"You're just saying that because you're jealous of me."

Katie frowned. If she was jealous, wouldn't she be mean rather than nice? "What exactly is there to be jealous of?"

"I'm getting married, and all you have is a paid escort."

Jackson leaned against the door frame. "You're paying me?"

"You haven't heard?" Katie asked, sounding more amused than hurt. "Hundreds of dollars."

"Is there a bonus for good behavior?"

"I was thinking I might give you a little something extra."

"I can't wait."

Courtney turned on him. "Shut up and stay out of this. None of this has anything to do with you."

He straightened and moved toward her. "On the contrary. It has everything to do with me because it has to do with Katie. Whatever your problems are with your fiancé, they have nothing to do with your sister. Katie has been supportive of you, which is more than it seems like you deserve."

Courtney's mouth dropped open. "You…you…"

"Your sister has no interest in Alex. If she did, he would be a very lucky man. But she has moved on. As has Alex. He's in love with you and wants to marry you. If you expect this marriage to work, you're going to have to grow up. You probably won't like acting like an adult, but it will be good for you."

Courtney glared at him. "I hate you."

"You're not my favorite person, either."

"You're not invited to my wedding. Don't even think about showing up," Courtney said as she ran out of the room.

He walked toward the bed.

"Should I go after her and apologize?" he asked.

Katie grinned. "No, but talk about great breakfast theater. That was amazing. And a long time coming."

"You shouldn't let her trash you."

"I know. Old habits and all that."

He was about to bend down and kiss her when the door opened again.

Janis hurried in, barely blinking when she saw him in Katie's room.

"Apparently the lovebirds have had a fight. I can't find Courtney, Alex is moping and it's not even nine in the morning. I knew they were going to make me wish we'd paid them to elope. They're both so immature, yet oddly right for each other."

"Courtney was just here," Katie said. "She's upset and emotional."

Janis touched her temple. "I can feel a headache coming on. I swear, there *will* be a wedding if I have to drug them and tie them up."

"At least that will make for interesting pictures," Katie offered.

"I'm ignoring that. How's your knee?"

"Much better."

"Thank God. That means you're out of excuses. Please get up and dressed. I'm going to need help today. And very possibly black-market drugs. I wonder if your father would write me a prescription." She drew in a breath and smiled absently at Jackson.

"Morning, Jackson."

"Janis."

"A word to the wise. Never have daughters."

The morning passed quickly. Katie was pleased to discover the swelling in her knee had almost completely disappeared. She wore low-heeled shoes, saving her moments on high heels for the walk down the aisle. There were a thousand details to see to and in an effort to take the pressure off her mother, she'd offered to take care of all of them. The cake was finished, the chairs set up. The florist was hard at work, stringing ribbons and setting out arrangements.

She left the room that would be used for the actual service, then made her way outside onto a side patio. The day was bright and sunny, promising to be warm. Perfect for pictures.

Courtney and Alex were nowhere to be seen, but she could only hope they were off somewhere having makeup sex. Anything to move the wedding forward.

"You're frowning," Jackson said as he came up behind her and put his arms around her waist.

"I'm thinking Courtney and Alex are crazy. Shouldn't they have worked out their issues *before* they decided to get married?"

"You'd think, but no." He took the clipboard from her hands. "How's the checklist?"

"I'm making great progress." She glanced at him, then away. "Ariel left."

He turned her until she faced him. "You have to let Ariel go. I did."

"But she's so…"

"Yes?"

It was impossible to think with him staring into her eyes like that. As if she was interesting and compelling and, well, wonderful.

"What were you like as a kid?" she asked.

"Reclusive." He tucked a strand of her hair behind

her ear. "I liked computers more than people and kept to my room. My mother tried everything to get me to play with the kids in the neighborhood, but I wasn't interested. I didn't know how to fit in or what to say to make them like me."

"Too many brains and not enough social skills?"

"Exactly. I was in college by the time I was sixteen."

"The summer we met," she teased. "When you were so charming."

"You bullied me."

"A moment of pride."

One corner of his mouth turned up. "If only I'd followed my heart back then."

She laughed. "Oh, please. You weren't interested in me."

"There was a spark."

"More like a laser beam of hatred."

"Maybe it would have been better if our mothers had waited to introduce us."

Katie nodded, then looked away. What would it have been like if she and Jackson had met when they were older? After she'd graduated from high school or during her first year of college. When she'd been thinner and prettier. More interested in boys.

"I would have been impressed," she admitted.

"Me, too."

He leaned in, as if to kiss her. She relaxed into his arms. But before she could give herself over to the moment, she heard a familiar laugh.

"Aunt Tully," she whispered against Jackson's mouth. "I'm supposed to find her and keep her away from Bruce."

Apparently the issues between the parents of the groom had not yet been resolved. Katie couldn't find out if there had been flirtation between Tully and Bruce or something more. To be honest, she didn't really want to know.

There were footsteps on the patio. Katie turned and saw an older couple in a passionate embrace. Even from several feet away it was easy to see their bodies straining, the deep kisses, the way the man's hands cupped Tully's butt oh-so possessively.

Katie's stomach flipped over. "Oh, God," she murmured. "That's not Alex's mother, is it?"

"Sorry, no. It's definitely Tully."

"What should we do?"

"They're adults."

Katie looked at him. "You're saying it's not our responsibility?"

"Something like that."

"So we should run."

"Quietly."

He took her hand and led her away.

Instead of returning to the hotel, they went around to the front, then across the driveway to the rose garden on the side. There was a gazebo, with a few chairs and benches. Jackson waited until she was seated on a bench before pulling a chair up across from her. He drew her feet onto his lap, pulled off her flats and began to rub her toes.

"How is your knee?" he asked, his long, strong fingers massaging her.

"Good. A little stiff, but I'm fine." She glanced over

her shoulder, toward the hotel. "I don't know about leaving Tully and Bruce like that."

"You really want to get in the middle of that conversation?"

"No. But Alex's mom is going to be pissed." She shook her head. "No. Not pissed. Hurt."

"You're assuming this is the first time."

Katie looked at him. "Tully does this a lot. Takes advantage of men."

"Sorry, no. She doesn't take advantage of them. They're willing partners in whatever she's doing. Maybe she shows them something they didn't know was there. Maybe they use her as an excuse. But either way, they have to take responsibility for their actions."

Something Katie hadn't thought about. "Everyone always says Tully is a force of nature. That no one can resist her."

"I did."

"You're different."

"No. Just scared."

Katie laughed. "You're saying she's not your type?"

"She'd probably kill me. I doubt I could keep up."

He continued to massage her feet. Warmth spread through her, making her want to confess her true feelings. But saying she was falling in love with him wasn't an option. If anything, it would frighten him off and that was the last thing she wanted to do.

"I think you could take on Tully and win," she told him.

"I appreciate the confidence but I'm not interested in that particular competition. I'd rather take on you."

"Good answer."

# *Ten*

After a few more minutes of massage, Jackson slipped Katie's shoes back on, then shifted so he was sitting next to her on the bench. He put his arm around her and she snuggled in close.

He felt warm, she thought. Safe.

"Tell me about where you live," she said.

"Outside of Los Angeles."

"Not Silicon Valley?"

"I avoided the cliché," he said. "There's plenty of talent in L.A. and when I was starting my business, I wanted good people."

"Have you lived there long?"

"Seven years. We're looking to move the company. We want something more low-key. Everyone's getting married and having kids. We used to talk about the latest game innovations. Now conversations are about parks and school districts."

Something fluttered in her chest. Hope, she thought, wondering if Fool's Gold could make the short list.

"Any contenders?" she asked.

"Not yet. We're just starting the process. What about you? You said you were a hometown girl. Is that permanent?"

"Yes. I went away to school, but I came back here. For a while I thought about moving to a bigger city— trying to get a job on a real paper. But this is my home."

He looked up at the mountains soaring behind the resort. "It's beautiful." He hesitated. "There hasn't been anyone to tempt you into moving?"

"A guy, you mean?" She glanced up at him. "Oh, please. You've met Alex. Not exactly my finest hour. I thought he was one of the good guys." She closed her eyes, remembering. "I'd always thought that he took one look at Courtney and was simply swept away. But now I'm not so sure. I don't think we were right for each other. Courtney was a catalyst, not a cause."

"And before him?"

"The usual suspects. A high school boyfriend who broke my heart. A guy in college who was intense and romantic and was ultimately too intense and boring."

He played with the ends of her hair. "So you're the girl who got away."

His voice was low and sexy and made her insides shiver. "Not exactly."

"That wasn't a question. You are."

*If only,* she thought, then cleared her throat. "What about you? Other near misses besides Ariel."

"A couple. I didn't have a girlfriend in high school. My first romantic encounter was in college."

"Let me guess. She was older, taught you every-thing you know."

He shifted to face her. "How did you know?"

"You went to college when you were what? Five?"

"Sixteen."

"Close enough. It would be difficult to find another college girl your age. Unless you waited until your senior year." She stared into his beautiful green eyes. "You might have been willing to stall, but I doubt they were."

One corner of his mouth turned up. "I was seventeen and she was nineteen. Spring break in Mexico. I hadn't wanted to go."

"She made you glad you did?"

"Oh, yeah."

"Good thing you were out of the country. In most states that relationship would have been illegal."

The smile expanded. "It was worth it."

She laughed. "Not you, Jackson. Her. You were a minor."

"Oh. You're right. Just as well, then."

"And between the cougar and Ariel?"

He chuckled and pulled her close. "I was waiting for you."

*If only that were true,* she thought with a sigh, surrendering to the moment and the man. Jackson was a temptation she couldn't seem to ignore. Everything inside her screamed that he was the one. An impossible reality, given how short a time they'd known each other. But everything felt right.

All her life she'd gone after what she wanted. Even though she'd been a disaster at sports, she'd found a way to translate her love of the games into a career. When Colleen, the curmudgeonly editor of the local paper, had refused to interview her for the sports writer job, she'd sent her an article a day for three weeks. Colleen had relented and she'd been hired.

She'd tackled tough interviews, developed a network of friends and been happy. Except romantically. There she'd always been cautious, mostly because she was afraid of being hurt. But pain or not, she was falling for Jackson. Maybe it was time to do something about it.

She shifted on the bench so she was facing him. "You head home in the morning."

"That's the plan. Unless you want me to stick around."

She stared at him. "As in…"

"You could show me the town. Invite me to a sleep-over." He cupped her face in his strong hands. "This has been great, Katie. I owe my mom, big-time. You're amazing. I don't want to lose you."

"I don't want to be lost," she admitted. "I'd love to show you around. I've enjoyed our time together. I never thought I could get involved with someone this quickly."

"Me, either."

She took one of his hands. "I've really enjoyed all our time together. You're exactly who—"

"*There* you are!" Katie's mom hurried across the grass toward the gazebo. "I've been looking for you everywhere. It's a madhouse. I say that because *disaster* is so negative, but trust me, it's not going well. Morning, Jackson."

"Janis."

Reluctantly Katie rose. "What's going on?" She checked her watch. "It's not time for us to be getting ready."

"No, you have a few hours before the stylist Courtney had flown in from San Francisco clucks over all of us. The big news is about Rachel and Bruce."

Katie winced, trying not to picture the older man in a passionate embrace with Tully.

"They're getting a divorce," Janis announced.

"What?"

"Apparently they've been separated for months, but Rachel didn't want anyone to know." Katie's mother lowered her voice. "It was Rachel's idea and she left Bruce for another woman."

Katie didn't know what to say.

Jackson moved next to her and whispered in her ear. "Are all your family events like this? I've got to tell you, it's better than dinner theater."

"Have you ever been to dinner theater?"

"You mentioned it this morning. It sounded fun."

Katie turned back to her mom. "Seriously? So it's okay that Bruce and Tully are involved?"

"I don't know if it's okay. Bruce isn't a young man. Tully will probably kill him, but he'll die happy. I saw them sucking face on the porch on my way to find you."

Katie winced. "Mom, do me a favor. Please don't say *sucking face.*"

"Isn't that the right term? You young people today, always changing the language. It's hard to keep up."

Katie linked arms with her mom. "I know. We do it on purpose. Now is there anything else I should know? Are Alex and Courtney speaking?"

"That is a question for the ages."

Jackson had to surrender Katie to the stylist at about one-thirty. He spent the next few hours exploring the

Fool's Gold city Web site and checking out real estate. From what he could see, the town was great and he could understand Katie's reluctance to move.

Shortly after four, he dressed in the dark suit he'd brought along, then went down to the lobby to wait for his mother. His father had gotten out of having to attend by a carefully scheduled business trip to Hong Kong.

He spotted his mom as soon as she walked in.

"You look great," he said, kissing her cheek.

"So do you." She put her hands on his upper arms and kissed his cheek. "Very handsome. And yet you're not the one getting married. Have I mentioned my need for grandchildren?"

"Sometimes you go a whole hour without mentioning it."

"Hmm, I must be slipping. How are things here?"

"Frantic," he admitted. "Trouble in paradise. Courtney and Alex are at odds. I have no idea where they stand now."

His mother winced. "No wonder Janis left me a voice mail telling me it would help if I drank before the wedding. I hope everything goes all right."

He agreed, although he wasn't sure what would define *all right*. At this point he would think the odds of Alex and Courtney figuring out how to be happy together were fairly slim, yet he agreed with Janis. The couple was oddly right together.

He glanced around to make sure they wouldn't be overheard. "Alex showed up at Katie's door, drunk, a couple of nights ago."

"What did he want?"

"Guess."

His mother shook her head. "Talk about a mess. What happened?"

"She called me, and I got him out of there." He wasn't going to mention how he'd then spent the night. Some details were best left undiscussed.

"So you've enjoyed your time with Katie," his mother said.

He led them to the bar and ordered them each a drink. While they waited, he faced her.

"Yes, Mom. You were right."

She sighed happily. "Hearing that never gets old. So you like her?"

"Katie's great. Funny and charming. Sweet, pretty, smart. We've had a great time. I'm sorry I waited so long to let you get us together."

His mother's gaze turned speculative. "Interesting. That's a little more enthusiasm than I was expecting. Are you planning to see her again?"

"Yes. She's going to show me around Fool's Gold tomorrow."

The pleasure bled from his mother's face. "Why would you do that? You don't have any interest in the town."

"I want to see where she lives."

"Is that all? Because I know you're thinking about moving your company. You can't move it here, Howie."

He did his best to keep from wincing as she spoke his name. "Why not? There's an educated workforce, great school and inexpensive housing."

"If you move the company here, Katie's going to think you're moving because of her. She's the daughter of my best friend. You can't do that if you're not one hundred percent sure of this relationship. I don't want you to hurt her."

"I don't want to hurt her, either."

"You never want to hurt them. But you do. You get involved to a certain degree and then you back off. I'm not saying you're wrong. I'm sure none of the young women you've dumped have been 'the one.' But Katie is different. If or until you know how serious you are about her, don't lead her on."

The bartender served their drinks. Jackson automatically handed the guy a twenty and waved off change.

He wanted to say his mother was mistaken. That he didn't have a pattern. Except looking over his past, he could see where she was right. He did get involved—to a point. But when it came to getting serious, when it came to getting married, he'd always backed away. He'd never been able to see himself spending the rest of his life with someone.

Until now.

Because while the thought of growing old with Ariel or any of the others would have sent him running for the impressive mountains behind the hotel, the thought of sixty or eighty years with Katie was appealing.

She would grow more beautiful with passing time. Her quirky humor and curious mind would challenge him. He found himself wanting to take care of her, make her feel safe. God knew he wanted to protect her from the few vicious elements in her family.

"Please don't take this wrong," his mother said earnestly. "I do love you, Howie, and I would love to see you and Katie together. But I don't want Katie to be hurt. You're amazing and the odds of her falling for you are huge. What woman wouldn't want you?"

"Spoken like a true mother," he murmured. "I get it."

"Are you sure?"

"I would do anything to avoid hurting Katie."

"Good. As long as you remember that."

# *Eleven*

Despite the drama, the crying, the sulking, Courtney was ready to walk down the aisle right on time. Katie had already checked out the groom and he was waiting in place, up by the minister. Both main players were excited, happy and telling whoever would listen how much they loved each other.

The nearly three hundred guests were in place—a number that made Katie's stomach flip over. At least she wasn't the one who had to deal with the crowd.

Or pay for it, she thought, wondering how much the wedding had cost her parents. She returned to the bride's room.

"I look perfect," Courtney said, turning in front of the mirror and checking out her reflection.

Katie did her best to shake off her irritation at Courtney's vanity. After all, it was her wedding day, and it was only a few hours, she reminded herself. She would get through this because Courtney was her sister.

But then it would be over and she could escape back to her regularly scheduled life.

"Everyone is waiting," Janis said as she entered the room. "Courtney, you look lovely. Your father is right here. Let's go."

Courtney adjusted her veil, picked up her flowers and smiled. "Hasn't this been the best weekend ever? Everything has been perfect, Mom. Alex and I really appreciate how you've made it so romantic."

"You're welcome."

Her mother took Katie's arm and pulled her out of the room.

"Thanks for all your help," Janis said. "I couldn't have gotten through this without you. I keep telling myself that in a few hours, this will all be over."

"That's what I was thinking. I swear, when I get married, I'm going to elope. Or have no more than fifty people."

"Your father and I will spend exactly the same on your wedding as we spent on your sister's."

Katie grinned at her mom. "Can I have the cash instead?"

Her mother hugged her. "With interest."

The ceremony was beautiful and went off smoothly. At the reception, the first dance made everyone sigh, the food was perfect and the cake had a place of honor in the corner.

The bride and groom had decided against a head table. Instead there was a special table just for them— under a fabric-draped archway, with twinkling lights.

Jackson pulled Katie close, moving in time with the

music. "Would you be mad if I asked how much longer we have to stay?"

She grinned up at him. "No, because I already have an answer. Fifty-seven minutes. I promised my mom we'd be here until nine-thirty. Then we're free."

"Good. Your room or mine?"

She tilted her head as she considered the question. The soft light spilled onto her beautiful face, illuminating the light dusting of freckles, the shape of her mouth and the humor in her eyes.

"Your room," she said at last. "Mostly because no one will look for me there."

"You're saying I'm little more than an excuse."

"Is that a problem?"

"Not at all."

She laughed, and he felt the sound clear down to his gut. The sense of rightness he felt when he was around her had only grown.

His mother's words still lingered, making him aware that he would have to tread carefully. He wanted to make it clear to Katie and everyone else that she was important to him. He wasn't playing games. She was the one and he intended to have her.

Courtney came up and tapped Katie on the shoulder. "I'm going to throw the bouquet. I'm going to throw it directly at you. You know, for luck." Then Courtney hugged her. "I love you, Katie."

"I love you, too."

Courtney released her and glanced at Jackson. "Thanks for coming to my wedding."

"I thought you hated me."

She giggled the laugh of the very tipsy. "Don't be

silly. Although you'd better be careful with my sister. I know all about you."

"What does that mean?" he asked.

Courtney turned her attention back to Katie. "I can tell you really like him. I mean, he's an arranged date and all but he's been nice. Still, be careful. You know how things go with guys. You're not very lucky."

Katie's expression went blank. Obviously she was really great at hiding her feelings.

Jackson wasn't willing to just take Courtney's crap anymore. "Listen," he began.

Courtney's eyes narrowed. "No. You listen. You slept with Ariel. She told me. So don't you hurt my sister. Come on." Courtney grabbed her sister's arm. "I'm throwing the bouquet."

Katie slipped away before he could stop her.

Jackson stood in the middle of the dance floor, watching the woman he loved being led away.

He hadn't slept with Ariel, at least, not in a very long time. Surely Katie knew that. She had to understand Courtney was lying or misrepresenting the truth. Or Ariel was. Katie had to know how much she meant to him. That he would never do anything to hurt her.

"Is everything all right?" his mother asked.

"Fine."

"Katie looked upset."

He had to fix this, he thought grimly. But how? There had to be some way to convince her that she was...

He put his hands on his mother's shoulders. "I need you to get Courtney to hold off on throwing the bouquet."

"What?"

"She's going to do it any second. I need you to get them to delay."

"For how long?"

"Until I'm back." He headed for the door.

"Howie—"

He turned around. "Mom, you have to stop calling me that. I'll explain everything as soon as I can. Just help me."

"All right. But I don't know what I'm going to say."

"You'll think of something."

"This is stupid," Courtney said, sipping champagne and pacing by the edge of the ballroom. "I want to throw the bouquet and get on with my life."

"Mom and Tina were really clear. They want us to wait."

"Fine. But only five more minutes. Then I'm doing what I want."

And damn the consequences, Katie thought wryly. Courtney had her moments of caring about other people. Unfortunately they were widely spaced.

"I'm hope you know I said what I did for your own good," Courtney said.

Katie stared at her blankly. "What are you talking about?"

"Jackson and Ariel. Did you look at her? You don't have a shot. I know that sounds cruel, but it's true. Better that you get over him now than he breaks your heart."

Katie told herself she would sleep better if she assumed the best about her sister. "I appreciate the warning, but Jackson and Ariel aren't together. They didn't sleep together."

Courtney's eyes widened. "Of course they did. Both nights."

"No," Katie said calmly. "They couldn't have. Jackson was with me."

Courtney flushed. Her mouth opened and closed. "Ariel said they did. She said she was telling me because she knew how much I loved you and thought someone should warn you. I've been trying to figure out how to tell you." Her expression cleared. "I'm glad it's not true."

Katie couldn't have been more surprised if the stemware started talking. "Um, me, too."

Courtney hugged her. "Now I really want you to catch my bouquet."

Still feeling slightly stunned, Katie got halfway across the dance floor when she heard Jackson call her name.

She stopped, her heart pounding hard in her chest. Love filled her. Love and hope and the knowledge that this man was the one. She turned toward him.

"Hi."

"I didn't sleep with Ariel."

He looked serious and worried, as if he'd genuinely been concerned. Which was exactly like him.

"I know."

"I wasn't even tempted."

"I believe you."

There were guests all around them. A few were pretending they weren't listening while others moved in closer.

Jackson pushed up his glasses as he stared at her. "I know this is fast and maybe a little crazy, but, Katie McCormick, you're the most amazing woman I've ever met. You're who I've been waiting for. It kills me that our moms were right, but we're going to have to live with that. At least I'm hoping we will. I love you."

Maybe there was other noise in the room. Music from the orchestra, a gasp or two, but all she heard were his words. Magical words that made her feel as if she could float.

"I've loved you from the second I saw you," he continued. "It's okay if you have to think about it, but please don't tell me no."

Then Jackson Kent, the most devastatingly handsome, sexy, wonderful man she'd ever known, dropped to his knee and held out a diamond ring.

"Katie, will you marry me?"

A thousand thoughts flashed through her mind. That if this was a dream, she never, ever wanted to wake up. That she hadn't known it was possible to love anyone as much as she did right now. That her sister was going to want to kill her. But mostly that every fiber of her being begged her to accept.

She crossed to him and crouched in front of him. After cupping his face in her hands and allowing herself to get lost in his green eyes, she smiled.

"Yes."

The room erupted in cheers and applause. Jackson stood, drawing her to her feet, then he pulled her close and kissed her.

"I love you," he whispered against her mouth.

"I love you, too. From that first second."

He pulled back long enough to put the ring on her finger. She stared at the massive diamond.

"Were you just carrying this around? Random diamonds in case you wanted to get married?"

"I got the hotel manager to get the jewelry store guy to open for me. We can get you something different, if you want. Maybe a little diamond football helmet or baseball."

She laughed. "This one is perfect. Just like you."

He swung her around, then kissed her again. "Not perfect. Just very, very lucky."

Katie hugged him. Over his shoulder, she saw her mother and Tina both dabbing at tears. Courtney hung on to Alex and waved her flowers.

Katie drew back slightly. "About the wedding," she began.

"I was thinking we'd elope."

"You read my mind."

\* \* \* \* \*

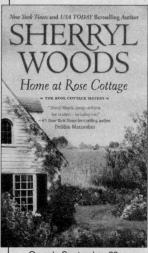
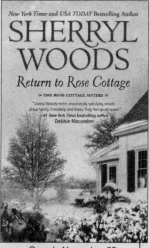

 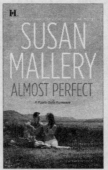 

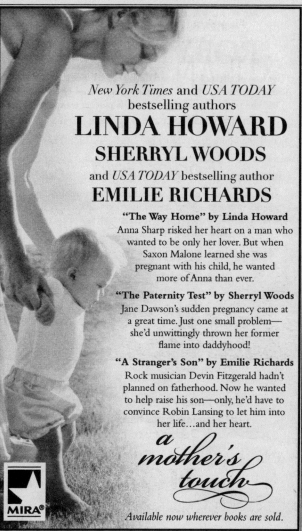

# REQUEST YOUR
# FREE BOOKS!

## 2 FREE NOVELS
## FROM THE ROMANCE COLLECTION
## PLUS 2 FREE GIFTS!

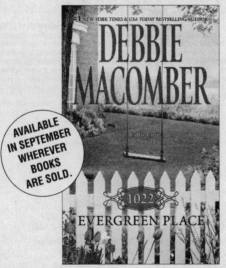